MORE THAN DUTY

CORINNE TESSIER

Contents

PROLOGUE

November 1806

The Winter Assembly

Claire Denham's innocent, excited eyes took in the grandeur, or what she perceived as grandeur, in the public rooms where the annual Ashwood winter assembly was taking place. Claire loved that she was now old enough to accompany her mother and elder sister to events such as these.

Being just those few extra years younger than Grace and Kate had meant that Claire had long been excluded from their few invitations. But now that she was finally seventeen, her mother had begun to allow her to attend these affairs.

Claire enjoyed being perceived as a grown-up woman. She desperately wanted to be seen as mature, amiable, and worthy. She had always been the little sister, the young girl, the child in comparison to Grace. Oh, how Claire had envied Grace when she had gone to work.

Of course, Claire did not envy Grace her position, only the location of her work.

Her mother, Mrs Denham, and Grace had secured positions as housemaids in the Slickson residence upon her father's death. This work had secured the family until her mother's fall.

While they worked for Mrs Slickson, Claire had made up every excuse under the sun to walk the few miles to the house. Perhaps Grace had forgotten her bonnet, or her mother a shawl. Anything to happen upon Arthur Slickson.

Claire could still remember the very moment she first saw Arthur Slickson. She had been eight years old and waiting outside of the schoolroom with her siblings before lessons. She had looked every bit a little girl, with a dress hemmed above her ankles.

Arthur Slickson had been sixteen, galloping through town atop the gelding he had been gifted as a birthday present. He had long been away at school, and Claire had never happened to meet him before.

Never had she seen such a beautiful man. And beautiful he was indeed. His hair was golden and curled like an angel's, his skin pale and smooth like porcelain. His eyes were a bright, piercing emerald green, and he was tall and lean. Claire could have sworn he looked at her and smiled, a grin that made her go weak at the knees.

It was then, Claire was certain, that she had fallen deeply in love with Arthur Slickson. Never would a man affect her so. Never could a man compare. At eight, her heart was stolen, and Claire became quite convinced that Arthur would be to her, what Adam had been to Grace.

Though Adam and Grace's understanding had fallen through, Claire was certain that when Arthur fell in love with her, it wouldn't end. It couldn't.

While her heart yearned for him when she was a girl, Arthur didn't look at Claire again for many years. It was not until she was fifteen, and finally allowed to wear her hair up in a fashionable style at church, did Arthur glance over at her.

Of course, Claire noticed this. She had not listened to a sermon in years. She used those precious hours in church to pray that Arthur might notice her and might see that she could be worthy of such a beautiful man.

Though she would never say so, it vexed her greatly whenever her family spoke negatively of him. Grace was often the naysayer. For whatever reason, she had seemed to form a negative opinion of Arthur while in his mother's employ, and Claire could not understand why. Grace seemed to think him terribly vain, but Claire had never sensed vanity about him.

Though, she supposed, any man who looked like Arthur did ought to deserve a little vanity. Regardless, Claire had never heard a cross word from him, and those few smiles and glances that she had collected over the years were utterly priceless to her.

Tonight, however, was the night that Claire was certain Arthur would return her affections. She was a woman, now, and dressed in her sister's very best blush pink gown. Grace had performed wonders with her often untameable raven locks, and she felt the prettiest that she had ever been.

Claire entered the ball on the arm of her sister as they followed their limping mother. She instinctively searched the room for seating and murmured to Grace under her breath that they ought to help their mother to a chair.

Both Grace and Claire were given dance cards, and Claire's excitement was quick to return. This was her first real dance card! She had never even seen one before! She quickly read down the list of dances that would be played and made a note in her head for which ones that she would most like to dance with Arthur.

All.

As Claire looked up to look around the ballroom, she could see the anxiety upon Grace's face. She knew that she was concerned about meeting the Beresfords. Claire was not even certain that they would make an appearance. Surely a village celebration was too common for the likes of them. Claire hoped that Grace would be able to enjoy herself.

No matter how she had once envied her sister, Lord, did Claire love her. Claire admired Grace above anyone else she knew, and she prayed for Grace to find peace. Even though she pretended that she had, Claire knew that Grace was still haunted by her demons.

Claire's eyes quickly found Arthur. It was a habit, really, but one she liked. Oh, Lord, he looked handsome. He was dressed every so richly, with a coat the shade of a deep burgundy. He'd had a haircut in the last week, Claire noticed, as his blond curls were not so much in his eyes anymore. He was dancing with a young lady, someone that Claire did not recognise, which made her think she must have been from another village around.

She felt the sparks of jealousy in the pit of her stomach.

Claire was forced to follow her mother and sister through the crowd, greeting friends and neighbours, before coming to a chair for their mother to occupy.

"I shall get you a refreshment, Mama!" announced Claire suddenly, and she left Mrs Denham and Grace before they could protest. Claire deliberately took the long way to the dining room, purposefully passing the lines of dancers so that Arthur might happen to see her.

As though God was on her side, the dance finished just as she passed by Arthur and his partner. Arthur's emerald eyes settled on Claire just as she had wanted them to. She smiled with satisfaction as she floated past him nonchalantly.

As though he was a duckling trailing after his mother, Arthur immediately followed her. She could have sworn she felt his hand brush the skirt of her gown, and a thrill tickled down her spine.

As they disappeared inside the dining room, and away from the possible attention of her mother and sister, Claire turned around to face the man she wanted to marry.

"Are you following me, Mr Slickson?" she asked innocently.

"Only because you want to be followed, Miss Claire," he quipped, a wicked, enticing smirk upon his chiselled face.

Claire felt her cheeks flush and her heart race. He was smiling such a devilish smile at her. Claire willed herself to be bold, enchanting. She would not be seen as a little girl who did not know how to converse with a gentleman.

Only, she did not know what to say! She was worried that the moment she opened her mouth again, she would accidentally profess her eternal love for him.

"My, how beautiful you look in that gown, Miss Claire," remarked Arthur appreciatively, his eyes slowly moving down her figure. "You are, for certain, the prettiest young lady here."

Claire felt her blush deepen. "Mr Slickson, please," she rebuffed.

"Did you wear such an ensemble for my benefit?" he wondered aloud, his wicked grin widening.

Claire's eyes flared with shock and embarrassment as he had seen her motives so plainly.

Arthur interpreted her silence correctly as he chuckled. "Well, I cannot thank you enough. What a sight you are," he praised.

While Claire's heart was singing, she had never before heard a man speak in this way, and especially not to her. He was appreciating her, he liked the way she looked, and Claire told herself that this was what she had wanted in her efforts to get ready.

Her heart quickly picked up speed again.

"So innocent," he murmured to himself, pleased. "So much to offer, and yet you have little idea of what to do with it." Arthur tsked.

Back in the ballroom, Claire could faintly hear the tail end of the attendant announcing the Beresfords' arrival.

Arthur looked upon Claire with a great intensity that nearly forced her knees to give way. "Have you ever been kissed before, Miss Claire?" he whispered.

Claire shook her head, fearing that she was about to start trembling with anticipation. Was he going to kiss her here? There were not many in the dining room, not especially since the Beresfords had been announced, but they were certainly not alone. However much Claire wished for her first kiss to be with Arthur Slickson, she could certainly not risk her reputation in front of others.

"I am promised for the next," he continued to utter quietly, only for her, "but I shall claim you for the one after. And before the night is out, you will not be shaking your head to that question."

Claire was so overcome with anticipation that she walked out of the dining room without a refreshment for her mother. She felt as though she was blushing all over, and looked every bit the innocent, frightened little girl she hoped she wouldn't be.

But ... but ... Arthur Slickson was going to kiss her!

Claire wandered a little aimlessly in the main assembly hall, not taking much notice of where she was standing. Her thoughts were far too occupied. So much so that when she felt a tap on her shoulder, she nearly jumped as she turned around.

She was greeted by a man, a young man, and one she did not immediately recognise. The first things she noticed were his eyes. They were hazel, brown almost, with hints of green around the iris. His hair was dark and unruly, and he had a handsome face, with a strong jaw and a straight nose. He was taller, much taller than her, which was not a difficult achievement, and he was smiling. Not a kind smile of introduction, but a grin that told her he was vexing someone.

He was dressed impeccably, wearing a navy ensemble that only deep pockets could afford. It was then that Claire noticed just whom were this man's party. Behind him stood Adam. Claire would know Adam anywhere. His sister, and his parents were all looking upon their interaction, though his mother was glowering.

Claire recalled the name of Adam's brother as Jack, just at the moment he extended his hand to her. "May I have the next dance, Miss?" he asked, seeming to be in a debonair attempt to charm her.

Regrettably, Claire felt her cheeks flush. "We have not been introduced, sir," she replied softly.

Jack looked over his shoulder to his siblings, and Adam, smirking, stepped forward.

"May I introduce Miss Claire Denham," said Adam formally. "Miss Claire, please allow me to introduce my brother, Lord Jack Beresford."

Claire heard the duchess say something nasty, but she did not quite hear it. She was informed enough to know that the duchess did not like her family. Poor Grace had always felt unwelcome as a girl.

"There now," said Jack confidently. "We are introduced. May I have the next dance?"

Claire looked over her shoulder briefly, and saw that Arthur was taking his place on the dance floor with his next partner. He had told her thus. Claire's eyes returned to Jack, and she knew it would be rude to refuse a gentleman, especially one of his standing, without a valid reason. "I would be honoured, milord," Claire uttered, curtseying to him as she placed her hand atop his and allowed him to lead her over to the dancers.

As they took their place in the line of dancers, only a few from Arthur, Jack uttered, "I am sorry to have ambushed you, Miss

Denham," sincerely. "But I am glad to stand up with you all the same."

Claire was almost so focussed on whether or not Arthur had noticed her dancing with another, that she had almost missed Jack's apology. "Oh, no matter," she said breathlessly, as the music began to play.

Claire realised that this was her first proper dance, and how she wished it could have been with Arthur. So much so that she nearly muddled several steps as she kept looking over at him. Much to her relief, Arthur seemed to be watching her at every opportunity, too.

When she forced herself to concentrate on her own partner, so as not to embarrass herself by tripping over him in the sequence, she noticed that Jack had a kind smile, a genuine smile, that made his overall appearance all the more pleasing. He was a good dancer, light on his feet, and he certainly was outdoing her in that moment.

When the music finished, the dancers applauded politely, and Jack took the few steps in to stand in front of her. "You are a fine dancer, Miss Claire," he complimented.

It was a falsehood to please her, though Claire knew that she could dance much more proficiently when not distracted. "You are too kind, milord," replied Claire breathlessly. Out of the corner of her eye, she saw Arthur leave his partner and start towards her.

"Would ... would you dance the next with me?"

Claire's eyes flicked back to Jack. He appeared even brighter, hopeful, and not as teasing as he had been when he had asked her to dance the first. He offered Claire his hand.

"I am afraid Miss Claire is already promised," interjected Arthur boldly, claiming Claire for his own.

Claire could not help the excited expression on her face as she suddenly found herself on Arthur Slickson's arm. For how many years had she dreamed of this moment!

Claire quickly regained her composure as she needed to refuse Jack. "Forgive me," she said softly, "but I have promised myself to Mr Slickson." She hadn't meant the words in any other context than dancing, but her mind raced with the possibilities.

She watched Jack's face fall as he nodded his head politely to Arthur, who returned the gesture.

"Do not trouble yourself," muttered Jack, before adding, "I am quite used to second place," under his breath.

"What have you done to me?" whispered Arthur seductively in Claire's ear as they went to take their place for the next. "I about came undone seeing you in another's arms. What spell is this?"

Claire felt the hairs stand up as Arthur's breath tickled her neck. "I haven't done anything."

"Oh, contraire," Arthur countered. "You do not yet know what you are capable of."

As they took their places opposite of each other, Claire sincerely believed she could see affection in Arthur's eyes. Could he love her already? She had loved him instantly, and from afar. Surely it was possible! Oh, she prayed he loved her!

As the music began, a blissful smile spread across Claire's face. She could see it in the not so distant future. She was going to be Mrs Arthur Slickson.

CHAPTER 1

September 29, 1809

Claire Denham was certain her arithmetic was correct. She had not needed to reach for the rags in her bottom drawer for six weeks. She was two weeks past when she had expected her monthly courses.

Claire felt a warm sense of fulfilment, bliss, as she stood in front of the mirror in her bedroom, the same room that she had once shared with both of her elder sisters. Though her stomach was still quite flat, and no one would ever guess that she was with child, she cradled her stomach protectively, knowing that she was carrying Arthur Slickson's precious son or daughter.

She could picture the beautiful child in her head. Of course, any child of Arthur's would be beautiful. Blond curls and green eyes, of course. She hoped their child did not inherit her features. A son would be tall, handsome and noble, a true gentleman. A daughter would be beautiful, elegant, and clever. She prayed the little child within her became exactly like their wonderful father.

Claire watched as colour filled her cheeks and tears filled her eyes. Lord, this had to be it! The time was finally here.

"Oh," she whispered excitedly, cupping her own cheeks as she smiled at herself. "Oh, happy day."

This coming November would mark three years. Three years since Claire and Arthur had entered into a secret courtship. It had to be kept secret as Arthur's mother was very particular about the ladies her son spent his time with. Despite her own social standing being raised with the elevation of Grace to duchess, Claire still lacked fortune. She now certainly had connections, but marriage to her would not bring land or dowry.

Arthur had told Claire as much when he persuaded her to keep their courtship quiet. Surprising his mother would not yield anything but a scandal and he would need time to encourage her towards the idea Claire.

In the meantime, both she and Arthur devised convincing cover stories for their families so that they could spend time with one another. Claire had told her mother that she had an interest in painting now that they had money enough to afford a maid to help with the household chores. Of course, Claire had no interest in painting, and had to produce an artwork every few months to keep up the ruse.

Mrs Denham always praised her, even though Claire was certain they both knew she was terrible.

Arthur Slickson had given Claire her very first kiss at the winter assembly and took pleasure in kissing her whenever he could. He had often chuckled at Claire's innocence and inexperience in the beginning, but Claire had learned, and she enjoyed feeling desired whenever Arthur's eyes found her.

Claire had thought that she loved Arthur before, but those had been the feelings of a girl. She had fallen deeply, passionately in love with Arthur during their courtship, and Arthur felt the same way about her. It was because he loved her that he kept their meetings secret. He pleased his mother by dancing with rich ladies at balls and assemblies in order to keep her on side, so that she would eventually approve of Claire. Claire had grown out of jealously and knew that nothing could come between them. With every kiss, with every touch, Arthur told Claire that he loved her.

Arthur had told Claire about the deeper intimacies of love, and how two people showed one another their affection. Claire wanted to make sure that Arthur knew exactly what was in her heart, and after months of suggesting on Arthur's part, Claire had finally agreed.

Arthur had been subtly working on his mother for three years now. With a child on the way, their engagement would be announced any day now ... once Claire told him, of course. Mrs Slickson would understand. When she learned that she and Arthur had been courting for three years, she would see how much they loved one another. She was going to be a grandmother. This was a happy occasion!

Claire nearly jumped out of her skin when there was a loud knock on her door.

"Claire, are you getting ready?" her mother called through the door. "We are to depart soon."

Claire wiped her eyes but could not wipe away her smile. She could not go to Ashwood House just yet. Arthur had to know about her pregnancy. They were due to meet up soon anyway.

"I thought I might get a little painting in first, Mama!" Claire called back. "The light is just lovely ..." Her heart suddenly stopped as she looked out the window and prayed for sunshine. God was on her side thankfully, as there was some autumn sun shining.

"What?" cried Mrs Denham. "Claire, this is not an ordinary party. It is Perrie's birthday!"

Claire couldn't help but nearly burst into happy tears again. Oh, Perrie was going to have another little cousin. She, Kate and Grace would all be mothers! Claire had always looked up to and admired her older sisters. Kate had been the first to marry for love, and how Jim Ellis adored her. And Grace had always been meant for Adam Beresford, no matter the obstacles they needed to jump between meeting in the schoolroom and meeting at the altar.

Just like her sisters, she was going to marry a man that adored her, and she would have a family of her own. She had thrown her sisters off the scent a few years ago and had been much better at hiding her affection for Arthur. Grace especially would understand now. She would understand that Arthur was her Adam.

"I will be along, Mama!" Claire promised. "I cannot forgo such weather! Winter will be dreadful for light. I won't be too far behind you. I shall walk. The exercise will do me well." Indeed, Mrs Denham would not know how well. Just yet, anyway.

She heard Mrs Denham sigh outside her door, but she did not protest. Claire had no plans to miss Perrie's second birthday. She knew it was a bit of a gathering, and Grace had spent a long while planning it. It was the setting of Jack Beresford's return, after all. Grace hoped that a large community of guests would provide Jack with enough cover to protect him from any offhand comments from his mother and he would feel welcome enough to remain at Ashwood House.

Claire could only recall a few details of Jack Beresford. They had danced once, but most of her attention had been on Arthur. She did not really remember if they had spoken. Of course, they were both in attendance at Grace and Adam's wedding, but he had been quiet and melancholy, understandably so, so soon after his father's death. Those were her only two encounters with the man.

Claire dressed herself in white, which was Arthur's favourite colour on her. She combed, fluffed, and pinned her hair, and listened out for the door and the sound of the carriage for when her family left for Ashwood House.

When they were safely away and she was satisfied with her appearance, Claire stole out of the house, too. During this time, Claire had become an expert in moving as clandestinely as possible. She knew the wood paths expertly and found her way quickly to the mossy clearing that had come to be known as their spot.

Claire's heart was beating quickly, and she felt a fluttering of nerves in the pit of her stomach. But they eased immediately when she saw Arthur leaning against a tree as he waited for her. Claire skipped into a run as she raced over to him, jumping into his arms as soon as she was close enough.

Arthur squeezed Claire tightly, pulling apart just enough to press his lips to hers hard. "I thought you might stand me up for the party," he murmured. His green eyes suddenly darkened, and

Claire knew his expression of desire. "But does this mean your mother's house is empty?" He arched an eyebrow curiously.

Her cheeks still reddened after all this time. "I am to follow soon," she replied softly. "It is my niece's birthday, after all."

Arthur pouted. "No," he urged. "Such an opportunity should not be wasted. Don't you love me?"

Claire's heart sank. "Of course!" she exclaimed, latching onto the labels of his coat. "Of course, I do. How could you doubt it?"

Arthur frowned and sucked in a breath. "I can't help it sometimes. I need to be shown."

As much as his insecurities hurt her, Claire would silence them with her news. "Arthur, please. I have something wonderful to tell you."

His interest was sparked immediately. "Oh?"

"This can all stop," she told him excitedly. "The lying, the sneaking about. We can finally be together properly. Arthur ... I am going to have a child."

Claire's smile was so wide it hurt her cheeks. Only it started to fade as she watched Arthur's reaction.

She had never seen someone turn physically purple before, and yet Arthur's contorting face was doing just that. Shock and anger flashed across his face so quickly, so interchangeably, that Claire needed to take a step back from him. What on earth was he doing?

"What?" spat Arthur, finally finding his tongue after a minute.

Claire felt her lower lip tremble, and her arm instinctively went across her stomach protectively. "Well ... well ... aren't you happy?" she worried. "We are going to have a child ... Arthur, we can be married."

Arthur swore, a crude, awful word, and he stormed about ten feet away, holding his head in his hands as he muttered under his breath. Claire was frozen, fear running through her veins as she was certainly going into shock.

Why was Arthur reacting this way? This was happy news! This was what they wanted!

"How can you be certain it is mine?" Arthur suddenly cried, marching back towards her, a cold, cruel look in his eyes that Claire had never seen before.

"Arthur!" she cried hysterically, her eyes welling up. "How could you say such a thing?"

"You opened your legs for me, you could have opened them for anyone," he snapped.

Claire gasped, all blood draining from her face. No, he could not have just said that. "Arthur, stop it!" she begged. "Stop it before you say something you cannot take back! You have said enough! Of course, this child is yours! What did you think would happen? You have wanted to marry me for three years! I know this is a shock, but it will be a blessing, I am certain!"

But Arthur laughed at her. Not a hearty, humorous laugh, but a cold, mocking laugh that made her feel truly terrified of the person who stood before her. "Marry you?" he scoffed. "In what world would I marry you. You took longer to persuade than others, Claire, but you did finally give in. And if you gave in to me, you could have given in to anybody."

Claire could not believe her ears, nor her eyes. Her emotions fogged her mind and made her lose all sense of reality as she fell to her knees. She felt a blinding pain in her chest, as though Arthur had driven in a knife, one cruel word at a time.

Where had this come from? What was he doing? She couldn't understand it, couldn't fathom it! He loved her! He had told her so!

Arthur came to kneel beside her, placing his index finger underneath her chin, forcing her to look into his once beautiful green eyes. "Do you understand me, Claire?" he whispered, his voice sounding almost tender. "Should you publicly name me, I will shame you. And who do you think will come out of the other side smelling like roses? Hmm? The gentleman, or the unwed girl?" He frowned, almost regrettably. "How I will miss you," he uttered, brushing his thumb over her bottom lip.

And as though she didn't matter at all, Arthur left Claire, kneeling on the grass, utterly and completely heartbroken and in shock at how her life had just imploded. Claire burst into violent sobs that shook her whole body. Her breathing escalated to the point where she was gasping for air in and amongst wailing in pain.

She couldn't understand what had just happened. How had Arthur flipped so suddenly, so cruelly? How could he do that to her when he had repeatedly told her that he loved her? They loved each other! It was a sacred bond! They were meant to be married! They were meant to raise a family together! Just like Grace and Kate, she was going to create a home.

Claire realised, to her devastation, that it was quite impossible for Arthur to be in love with her. One did not destroy their love. He had lied, and that realisation in itself burned her very soul as she cried into the empty clearing.

Claire didn't know for how long she cried. She didn't know what time it was. She felt raw and empty, only she wasn't. She was still with child. A child who, up until now, she had believed would have a devoted and loving father.

Now, this innocent child, would be born to a shamed, unwed mother. It would be a bastard, and Claire would be ruined. Her family would be ruined. Oh, her mother! What would Mrs Denham say? Mrs Denham was so proud of both Grace and Kate, and the families they had made. Claire could not bear the thought of her mother thinking ... her mother knowing ...

Claire couldn't stay. She had to run away. People went missing all the time. It would not be difficult to start towards London. It would be easy to disappear in London. She could have the baby and leave it ...

The second the thought crossed her mind, Claire sat up straight, the shock of it bringing her back to earth. She had no idea what she was going to do, but she could not do that. Maybe, maybe this had been a shock to Arthur, too. Well, of course it had! Perhaps, once he'd had enough time to come to terms with it ...

Claire clapped her hand over her mouth to stifle another sob. No. She had been fooled. And she was now left with the consequences. She couldn't run away. And as much as she never wanted to see such an expression of disappointment from her family, she would have to tell them.

Claire rose to her feet, shaking on unsteady legs, and started off towards Ashwood House, feeling frightened, lost, and excruciatingly heartbroken.

CHAPTER 2

The deepest glory for all gentlemen, titled or otherwise, is to sire a son. An heir. A namesake for which to pass on their legacy, to carry the family name into the next generation, and to keep land, fortune, and titles within the family.

But ... what if tragedy struck? What if smallpox spread through the estate? What if fever took hold? What if he fell from a horse? What if he ate spoiled game at suppertime and succumbed to poisoning?

The death of a son could spoil a legacy, just as much as it could spoil a family.

And thus, someone, somewhere, had coined the term "spare". The spare. The second son. The insurance. Should anything tragic happen to the first, the second was there.

It was not from his own parents that Jack Beresford had first heard himself called a spare, though it was not difficult to surmise why onlookers viewed him in such a way.

Adam was the first, the eldest, and his parents had spent much of his life preparing him for life as a duke. Adam was educated, drilled, lectured, and almost married to fulfil the role he was born to play. Jack, of course, was educated as well. Should he ever need to inherit, he ought to know how to read and write. Though Jack was not educated to inherit. Jack was kept, supervised by teachers, before he could take his place in one of the few options available to mere second sons.

Jack had been a naturally boisterous child. He had been energetic and playful, and not the sort of quiet spare his mother had hoped for. Jack hadn't known exactly the moment his mother had tired of him. Perhaps she had never really warmed to him. They were very different people, and Cecily Beresford liked things her way. Jack was not a boy who could be easily moulded.

His father had been kinder, though as warm as a father of his status could be. Peregrine was not the type of man to play with his children. But Jack had loved him, and perhaps even more so seeing as he never really found middle ground with his mother.

Cecily had meant Jack for the church from a very early age. Jack had soon got into the habit of doing the exact opposite of what his mother wanted. As an adult, Jack realised, that in rebelling, it really was the only time that Cecily paid him any attention.

Jack was clever, but reckless, and was often the student with the best marks and the most welts from the cane. The letters from his mother, scolding him for being an embarrassment, had once amused him, encouraged him to go further. But when he reached university, the amusement waned quite quickly.

Being only two years younger than Adam, Jack did spend quite a bit of time with him while they were at Cambridge. The differences he noticed between them began to really affect him or take its toll. They had always affected him. The letters Adam received from their mother were full of hope and plans. Cecily spoke of his future, the ladies she wanted him to meet, to ask when he would be home to see Susanna.

The letters Jack received were often short, curt, scolding him for one thing or another.

One could only read I am so disappointed in you so many times before it became a part of their identity. He was a disappointment, and he had been from the moment he could talk. Jack was the spare, and that was all he ever would be.

Second best and second place.

Rebelling, as his mother saw it, was no longer humorous to Jack. At nineteen or twenty, a time in a young man's life when they were truly becoming men, Jack realised that he had never really known what it was like to feel wanted, to be valued, to be loved. He had never been held before, never been comforted by someone. He had never known what it was to make a mistake and not be called a fool. He had never known a place where he belonged.

And Jack had spent the next five years of his life trying to feel something. Oh, had he made mistakes, and oh, was he reminded and scolded for them. He had drunk himself in oblivion on countless occasions. He had bedded numerous women, hoping that one of them would be able to make him feel whatever it was he'd been craving for a quarter century.

But every day he woke up, and he still felt the same. At the core of his being, he was just a spare.

When Jack's father had died, he had felt a kind of pain he hadn't thought possible. And it was not a pain he could endure in that house. Not with his mother there. Cecily had a gift when it came to putting Jack in his place. And so, he had run away to London.

Jack had been searching for a feeling and some sort of purpose but had found neither. He had spent the last few years drinking, gambling, and spending time with whatever woman would pay him attention. It was no surprise that his vicious circle of bad habits drew him no closer to how he longed to feel.

To be certain, the only semblance real pleasure he had ever found in his life was books. Perhaps it was because the library at Ashwood House had often been a sanctuary for him. His mother never seemed to venture in there. Jack adored the written word and envied the talent of those who had the power to take a reader to another place. More often than not, those places he had visited in books had been his saving graces.

Jack had lost count of how many books he had read years ago. When all the world was crumbling around, in a complete inferno, it was easy to be transported to another place in a book. Especially in the last few years, it had been necessary.

Jack truly wished he was back in London, nose deep in a book, or in a bottle of whiskey, rather than standing outside of the enormous walls of his childhood home.

Adam had travelled to London several times over the last few years, and Jack truly had enjoyed his brother's visits. It would be easy to assume that Jack would have resented Adam, or had a cool relationship with him, owing to the differences in their positions, but it was not the case. Jack greatly admired his brother, and never forgot all the times Adam had intervened on his behalf.

Perhaps what Jack admired most about Adam was his loyalty, his constancy. He was loyal to a fault. To Jack, to Susanna, to their mother eventually, and to, of course, his beloved wife, Grace.

A small smile hinted at Jack's lips as the memory of marrying Adam and Grace popped into his mind. What could have been a childish joke was never forgotten by Adam. How on earth he had managed to convince their parents of the match with Grace, Jack would never know.

Adam had begged Jack to return to Ashwood, guilting him with a miniature of their now two-year-old daughter, Perrie, whom Jack had not yet met. Jack had tried to convince Adam to bring Perrie to London, but a thirty-mile journey was not ideal for a girl of her age.

And so now Jack found himself ascending the steps of Ashwood House, not knowing how on earth he would need to prepare himself for his mother's remarks. Perhaps a stronger man could take them, but Jack had been put down one too many times. He was certain Cecily would know all that he had gotten up to in London. She always knew.

The door was opened for him, and the house was abuzz with guests, as was evidenced by the stationary carriages and carts outside the house.

Jack had hoped to slip inside, to remain unnoticed so that he might subtly meet with Adam and Grace, but no sooner had the thought crossed his mind, their old butler, Cole, announced, "Lord Jack Beresford has arrived!"

Jack practically winced and looked away from the surprised gazes of the guests who were gathered about the house. "Cole, how are you?" he murmured quietly.

"Well, thank you, milord. And you?" replied the butler politely.

"Loving every minute," he muttered. "Where is my brother?"

No sooner had asked the question, did a flash of blonde hair streak towards him, and a pair of arms flew around his neck in a vice grip.

"Jack!" cried Susanna.

Jack felt his heart settle as he returned his sister's hug. It had been June, perhaps, since Susanna had last visited him while in London for the Season. She looked a little taller, though every bit the lady Cecily raised her to be. Though, at two and twenty, he was surprised that she had managed to ward off the potential husbands their mother was no doubt throwing at her. Jack wondered for a moment just whom would persuade Susanna into matrimony.

"I really did not think you would come!" Susanna continued, pulling away so that she could look up at him. She cupped his face with her hands, feeling to make certain he was real, no doubt.

Ever since he had agreed, albeit reluctantly, Jack had not been certain himself. It had been a constant battle to ward off the temptation to send Adam a cancelation note.

But Jack had a niece, a niece whom he had never met, and that had never sat right with him. He was looking forward to meeting the young Lady Perrie Beresford.

"I've missed you, Susanna," Jack said earnestly. "Are you well?"

"Yes, now that you are returned," she declared.

Jack did not like the finality in the word "returned". It was highly likely he would be returning to London in the morning depending on how this day went.

"Where are Adam and Grace?" he asked.

Susanna frowned and looked around. "Oh, I did see them before. I think they were in the dining room. I think Mother and Mrs Denham have Perrie if you would like to see her."

Jack felt the colour drain from his cheeks. He wanted to avoid that confrontation for as long as possible.

Susanna suddenly hugged Jack again, tighter this time, as if it were possible. "Oh, Lord, it is good to have you home," she said quietly. "Please don't leave again."

"Susanna ..."

"Jack!"

Jack looked up in the direction that he had heard his name, and watched as his brother walked proudly towards him, arms extended and a bright smile on his face. Adam looked every bit a duke with his fine, tailored coat and breeches, his golden pocket watch, and the very fact that people bowed and curtseyed to him as he passed.

"You came!" Adam beamed as he received Jack in a hug, Susanna stepping back.

"Did you doubt I would?"

"Absolutely," confirmed Adam, chuckling, "but I am glad to be wrong. Welcome home."

It felt oddly normal to be standing, conversing with his siblings again. In them he had allies and friends, though he knew it would be too good to be true. Twenty-five years of history told him that.

"I feel odd telling you to come into your own house, but come in," urged Adam. "Grace is anxious to see you."

Adam pulled Jack towards the dining room, and Jack found himself forcing smiles at the people he had once been acquainted with years ago. Some he did not know at all.

The dining room itself was extravagant, laid out with every possible refreshment and treat imaginable. Poor Mrs Reynolds must have been cooking for days on end. Jack did, however, notice several of his favourite dishes on the table, and he did not think it at all a coincidence.

As soon as he had stopped staring at the food, Jack realised that he had been led over to Grace. The last time Jack had seen Grace was the summer before she had given birth to Perrie, and she had not changed very much since then, except for the fact that she was not harbouring a melon under her chemise. She was still small in stature, and elfin in appearance, with the same eyes that Adam had once obsessed over. She was draped in an elegant gown that was certainly not a housemaid's uniform and was wearing quite a few pretty baubles. Perhaps the only real difference was the way in which she carried herself. She stood with a posture of pride, something one certainly needed in a crowd of aristocracy.

"Grace," uttered Adam tenderly, placing a soft hand on the small of her back.

Such a simple gesture, Jack noted, and one that affected him. Adam had not been free from their mother's criticism as a boy and young man. But the difference between them was right here. Perhaps that was what Jack truly envied. What his brother had found with Grace. She was the reason he had survived their mother's pressures. With her by his side, anything was possible.

Grace turned around, and her blue eyes widened when she looked upon Jack. She smiled, though not fully, and Jack could see concern upon her face. Adam saw it, too. "Jack!" she gasped. "Oh, one moment, please!" She held up her finger to hold him, before turning around again, and it was then that Jack realised that Grace had been talking to someone, someone trying to conceal herself on the fringes of the dining room.

Her dark hair was pulled up in a twist, though several tendrils had come loose and were curling naturally in a charming disarray. The skin on her heart-shaped face was pale and her full lips were the colour of a pink rose. Her dress was white, and suited her slender silhouette well, though he could see slight staining on the skirt, as though she had fallen, or been kneeling on the ground. But her eyes ...

The minute he saw her eyes, Jack understood why Adam had been so obsessed with Grace's. Her eyes were beautiful. A violet blue so unique, and yet so haunted, filled with emotion that made Jack feel on edge.

Jack knew her immediately to be Claire Denham.

"I need a moment," Claire murmured to her sister, hurrying out of the dining room before Grace had a chance to protest.

Grace huffed; her brows furrowed as she looked up at Adam. "She won't tell me what's wrong," she uttered. "She looks terrified! What could have happened to her?"

CHAPTER 3

Jack stayed in the dining room for much of the party, definitely indulging in the treats that had been prepared, but mostly in an effort to avoid a public confrontation with his mother.

His brother, the good supervisor that he was, stayed with him, but when he was taken in conversation by his guests, Jack's mind did stray. Lord, it had been a long time since he had laid eyes on Claire. Adam and Grace's wedding day to be exact.

While he had only ever spoken to her a handful of times since their first meeting, someone as lovely as Claire certainly did leave an impression. A wound really, on an already terribly bruised ego. It was not the first time he had been rejected, and it would certainly not be the last. Claire had been a beautiful young lady, and of course he was not her first choice.

Of course, she was still a beautiful young lady, though he would agree with Grace. Something was definitely amiss.

Jack, however, did not see Claire again for the remainder of the afternoon, and Grace had seemingly given up searching for her at the behest of Adam, who seemed to be hovering a little whenever she joined them. Adam convinced Grace that Claire must have returned home, and that if something were really wrong, she would have told Grace.

Grace acquiesced, though Jack could see she was not settled. Towards the end of the party, the guests all gathered, and Perrie was carried into the dining room by Cecily.

While Jack wanted to focus on his niece, he couldn't help but feel a sense of foreboding. He had not met with Cecily yet. He always felt as though he were eight years old around his mother, and that nothing he could do would ever please her. It was entirely demoralising.

Perrie was dressed in a pink dress, covered in frills, flounces, and ruffles, with ribbons fixed in her dark hair. She yawned, clearly tired, and rubbed her eyes with her little fists. She was very delicate and sweet and was very much like her mother in looks.

Jack watched as Grace and Adam flanked Perrie, cooing over her as Perrie was toasted and the cake was served. He couldn't help but smile at the sight. His brother was so happy, and he definitely had what he deserved.

Yes, Jack realised. This was what he envied. He wanted that. He wanted a family of his own. A wife who chose him, who wanted him, who loved him. A child, children, to whom he would be a loving father. Never would he allow a child of his to feel less than beloved.

Jack's eyes flicked back to him mother, and he noted how she had not changed much in appearance in the few years he had been away. She was dressed as elegantly as she always did, though she was wearing something Jack was entirely unused to. A smile. Cecily did look genuinely besotted with Perrie.

Could she ... perhaps ... have changed?

But she had never written him. Jack, in turn, had not written to her either. For better or worse, he supposed he was about to learn.

The guests began to filter out, saying their goodbyes around sundown, and the servants were quick to return the dining room to its usual state. The footmen set the table for a normal meal, and Jack soon found himself standing in the same room as his immediately family.

It was not long after the cake was served that Cecily had noticed Jack, and she had given him a nod and a smile in acknowledgement. Jack had managed to return the gesture stiffly.

When it was finally just family, Adam held Perrie in his arms and brought her over to Jack. In seeing her from this close, Jack could now see how large her blue eyes were. They were like saucers and were focussed entirely on him. Jack suddenly felt nervous. He had never really been around a young child before.

Out of the corner of his eye, Jack could see that Mrs Denham was distracting Cecily in conversation, and Jack thanked God for her in that moment.

"Perrie, this here is your Uncle Jack. Uncle Jack, this is Perrie," introduced Adam softly.

Jack couldn't help grinning. "You're a father," he observed, almost in disbelief.

"I know, we cannot get rid of her. We tried putting her outside, but she kept coming back," Adam said teasingly, and Jack nearly snorted, and it felt good to feel a spark of amusement.

"You're horrid," accused Grace in false admonishment.

Perrie, meanwhile, stared at Jack curiously. Adam moved his hands to under Perrie's arms and held her out to Jack, motioning for him to take her. Jack, who had never held a child before, awkwardly replaced Adam's hands with his and took the sudden weight of Perrie.

The moment her father released her, Perrie started to wriggle and complain, her lip trembling as though she was about to start crying and moaning. Jack panicked and thrust her back at Adam.

"Oh, she doesn't like me," he noted quickly.

"She just doesn't know you yet," replied Adam, accepting Perrie back. She settled immediately and chirped something to him about a doll.

Perrie was put to sleep a little while later, and Jack found himself seated at his family's dining table. He sat between Adam, who was at the head, and Susanna, strategically, he though, and Cecily was seated opposite Adam at the other head. The Denhams filled the remaining chairs, though Claire was an obvious omission.

Jack heard Mrs Denham quietly grumble to Kate that she was going to give Claire a stern talking to when they returned home. She was clearly displeased with her failure to appear, and perhaps had not seen Claire's state when she had been in attendance at the party.

Jack hoped that whatever the reason, Mrs Denham showed her mercy.

As dinner was served, and Jack speared an asparagus stalk with his fork, Cecily finally broke her silence, and it set Jack's teeth on edge.

"So, Jack, are you permanently returned to Ashwood?" she asked nonchalantly.

Jack met her eyes briefly. "I don't know," he replied. It was honest.

"Mother," Adam said tersely.

"What?" exclaimed Cecily. "It was a simple question. Are you not curious?"

Adam jaw tensed.

"Jack was finding himself in London, you see, Mrs Denham," explained Cecily, in a condescending tone that Jack knew all too well.

"For God's sake," hissed Adam under his breath. "I asked for one day."

"Adam," Grace uttered as she placed her hand on top of his to calm him.

Jack knew that Cecily would not approve of his behaviour, and she would never understand his motives. Even if she had changed by including families like the Denhams into their circles, she was a well brought up lady and Jack was a well brought up disappointment to her.

"Oh, well, London," said Mrs Denham awkwardly. "Now, I have never been. Is it exciting?" she asked Jack.

"Terribly, Mrs Denham," confirmed Jack quietly.

"Though I do not believe that you would frequent the establishments that my son familiarised himself with while in town, Mrs Denham," interjected Cecily as she sipped her wine. "We lived there for some years, after all." Cecily's eyes flicked to Jack. "I have many friends, and by all reports, Jack spent little time studying or bettering himself. I do not quite understand how one finds their purpose when their tongue is inside a –"

"Mother!" shouted Adam, standing up from the table, causing the crockery to rattle and the table to shake.

Jack couldn't take that. He threw his fork down on his plate, creating a loud clatter, and he shoved his chair back so forcefully that it fell over behind him as he stormed out of the dining room. Behind him, Jack could hear Adam scolding Cecily, but Jack was not going to listen to her protests.

His legs took over his racing mind and brought him to what once was his place of refuge. The library had not changed much at all, and the smell of books was instantly comforting. The library was dark, save from the glow of the fireplace, and the few candelabras that were lit.

Just as Jack was about to go over to the shelves and choose a title to lose himself in for an hour before he found the willingness to show his face again, he heard a whimper.

"Who's there?" came a soft, female voice.

Jack turned his head towards the voice, and he saw a small, shadowed figure lean out from behind one of the sofas. "Jack ... Beresford," he replied quietly. "Who are you?"

When she stood up, the glow of the fire illuminated her face, and Jack realised that this was where Claire had disappeared to. Even from where he stood, he could see that her eyes were swollen from crying, and her face was flushed with emotion.

"Miss Claire," Jack realised softly. "Would you like me to fetch Grace? Or your mother?"

"No!" cried Claire, so loudly that she clapped her hand over her mouth quickly after. "No," she said again, adjusting the volume of her voice. "No, please, do not say that you have seen me ... I can't ..." A sob suddenly ripped through Claire's chest and she buried her face in her hands.

Jack went to her, not knowing at all if it was the right thing to do, or if he should ignore her wishes and fetch her sister. All he could think to do in that moment was to pull a clean handkerchief from his pocket and touch her arm gently so that she might look up and see it.

Tears streamed down Claire's face as she accepted the hand-kerchief. She immediately wiped her eyes, though they were red and raw.

"Are you ill?" Jack pressed. "Do you need a doctor? Please, Miss Claire, what is wrong with you?"

"What is right with me?" Claire miserably countered in dis-belief. "I thought everything was right ..." She blew her nose, the tip of it becoming pink. "If Grace knew ... if my mother knew ... oh, but they will," she worried to herself in a shaky, frightened voice. "Everyone will know ... and Grace will have been right. What will she think of me? Oh, she will hate me! Mama will hate me!" Claire was practically trembling, and Jack didn't know what to do or say to stop it. All he knew was that something terrible had happened and Claire was terrified. What could possibly scare her so much?

"Claire," Jack said firmly, placing a hand on her upper arm to steady her. His tone brought Claire out of her thoughts and her frightened blue eyes looked up at his. Lord, he could see her fear as clear as day. Jack felt an overwhelming urge to take it away, however he could. No woman should be as frightened as this. "Tell me what has happened to you," he demanded, quite forcefully indeed.

Claire's lower lip trembled, and her brows furrowed as her eyes filled with tears once again. "I ... I ... I am with child!" she whispered fearfully, helplessly.

Of everything that Jack might have considered, this was certainly not what he had expected. But as soon as Claire said the words aloud, he understood her terror. She was a young girl, compromised ... unwed. Her reputation would disintegrate ... her family shamed ... his family, too. This would be a scandal that would never leave her, and she would never marry, of if she did, it would be disastrously beneath her. Her life was over before it had even begun.

As the images of society headlines left Jack's mind, his attention resettled on the frightened girl before him, shaking so much she might have damaged her teeth. She was not the only one at fault here. A man, whomever he may be, was responsible for her.

"Mama will never speak to me again," realised Claire, her voice so quiet that Jack barely heard it. "Grace will never speak to me again. Kate will never speak to me again. Both of them married with children of their own, and I ..." Claire whimpered.

"Who is responsible for this?" Jack demanded to know forcefully. "Tell me so at once." No man, no decent man, allowed such a series of events.

"I can't," stressed Claire. "He ... he won't ... he has ... abandoned ... he doesn't love me." She looked to have shocked herself with her own words.

Jack had to let go of Claire's arm as he felt his hand clenching and he didn't want to hurt her in anger, but he felt his blood boiling. She wasn't attacked. She was tricked. Claire's innocence had been preyed upon by a lecherous scoundrel and he had left her in this state. A vile blackguard indeed!

"For God's sake, tell me his name!" Jack demanded, though Jack did not know whether he would force the rake to marry her, or if he would challenge him to a duel with how angry he was feeling.

"I can't ... he said ..." but Claire couldn't finish her sentence.

Jack did not need her to. He had imagination enough for what the bastard might have said. He tried to push his anger out of his mind so that he might begin to think about what to do for Claire. She was in a very serious, very precarious position. He had never before seen a woman so afraid in his life, and every fibre of his being wanted to take her fear away.

"I thought I could face them, but I can't," whispered Claire. "I can't have them disappointed in me. I can't know what that feels like."

A pain from deep within Jack throbbed.

"I don't know what to do."

Claire's eyes were closed as Jack looked down at her frightened face. He knew the exact pain she feared, and yet Claire was going to be faced with far worse than her family's disappointment. Her life would never be the same again, and this man, the man who was responsible for this, had threatened her, most likely, and would get away with it. Jack had lived for a very long time with his woes, his troubles that he could never seem to mend properly. Nothing he seemed to do was right.

Except for this. This was right. Claire was an innocent, a victim of a dishonourable man. She would be disgraced for believing the lies he told her. He could not in good conscience allow Claire to fall. Jack had the power to take her pain away, and maybe ... perhaps by the grace of God, it might take his own pain away someday, too.

CHAPTER 4

"Please," begged Claire suddenly. "Please, you mustn't say a word." Claire could not believe that she had opened her mouth thus. How could she have been so foolish? And to confess such a thing to a gentleman?

The walls of her life were already caving in, but Claire felt as though she were about to be buried under the rubble. It would be moments, mere moments before her mother, her sisters, the whole family found out the truth. They would know what she was, and Claire felt petrified at even the thought.

In a panic, a grief-stricken panic, she had unburdened her heart onto Jack Beresford. Logically, Claire knew that she could not keep such a secret hidden for long, but surely, she would have a little more time. She needed to come up with a story, and excuse, for her pure and utter stupidity at believing ... Claire could not even finish the thought. Thinking about him, seeing his beautiful, cruel face in her mind, hurt her very soul.

For a brief, a very brief moment, Claire believed that she, Grace, and Kate were all going to be happily wed mothers. To have three daughters married and settled, Claire knew that her mother would be so proud to have achieved such a feat without the assistance or dowry from their late father.

Oh, he dear papa. Claire knew that in years to come, she would be glad that her father was not alive so see her like this. But her mother was, and this would kill her. She would die for the shame. Claire was going to disgrace her entire family ... and in a matter of moments.

Claire dared to look up into the hard, hazel gaze belonging to Jack Beresford. She couldn't see his thoughts but for the fixed scowl on his face, and Claire immediately wanted to vanish, to fall through the floor. What he must think of her. He had to be thinking about her stupidity. She was another foolish girl to be so easily deceived into believing a man so far above her might actually be in love with her. Oh, Claire felt wretched, and she couldn't look at Jack for another minute knowing what awful things must have been going through his mind.

She was not oblivious to what Jack Beresford got up to in London. Grace worried about him all the time because Adam worried about him all the time. He, no doubt, probably knew all about girls like her.

"Please," she begged again. "Please, I know what you must think of me," her voice broke, "but you cannot say a word. I will tell them ... but you mustn't out me ... not yet. I need to ... to ..." To what, she didn't know.

"You need to be married. Immediately."

Jack's tone was sharp, quick, determined. So much so that it all but made Claire jump backward in surprise. But it made Claire want to cry again. Yes, that had been what she thought would happen! But he, Arthur, had no intention of marrying her.

"He won't have me," Claire whispered, heartbroken. "No one will. Not now."

"Will you marry me, Claire?"

Claire was quite certain that her heart had stopped beating, her brain had all but melted, and her ears had deafened, for she certainly had not just heard a proposal from Jack. She met his gaze again, staring up at him in utter disbelief.

While Jack's eyes were still hard, Claire did believe that she saw concern and sincerity beyond the anger. Perhaps ... could it be ... that he was on her side?

Was he ill? Why on earth would he offer his hand to her when he could have anybody? He could have a proper lady, and not a foolish village girl who fell for the first handsome man she had noticed.

After these thoughts crossed her mind, Claire became quite certain that she had misheard him, or her had misunderstood her. There was absolutely no possibility that a man like Lord Jack Beresford would ever offer to marry a girl like Claire, even if she were not in the family way.

Grace was the exception, but Adam had been hers since the schoolroom.

Jack was not in love with her.

"You misunderstood me," she insisted. "I asked you not to say anything," she repeated fragilely. "I promise, I will tell my family, but I cannot have you out me, please."

Jack frowned, his brows knitting together. "Out you?" he repeated. "Claire, I am offering to marry you," he repeated. "You need a husband, and I am not married."

Claire needed to sit down, and for the lack of sofas in her immediate vicinity, she sank to the floor, her hands out in front of her. She clung onto the pile of the rug for fear she might float away.

What in the world was happening? This had to be a sort of joke, a trick. Claire felt as though she was being hoodwinked for the second time that day, and her poor heart could not take it. "This is not funny," she said, meaning to whisper, but her voice sounded more like a vicious hiss.

She saw Jack sink to his knees, before crossing his legs on the floor as he sat down in front of her. Claire looked up at him, wanting to find falsehoods in his eyes, but she doubted her ability to spot them. She had already failed dismally in this area.

He looked so like his brother. The eyes, the shape of the nose and his mouth, the strength in his shoulders. His hair was darker, slightly curlier, than Adam's, and a few wayward curls fell into his eyes as he peered at her. He was a handsome man, one whom could have any woman of his choosing.

"I am not laughing," murmured Jack in reply.

"I am carrying the child of another man." She had not meant her words to sound like an insult. Really, they tasted horrid on her tongue. It was astonishing to believe her capable of such a truth.

"Yes, I am aware. You told me. I understand how human biology works, Claire," Jack replied dryly.

"Why then?" she asked in disbelief. "Why would you ever want to marry me?"

Jack was quiet for a moment, and Claire held her breath. She had met Jack Beresford all of a handful of times and had not seen him since Grace and Adam's wedding nearly three years ago. What sort of man offered to marry a woman with whom he was so little acquainted?

"What do you gain?" Claire pressed, before Jack answered her. "My family have no money. Adam married Grace without a dowry. I have nothing for you. My mother's house will go to my brother ... I have nothing!"

Oh, how could Arthur do this? Surely, surely there had to be a mistake. Three years could not be abandoned so easily. One had to be truly heartless and she could not believe he was so! Was he scared? Claire certainly was! Did she need to give him a moment to be frightened before he came around?

"Claire, you are a victim of someone," Jack said simply, sympathetically.

The word "victim" made her lower lip tremble yet again. How she didn't want to be. And yet, Claire knew in her heart that Jack was right.

"And this is the right thing to do," Jack insisted. "I have my reasons, but you have very little choice. Your family ... well, you family may come around to the idea. They would probably be the first to come around to such an event, but stranger things have happened. But the country is unforgiving. Word will inevitably get out, and you and this family will be forever tarnished. I hate it, but it will happen. Believe me, I have had my fair share of scandals. But one like this? You shall never escape it."

Claire hated that possibility, and she knew there was a possibility that her family would never come around. "You could have anyone," she whispered.

Jack pressed his lips together. "What does it matter?"

Claire lifted one of her hands off of the rub to rest on her belly. She watched as Jack's eyes flicked down to it momentarily, and she wished she could have read his expression. "I don't believe that you, that any man, could raise another's child."

"Life is hard enough, filled with enough people to constantly remind you that every one of your choices is wrong. To then additionally punish a child with the burden of illegitimacy?" Jack shook his head. "My conscience won't have it, even if his can."

Claire knew that he was referring to Arthur, even though he did not know the identity of the child's father.

"If we marry Claire, the child will be mine. It will bear my name. Be raised as my blood." He took a breath. "No one need ever know. No one."

Whatever foolishness was left within her, Claire used it to believe Jack. She believed her was sincere, and that he would truly marry her and take responsibility for Arthur's son or daughter. Jack, by some miracle, was sitting before her, offering her a miracle on a silver platter.

And Claire knew that she had no other choice, no other option to save herself and her family from disgrace. She had to become Jack Beresford's wife. She would be one of many girls, most likely, who were forced to marry for getting into such trouble. Forced to marry men whom they did not love to prevent scandal.

Claire had spent the last three years of her life imagining what it would be like when she and Arthur could finally be wed. She had imagined a life filled with love and children. She imagined loving him until they were old and grey. Hers would be a happy life, and a happy marriage. They would be faithful to one another, and raise dear, darling children.

In an afternoon, that future had vanished, and her only option was a marriage of convenience, like so many before her. A life shared between a couple who did not love each other. A couple who did not really know each other. And what would Jack expect from her? The notion made her stomach churn.

"I will look after you, Claire," Jack promised. "Will you marry me?"

Claire willed herself not to sob again, but she couldn't help it as her eyes welled up as she nodded. She knew it was the right thing, and the only thing she could do. She only wished that the idea of being married off in such haste did not make her want to curl up in a ball and never wake up.

Jack nodded once, formally. "Alright," he said. "I will have to seek a special license from the bishop in order for us to marry quickly. We will also have to come up with a story, something feasible that our families will believe."

As soon as he started speaking of plans, Claire felt numb. She wondered if she ought to condition herself to feel this way.

"Or would you rather tell them the truth, but protect yourself with this marriage?" Jack suggested tentatively.

Claire stiffened. Lord, if she did not have to confess this to her family, then she wouldn't. No matter her indifference towards him, she prayed for God to bless Jack's decency. "No," she uttered. "If there is a way for me to stay good in their eyes, then I want it."

CHAPTER 5

J ack surprised himself with how easily, and how quickly, he formed a plan to make such a union believable. With every word he spoke, he felt himself reaching toward something, a future unknown, but one that had to be better than the endless abyss he was currently living in.

But he only needed to look down at Claire to convince himself that this was the right decision. She was so hurt, so vulnerable, and she needed him. Jack could not recall ever being needed, and after years of walking in circles, this could well be his first honourable decision.

"Wait!" cried Claire, her voice barely above a whisper as they approached the dining room together. She seized Jack's forearm to stop him mid-stride. "No, this is madness."

She was trembling. Jack wondered if she was going to go into shock. "Claire," he said softly. "Everything will be alright," he promised.

"But what if they hate me?" Claire worried, and Jack could see in her eyes that she genuinely thought her family would hate her. Hate her for getting married? Or hate her for marrying him? Jack didn't know.

Either, or, Jack knew that Claire would never be hated by her family. They were loving, decent people. He had always envied Adam's friendship with Grace as a boy. Not because he wanted to be her friend, but because Adam had an open invitation into the Denhams' house. Theirs was a true family home, and it was no wonder Adam spent so much time there.

"Your family could never hate you, Claire."

His family, on the other hand ...

Jack knew his brother would never give up on him. Adam was terribly persistent. Susanna saw the best in him, though she was innocent enough that she did not know half of what he had been up to in London. Their mother, however, knew all. Jack knew that he had not done much to endear himself to Cecily Beresford, but ... once in a while ... being given the benefit of the doubt by that woman ... well, it would mean something.

Claire nervously nodded her head.

"For God's sake, smile," he urged, his voice soft. "You're engaged. We're happy."

Claire exhaled shakily as she forced herself to smile, though it looked more like a grimace. Jack reached up tentatively to brush the tears from underneath her eyes away with his thumbs. He didn't react when Claire flinched at his touch, though he couldn't deny that it was a little disheartening.

But he knew this wouldn't be simple. He didn't know if it would ever be simple. Would they one day have the sort of bond that Adam shared with Grace? Jack didn't know. Perhaps that was a once in a lifetime miracle.

"Alright." Claire nodded, exhaling, her voice decidedly less shaky. She curled her arm around Jack's, trying to make the movement as natural as possible.

Jack pushed open the door to the dining room, and he heard the sounds of silverware hitting plates as the diners viewed the sudden intruders.

Jack's eyes met with Adam's immediately, as he was sitting directly opposite him at the head of the table. He was slumped in his chair was a foul expression on his face, though the moment he saw Jack, he straightened his posture. His expression grew cautious when he saw that Jack was leading Claire into dinner.

And he was not the only one.

"Claire!" cried Grace. "We had wondered where you'd got to." She rose to her feet, and Adam did as well. Jack could see the look of concern on his sister-in-law's face.

"Mother has something to say to you, Jack," Adam said next, clearing his throat and motioning for Cecily to speak.

But Cecily's perceptive gaze was focussed on Claire's arm, and how it was wrapped around Jack's in a familiar way.

"Everyone," announced Jack. "I have asked for Miss Claire Denham's hand in marriage and she has accepted."

Jack did not think he had ever seen a room full of jaws collectively drop before, though he had not entirely imagined what this reaction would be in the twenty minutes between discovering Claire in the library and announcing their engagement.

Adam was truly astonished. Grace was in utter shock. Mrs Denham was less so, though her bewilderment was less so. She appeared to be ... pleased, perhaps? Cecily looked furious, and Jack could not have predicted anything less.

Susanna, dear Susanna, leapt up from her chair to come over to them, kissing both Claire and Jack on the cheek.

"Oh, my warmest congratulations!" she cried. "How ever did you both keep such a secret?"

"Yes, I should like to know," Cecily almost growled. "Considering how you have been carrying on in London, one would have never guessed an engagement was on the horizon. And to Miss Claire, no less."

Jack glared at her. He did not know if that was a slight against Claire, or indeed him, but he knew that Cecily was displeased. She and Mrs Denham had become friends, of sort, before he left for London and he wondered if she would openly insult her youngest daughter. If not, then it was directed towards him.

"Claire and I have been corresponding in secret ever since I returned to London," lied Jack coolly. "We both agreed that upon my return for Perrie's birthday, that we would discuss marriage. And luckily for me, Claire agreed. We want to be married right away, and so I plan to seek a special license."

They burned the letters so as not to be discovered prematurely before anything was decided. That was the next answer should anyone inquire after the correspondence.

But they didn't.

They continued to simply stare in shock.

"I am ... very pleased," Claire said, speaking for the first time since entering the dining room. Much to Jack's chagrin, she sounded less than pleased. He willed her to make it more convincing. "I was nervous upon coming here today, knowingthat my possible betrothed would be here. I am sorry for keeping this correspondence a secret." The latter part of the speech as slightly more convincing.

Though Grace did not appear fooled at all. Her brow was deeply furrowed as she studied her younger sister. Jack wanted to step in front of Claire to stop this assessment lest she discover the truth.

"Well, Jack," remarked Adam. "I am bemused, as is much of our party this evening, I believe. However, you have certainly made a fine choice, and I am pleased that you are taking such a positive step forward. I offer you congratulations." He nodded approvingly.

Much to his surprise, Jack felt an odd sense of pride at receiving such an approval. He stepped forward with Claire on his arm as Adam called for champagne. Jack pulled out her chair before sitting down beside her.

Claire avoided Grace's inquisitive gaze for the entire evening. Slowly but surely, the entire party seemed to accept what had transpired. Congratulations were offered, plans were made, and before Claire knew it, it was quickly decided that they both should spend their honeymoon in London before making their home at Ashwood.

Jack was better at this than she. Deception, that was. He seemed to lie easily, to convince his family of falsehoods. Claire, really, ought to have been better at it as well considering she had been telling her own falsehoods, but she supposed to motivation of what she thought had been true love had helped her along. Tonight, it was better if she kept her mouth shut and nodded whenever someone asked her if she was happy or excited.

Claire wondered why Jack was so practised in falsehoods.

Weddings were exciting affairs, and there was much to organise in such little time. Claire could see that her mother was getting more excited by the minute. She imagined that Mrs Denham truly believed that she had been lucky enough to have three daughters marry for love. This morning, Claire would have thought this to be true.

Oh, the horrid thought entered her head without her realising, and Claire was minutes away from bursting into tears. She willed herself to think of happy things, but her mind was still filled with her own pain and heartbreak.

Regretfully, Claire knew that her lapse in control had been noticed by Grace.

At the end of the evening, Grace would not hear of a carriage been called, and insisted on them all staying the night. Claire knew her sister was normally kind enough to make such an offer, but she also knew of Grace's ulterior motive.

She feigned severe fatigue after such a day to deter her mother's entering into her bedroom for a debriefing, but no such excuse would work on Grace. Claire was alone in her bedroom for all of three minutes practising her responses before the door was opened rather forcefully.

Grace had not even changed out of her gown. She must have come straight from the nursery.

"What on earth is going on?" Grace demanded to know, shutting the door behind her.

Claire looked at her eldest sister and prayed that her expression was neutral. She had always looked up to Grace. Grace was six years older than Claire, and always making decisions for the benefit of others. When their dear father had died, she had taken it upon herself to support the family. Claire could only ever aspire to be like Grace.

And how was she to know that her very own love story, one that would mirror Grace's marriage to Adam, would end in utter ruin? Claire then supposed she should have known, but she could never confess such foolishness.

Not to Grace. Not when she had been the one to speak against Arthur Slickson from the very beginning. But had Claire listened? No. She certainly had not. She had merely convinced herself that she saw something in Arthur that Grace couldn't see.

"I don't know what you mean," uttered Claire as nonchalantly as she could muster.

Grace shook her head, but she wore a sympathetic expression as she crossed the bedroom to join Claire. "Claire, I am worried sick about you right this minute," Grace stressed. "Where did this come from? You can't have been corresponding with Jack all this time. We would have known."

"No, you wouldn't have," retorted Claire. They hadn't known she had been seeing Arthur all this time, and so that was not a lie. "We kept it well hidden. You needn't be worried about me."

Grace scoffed. "Claire, be serious," she appealed. "Even you have to admit this is sudden. And a special license? You are not even having a moment to think about this!"

Claire did not have moments. Every day that passed was a day further into her pregnancy.

"Claire, I'm terribly worried about you, and I do not like that I am feeling this concern. When you arrived, it was not nerves that I saw on your face. Darling, I have known you your entire life. I know your every expression. I know when you are happy, and I know when you are sad, and I know when you are in pain. And Claire, my dear, Claire, you were in pain today." Grace grabbed hold of Claire's hands and sat down with her on the edge of the bed.

Claire was holding her breath. Every fibre of her being wanted to confess the truth to Grace. She wanted to confide in her. But she could see it in the concern in Grace's clear, blue eyes. If she knew what Claire had done ... if she knew how far Claire had fallen ... she could not disappoint Grace.

"You can tell me, you know," Grace urged softly. "Whatever it is, you can tell me."

Claire wouldn't cry. She willed herself not to cry. Not this. She couldn't tell Grace this. "I'm sorry for not telling you about Jack," she uttered quietly.

Grace's face fell, and she recoiled slightly. Claire heard her swallow loudly as she thought of what to say next. "Claire, my eyes were not deceiving me. Something isn't right," she persisted. "If you are in pain, I want to know. I want to help you. I don't understand how you can be in pain one minute, and then engaged the next. You don't look happy. How did this happen? Will Jack make you happy? Is this what you really want? Because if you have changed your mind, it is alright. I will help you whatever it is." Grace was rambling in her concern, firing question after question.

"Jack is a very good man," Claire said, with as much confidence as she had had all evening. She vehemently believed these words. "And marriage is what I want."

Marriage to whom, however, was a different question altogether.

Grace wasn't satisfied. "As much as the duchess can be very
good, you know how she can be quite blunt. She speaks the
truth, though. Darling, Jack has not led a chaste life in London.
Are you aware of this?"

"I am aware of the follies of men, Grace," Claire murmured.

All too well.

Grace frowned in disbelief. "Well ... well, how can you accept
it?"

"Perhaps you and I are different, Grace," Claire remarked,
knowing her sister could never know how different they were.

CHAPTER 6

Jack was successful at procuring a license from the archbishop. How he had managed it, Claire hadn't known, but she was glad of it. A license meant that their impending marriage was not subject to the traditional three Sundays of banns. She could not afford to wait three weeks.

That success, however, did not mean that their engagement was not announced to the parish. The announcement was made just as soon as the license was procured, and the news spread like wildfire, as often swift marriages did. Theirs was even more astounding given their dramatic differences in situation.

Just how had another one of those Denham girls done it? Such was the question on every curious villager's lips.

It was the Wednesday after Perrie's second birthday, and the wedding was scheduled for Sunday. There was to be no grand affair, with only a wedding breakfast provided for their immediate family. Claire couldn't stomach the idea of onlookers watching her every move and suspecting something was wrong. What was bad enough was Grace already knew something was wrong, and Claire had not yet confessed it.

She never could. Claire sat at the small dressing table in her bedroom, the tired mirror resting on the tabletop. She had stopped brushing her hair to stare at herself, almost astonished that she barely recognised the face staring back at her.

Had there been a day in the last three years when she was not smiling? The muscles in her face seemed to have forgotten how. Smiling seemed like the hardest thing in the world, and yet she knew an even more troubling feat lie ahead on Sunday.

Bless Jack Beresford. She would pray that God blessed him for his decency. But never could she have predicted she would be marrying a man she did not love, or even know.

Her eyes, which had always been bright and wide, were startlingly icy and hollow, the shadows underneath indicative of the trouble she was having sleeping. Despite the fact she was growing, or would be, her face looked thinner, as though in the days since Arthur had revealed himself, she had lost weight. Claire realised that she had barely eaten anything, food having since lost its lustre.

Claire was startled by a knock at the door, and her mother appeared soon after. She struggled into the room on her cane, and Claire leapt to her feet to assist her.

"I'm alright," Mrs Denham assured her, holding up a hand to stop her. "Jack Beresford is here," she revealed. "Downstairs. He has come to ask you to walk with him. I have given him permission." But as she looked upon Claire's face, she frowned with concern. "Oh, Claire, what is it? You look tired. Is it nerves?"

Mrs Denham had not disapproved of the match at all. Nor had she questioned it. Perhaps she believed Claire romantic enough to not ever accept a man without love, and so she believed the tale of their secret correspondence. Claire hated how much she had lied to her mother. Not only with regards to Jack. Really, Mrs Denham had not known what was in Claire's heart for a long time.

"Yes, Mama," confirmed Claire breathlessly. "Just nerves."

Mrs Denham smiled. "Everyone is a little nervous before their wedding," she assured her. "Even those who have been concealing their attachments," she chided teasingly, bending over to kiss Claire on the cheek. "Come now, let me help you to ready yourself as the poor man does not want to wait forever."

"I thought I ought to call," Jack said quietly as he and Claire walked together down the main street of the village. He kept his voice low as everyone they passed looked upon them inquisitively. "I know our engagement was only announced yesterday, but how would it look if I did not call between then and our wedding?"

Claire involuntarily shuddered and she hoped that Jack didn't notice. If he did, he certainly did not say anything. "No, quite right," Claire agreed. "Very astute of you."

"Then, perhaps you might take my arm?" Jack lifted his forearm and Claire jumped, before staring at it for a moment. "You are going to need to stop flinching away from me as though I have leprosy, Claire," Jack uttered dryly.

"I am sorry," muttered Claire as she took Jack's arm.

"Your sister won't speak to me, you know," Jack informed her as they continued to walk.

Claire's eyes widened. "What?"

"She doesn't believe the lie, and she thinks me some sort of villain who had pressured you. She has not said any of this, but it is quite simple to deduce," Jack continued.

Claire bit down on her bottom lip. Jack didn't deserve that treatment. Not at all. "I am sorry," she said again, only this time much more sincere. "Grace, she –"

"She is a protective elder sister, fear not," interjected Jack. "I have been called much worse than the words that are floating around in her head."

As much as Claire did not want to say the next words, her conscience wouldn't allow her to stay quiet. "It's not too late, you know," she said softly. "If you didn't go through with it ... you don't have to. You don't deserve unkind treatment from my sister, from anyone. You deserve more than ... well, me."

Jack stopped, his abrupt movement drawing attention from observers. He seemed to notice that, and so he kept them moving. "I will not abandon you," he promised. "I knew the moment you confessed this to me that this was the right thing to do. But, if it makes you feel better, I suppose I have realised my motives are not entirely altruistic."

Claire frowned. "How so?" she asked.

"Well, as you must know, my mother and I do not share a particularly loving relationship. Pigs will fly before that woman found anything to approve of with regards to my life." Jack's jaw clenched for a moment as he brushed off the tense emotion he felt. "I know she has plans for my redemption. In her eyes, of course. My marriage to some extraordinarily rich and insufferable debutante. I know that you would not be her choice for me. And I suppose that pleases me a little."

Claire could believe that, certainly. Grace had spent months, years really, afraid of that woman. They seemed to have formed an understanding in years past, but she was definitely a tricky woman to please.

"I don't know what the future holds, but we are both uniquely motivated to make this choice," Jack continued, his voice trailing off a little, giving Claire an impression that there was something that he was leaving out. "Don't question me." It was not a demand, but an appeal, and Claire nodded. "Now, I don't want you to take this as an insult, but you look tired, thinner even. Are you well?"

They were now insight of the forge, and Claire wondered what Kate would have to say now that she had had a few days to mull over the idea of Claire's sudden engagement. No sooner had the thought popped into her head, she noticed a very familiar man leaning up against the side of the forge.

Arthur looked as though he was waiting, glaring, and as soon as he had captured Claire's attention, he walked off into the wooded area behind the forge, motioning for Claire to follow him.

Claire froze.

Jack tensed immediately. "Really, I did not mean it as an insult," he insisted. "I apologise. I only wonder after your health, and the health of ..." he trailed off.

Claire felt her heart, her stomach, and everything else inside of her tense, squeeze, and then shatter all at once as the overwhelming pain, shock, and grief that she had been trying to conceal bubbled to the surface, threatening to explode.

Arthur wanted her to follow him. What could he possibly have to say after he had treated her so ill? Did he have more cruelties to sling at her?

Or ... or ... did he want to apologise? Did he realise his mistake? Did he want to make amends?

"Please," Claire whispered. "I need to go and visit with my sister. She lives just there at the forge." Claire pointed ahead.

Jack looked very remorseful, truly believing he had offended Claire. "Allow me to escort you," he offered. "Perhaps I could meet her and her husband outside of a tumultuous Beresford dinner party."

"No," Claire said, all too quickly. "I can manage." She removed her hand from Jack's arm.

"When I said 'tired', I meant ..." Jack sighed, placing his hand on his forehead. "Tell me I have not dreadfully offended you."

"You haven't," promised Claire, her voice shaking, and giving her anxiety away. She was nearly breathless as the nausea rose in her throat in anticipation. "Please, I can manage. My brother-in-law will see me home."

Jack nodded, seeming to accept her words of assurance. He bowed his head, and uttered a goodbye, before turning and walking back up the street they had walked down.

Claire waited until he was well up the street before she turned on her own heel and hurried after Arthur. She bypassed the forge and entered into the woods, scanning her surroundings desperately, her heart growing with longing every second that passed.

Claire nearly yelped with fright as her hand was grabbed from behind her, and she was pushed up against a tree before she had

had a chance to breathe. She barely saw the green of Arthur's eyes before he kissed her deeply enough to take her breath away.

For a moment, for a brief, blissful moment, Claire forgot her pain. For a moment, she allowed herself to love, and feel loved. But her illusion was quickly shattered when Arthur pulled away and murmured, "I'd wager your fiancé doesn't kiss you like that."

His voice wasn't tender or loving. It was possessive, rife with jealousy and rage, and it filled Claire with a sickeningly dirty feeling that she was entirely unfamiliar with.

"What do you want?" she demanded to know; her voice as fragile as glass. She dared to look up into Arthur's eyes, the emerald eyes she'd always thought were beautiful.

Only now they were hard, wild, and unpredictable. Jealously could warp a man like nothing else. "How dare you," he accused. "How dare you flit into bed with another man."

Claire's mouth dropped open in shock, her words escaping her.

"I don't think I meant it before, but I can see now that I was right. You would open your legs for anyone. Only, don't you know the stories, Claire? Don't you know his reputation?"

"I ... I never!" Claire stammered. Her heart was thundering in her chest, and she didn't know whether to scream or cry. What was he doing? What was she doing? "What do you want from me? You sent me away. You laughed at me. You broke my heart!" Her voice finally cracked, shattered. "You fooled me into thinking you loved me. I thought you would marry me, but you left me. Arthur, you are dishonourable." How Claire wished she could sound strong and powerful as she spoke, instead of sounding like a weak, heartbroken little girl.

"Dishonourable?" repeated Arthur, a laugh escaping him. "Dishonourable? Yet you are to marry the Rake of London?"

Claire closed her eyes to attempt to regain any of her composure. No matter Jack's reputation, he certainly was not dishonourable. But Arthur took her lapse in concentration as an opportunity, and he brought himself closer to her again, cupping her face with his hands.

"You will have to accept it, dear Claire. I will be the only man to have you, no matter who you marry." He leant his forehead against hers.

Claire trembled, hating his words, which she knew were fuelled by jealousy and not affection, but loathing herself more, for missing his closeness.

"Marry him if you will, but you will always belong to me. You know that in your little head. You would do anything for me. I know from experience."

Claire's eyes were clamped shut as she held in tears, but they burst open at the sound of a twig snapping under foot, and the sudden realisation that they were not alone.

"Kindly take your hands off of my fiancée, or the next time we meet, you shall be staring down the barrel of my pistol from twenty paces away."

CHAPTER 7

Jack had started away from Claire, but something inside him was pushing him to turn around. Perhaps it was his conscience worrying over the fact that he had said something unintentionally rude. And the minute he had, he saw Claire scampering away into the woods, and not toward the forge as she had claimed.

She had lied to him.

The very notion unsettled him greatly. Jack wondered in the moment, perhaps, if that was hypocritical of him, considering that they, together, were lying to both of their families.

But they were not lying to each other.

Jack followed Claire quietly, hesitantly curious as to what might have persuaded her to attempt to deceive him. When accosted with the sight of his fiancée in the arms of another man, Jack realised that he should have been able to guess her motive.

He stood frozen, hidden by brush, watching as a man he recognised ravished Claire. She was not an unwilling participant. How ... how dare she? How dare he? Who was he? Jack knew him. What was his name? Where did Jack know him from?

When the man pulled away from Claire, Jack was about to intervene, shout something, do anything, but his legs would not move. He didn't know quite what he was feeling in that moment, but a burning fury was igniting in his belly.

"I'd wager your fiancé doesn't kiss you like that."

The man's words were cold, taunting, and possessive, like those of a scorned lover, and Jack knew for certain that this blackguard was responsible for Claire's condition.

He was responsible ... he had left her ... he had made her cry ... and yet she still went to him? What wicked spell had this lout cast upon Claire?

"What do you want?" Claire asked, her voice as soft and hesitant. Jack watched as she looked up at him in an attempt to be brave.

Lord, he wanted to go to her, to take her, but he needed to see this. He needed to see what hold this man had over her. Claire was entirely at his mercy.

His voice whipped her like a cat o nine tails, as he seethed, "How dare you! How dare you flit into bed with another man."

Shock filled Claire's face at the false accusation. She was silent, and Jack yearned to know what she was thinking.

But he continued. "I don't think I meant it before, but I can see now that I was right. You would open your legs for anyone. Only, don't you know the stories, Claire? Don't you know his reputation?"

In and amongst his fury at hearing such an accusation made, Jack suddenly remembered where he had last seen this man. The winter ball three years earlier. It was where he had first met Claire ... and he was the man to claim her for the dance after Jack. He could remember seeing the look of elation on Claire's face as he accepted defeat and stepped away from her. This was the man she had spurned him for, if that was what it could be called.

Was this how long their tryst had been going on? This man had spent three years seducing an innocent young woman, only to leave her when it mattered?

"I ... I never," stammered Claire. Her voice was frightened, fragile, and filled with emotion. "What do you want from me? You sent me away. You laughed at me. You broke my heart!" Her voice finally cracked, shattered. "You fooled me into thinking you loved me. I thought you would marry me, but you left me. Arthur, you are dishonourable."

Arthur. That was it. Arthur Slickson, Jack recalled. That cruel, evil, lying ...

Jack continued to listen to their conversation until he couldn't anymore. He listened as this man laid on another layer of manipulation into the web of dishonesty that he had spent three years weaving in Claire's head. Somehow, he had made a once bright and innocent young girl believe that she was deserving of this treatment.

Jack snapped, quite literally as a twig broke under his foot as he lunged out, when he heard Arthur utter, "You would do anything for me. I know from experience."

Arthur's hands were on Claire's face, but her wide, reddened yet expressive eyes were on Jack.

"Kindly take your hands off of my fiancée, or the next time we meet, you shall be staring down the barrel of my pistol from twenty paces away."

Jack meant it. With the pure and unadulterated fury he felt, he would have challenged the man right then and there. Now knowing what he did, knowing what he had done to Claire, Jack knew that he ought to challenge him for Claire's honour, to force him to marry her.

But that couldn't happen. Claire did not deserve to be his victim forever. Jack wouldn't allow it. She deserved a good marriage, and a good man. Jack did not know if theirs would be a good marriage, but he hoped that he was a better man than the scoundrel who was standing between them.

To Jack's surprise, Arthur's hands fell, and he turned his body to properly face Jack. He had not changed much in his appearance in the three years since Jack had last seen him, perhaps only the smug expression was new.

"So, you have learned Claire's scandalous little secret?" taunted Arthur.

Jack's eyes looked past Arthur at Claire, who seemed to fold into herself, as though she was trying to appear as small as possible.

Jack could not bother replying to such a remark. "Claire," he said with quiet authority. "Please come."

Claire complied immediately, walking straight past Arthur without daring to look up at him. She came to Jack's side, and he instinctively stepped in front of her.

"Go and wait for me by the forge," Jack instructed.

"What are you going to do?" she whispered, so quietly that even Arthur might have missed it.

"Go," he repeated, and this time, Claire did not question him. She turned and left them standing there.

"Do you want to kill me?" Arthur mocked when they were alone.

"I won't deny that the thought has crossed my mind in the last quarter hour or so," replied Jack stiffly. He stepped forward, close enough to Arthur that should he have reached out his arm, he would have brushed the lapel of Arthur's coat with his fingers. "But I will tell you that you have spoken with Claire for the final time." Jack found that his voice took on a new tone, a dark, authoritative tone that he had not heard from himself before. "You are never to come near her again."

Arthur let out an amused exhale. "You confuse me," he murmured. "You could have anyone. Your connections, your name, your rank … and yet you settle for my spoiled goods? Didn't your father ever teach you that you bed those sorts of girls, Beresford? You don't marry them."

"Somehow, I do not think civilised conversation is going to get my point across," realised Jack.

Just as Arthur's brow furrowed, Jack's clenched fist connected with his jaw, projecting such force that Arthur flew back a few feet before hitting the ground. Jack shook his hand out and flexed his fingers, checking for injury, as he watched a dazed Arthur try to sit up.

As he spat blood, and perhaps a tooth, Jack leaned over him. "Come anywhere near Claire again, and I will end you," he threatened, before turning on his heel to walk away.

As he did, Arthur shouted after him in a voice marred by slurs, "You'll always know I was there first! You'll always know her bastard isn't yours!"

Jack kept walking.

He found Claire by the forge, where he had told her to wait, pulling at her handkerchief nervously. When he joined her, she gasped. Had she not been expecting him to return?

"Are you alright?" Jack asked patiently.

Claire nodded helplessly.

"Good." Jack inhaled. "I can take a lot, Claire. I have done. But I won't be lied to. You lied to me before, and that can't happen if we are to enter into this together."

"I know," whispered Claire.

Jack wanted to say a lot more. He wanted to ask her why she accepted that. He wanted to ask her if she believed she deserved his cruelty. He wanted to ask how she could love a man who treated her so ill. He wanted to ask if she knew that she was being manipulated. But it was not the time.

"Why don't you scold me?"

Claire's question caught Jack off guard, and yet it really should not have. It was what she expected, what she thought she deserved. Did he scold her? He probably told her she was stupid if ever she made a mistake, among other ungentlemanly manners.

"Because you are not a child," Jack replied, "and I am not your possessor. All I ask is honesty and transparency. It is vital if this charade is to work."

"I ... I can't believe you will still honour your proposal," said Claire tentatively. "I ... I am such a fool ... I can't believe I let him fool me again ..."

What must it have been like, Jack wondered, for Claire to tell the man she had been secretly ... courting perhaps was the right word, that she was with child, only to have him laugh at her? He had seen how very broken she was in the library the other night, and she was still so now. Jack would need to tread carefully.

"He fooled you, yes," agreed Jack, "but you saw the best in him, or at least you wanted to. And that is a very good quality, indeed. To have someone view us as our best selves is quite the ideal."

Claire dried her fresh tears with the handkerchief that she had been pulling apart. Jack reached into his pocket and produced his own. Claire accepted it with a grateful whimper.

"I will take care of you, Claire. Of you both. But you must promise me something. I ask only one thing in return."

"Yes?"

Claire's hands were trembling as she wiped her eyes, so Jack covered them with his own, helping her to dry her face.

"You cannot ever see him again," he said calmly.

If Claire was ever to be seen with Arthur Slickson, their entire marriage story would be discredited. The child outed. Their families ruined. And Jack ... well, Jack did not know if he had the stomach to ever view what he had just seen again.

"I accept your condition," Claire promised, nodding her head as her eyes watered over once more.

How protective he already felt. He could not fathom what he would feel if Arthur somehow managed to snake his way back into Claire's head. Considering his stomach had already contorted itself into painful knots, Jack wondered if he ... if they ... would survive it at all.

CHAPTER 8

Claire had a book open on her lap, but she was too nervous to read, it being her wedding day in a matter of hours. This time tomorrow night, she would be a wife. And she would not be Arthur's wife, as she had so long dreamed. She would be the wife of Jack Beresford, a man who was indeed still a great mystery to her.

Claire had kept her promise to Jack in the few days since their last meeting, though it was not hard to avoid Arthur Slickson when one kept to their bedroom. Mrs Denham, again, attributed it to nerves, and even Claire was surprised at how easy she was able to fool her mother. How good she had become at lying. It was not a talent that Claire had ever aspired to.

But late that Saturday night, Claire was disturbed by a knock on her door.

"Yes?" she called.

Mrs Denham quietly opened the door and hobbled inside, having abandoned her cane for the evening. She made quick work of shutting the door behind her and making her way to the edge of Claire's bed.

Claire abandoned her book, not that she had been reading it anyway. "Are you alright, Mama?"

Mrs Denham smiled awkwardly. "Yes, Claire," she murmured.

She did appear to be struggling with something, which made Claire terribly nervous. Did her mother bear her bad tidings? For a dreaded second, Claire suddenly thought that perhaps Jack had changed his mind.

"Oh, one would think by the third daughter, this conversation would be a little easier," Mrs Denham said under her breath. "My dear, I have come to explain things to you, to help you know what to expect tomorrow night ... your wedding night."

Claire immediately paled. Oh, dear Lord, how Claire wished she could tell her mother such a conversation wasn't necessary, for she had learned the hard way already. But to say such a thing would be to break her mother's heart, among other ruinous things.

Claire then realised that not only was it her wedding day tomorrow, but it was also her wedding night. No matter their circumstances, Jack would expect ... Claire felt green.

"You needn't appear so frightened, dear," Mrs Denham assured her. "It ... it is an act of love, after all. One which creates life."

A rogue sob escaped Claire's chest as the realisation that her mother was entirely incorrect settled within her. Life was not only created through an act of love, but also an act of deception.

"Oh, dear, my darling," cooed Mrs Denham, shuffling closer to Claire on the bed, near enough to take her youngest daughter into her arms. Claire rested her head against her mother's chest and wept. Mrs Denham stroked Claire's back comfortingly, hushing her soothingly. "Claire, I implore you to tell me why you are so upset," she begged. "Surely this cannot be just nerves."

How Claire wanted to confide in her. But she would not let herself. "I am sad to leave you, Mama," whimpered Claire, without a word of a lie. Among every emotion that was flowing within her, Claire was truly upset at the fact that her silly actions had resulted in her need to leave her mother's house.

"Leave me?" Mrs Denham chuckled quietly. "My dear, I would never let you leave me." She lifted Claire's chin with her index finger. "Your getting married does nothing to sever my love for you, just as it did not for your sisters." Mrs Denham kissed Claire's cheek. "How I wish your father was alive to give you away tomorrow. You are going to be the most beautiful bride."

When Claire had calmed herself, Mrs Denham persisted with her original reason for visiting Claire's bedroom. She explained, in as delicate and ladylike detail as possible, exactly what Claire was to experience the following evening. And in that moment, Claire was far too embarrassed to be upset. When she had no questions, Mrs Denham had expressed her surprise, adding that Kate had prepared a whole list of them. That was knowledge that she could have quite happily gone on living without.

When it came time for Mrs Denham to leave, she asked, "Is this what you truly want, Claire?"

Claire was unprepared for the question, but her emotional state masked her apprehension. "Yes, Mama," she breathed. "I am sure." She was left alone to cry soundless tears into her pillow before sleep eventually overcame her.

"Dearly beloved, we are gathered together here in the sight of God, and in the face of this congregation, to join together this Man and this Woman in holy Matrimony; which is an honourable estate, instituted of God in the time of man's innocency, signifying unto us the mystical union that is betwixt Christ and his Church; which holy estate Christ adorned and beautified with his presence, and first miracle that he wrought, in Cana of Galilee; and is commended of Saint Paul to be honourable among all men: and therefore is not by any to be enterprised, nor taken in hand, unadvisedly, lightly, or wantonly, to satisfy men's carnal lusts and appetites, like brute beasts that have no understanding; but reverently, discreetly, advisedly, soberly, and in the fear of God; duly considering the causes for which Matrimony was ordained.

"First, it was ordained for the procreation of children, to be brought up in the fear and nurture of the Lord, and to the praise of his holy Name.

"Secondly, it was ordained for a remedy against sin, and to avoid fornication; that such persons as have not the gift of continency might marry, and keep themselves undefiled members of Christ's body.

"Thirdly, it was ordained for the mutual society, help, and comfort, that the one ought to have of the other, both in prosperity and adversity. Into which holy estate these two persons present come now to be joined.

"Therefore, if any man can show any just cause, why they may not lawfully be joined together, let him now speak, or else hereafter for ever hold his peace."

There was silence in the church, and Jack had half expected Arthur Slickson to come barging through the doors revealing everything, but he didn't, and Jack felt foolish to even think him capable of doing anything honourable.

Jack stole a glance down at Claire, whose blue eyes were solely fixed on the vicar, her lips pressed firmly together, as though the force between them would stop her whole body from trembling.

Beyond her expression, she was a vision. Her gown was a pale shade of rose pink, and Jack had recognised it instantly. It was the gown she had worn to the ball three years earlier, the one she had worn upon their first meeting. It still suited her remarkably. She wore a bonnet affixed with flowers, and carried a bouquet emitting a pleasant perfume. She looked every bit the bride until one looked at her face.

The vicar continued to waffle, enjoying the sound of his own voice it seemed, before he suddenly surprised Jack by stating his full name.

"John Anthony Edward Beresford, wilt thou have this woman to thy wedded wife, to live together after God's ordinance in the holy estate of Matrimony? Wilt thou love her, comfort her, honour, and keep her in sickness and in health; and, forsaking all others, keep thee only unto her, so long as ye both shall live?"

Jack had attended one wedding in his lifetime, and it has been his brother's. The man who had been so dreadfully in love since his was barely out of the nursery had meant his vows whole-heartedly. Despite knowing it was the right thing to do, he felt a little uneasy in responding, "I will." Comfort her and keep her, yes. But love her? Would it be like that? Could it be like that? Would Claire ever allow that?

"Claire Frances Denham, wilt thou have this man to thy wedded husband, to live together after God's ordinance in the holy estate of Matrimony? Wilt thou obey him, and serve him, love, honour, and keep him in sickness and in health; and, forsaking all others, keep thee only unto him, so long as ye both shall live?"

Jack wondered if his very thoughts were running through Claire's mind. Or, was she wishing she were standing beside the vile man who had tricked her? Lord, the latter thought made him sick.

Jack did his best to mask his surprise when he heard Claire's soft voice utter, "I will."

The vicar looked up to Peter, who was stood beside Claire. "Who giveth this woman to be married to this man?"

"I do," replied Peter, as he placed Claire's hand in the vicar's.

The vicar then took Jack's right hand, before placing Claire's within it. It was then that Claire finally looked up at Jack. Her brows very furrowed slightly with anxiety, and he saw her lips wobble, but only for a moment. She was frightened, and Jack squeezed her hand, it being the only thing he could do in that moment.

Jack heard the vicar begin his vow, and he repeated, "I, John Anthony Edward Beresford, take thee, Claire Frances Denham, to be my wedded wife, to have and to hold from this day forward, for better for worse, for richer for poorer, in sickness and in health, to love and to cherish, till death do us part, according to God's holy ordinance; and thereto I plight my troth."

Their hands dropped momentarily before it was time for Claire to take him by his right hand.

Claire's voice was shaky, indicative of nerves and apprehension as she repeated after the clergyman.

"I, Claire Frances Denham, take thee, John Edward Anthony Beresford, to be my wedded husband, to have and to hold from this day forward, for better for worse, for richer for poorer, in sickness and in health, to love, cherish, and to obey, till death us do part, according to God's holy ordinance; and thereto I give thee my troth."

As their hands dropped, Claire whispered, "I mixed up your names!" in a voice so soft only he would hear.

Jack breathed a chuckle. "How many names does one need? I do not go by any of them anyway." To laugh, even quietly, and to see such a brief expression of amusement and relief on Claire's face filled him with pride.

As the vicar blessed the ring, Jack took Claire's left hand in his and let the ring linger at her knuckle. "With this ring, I thee wed, with my body, I thee worship, and with all my worldly goods, I thee endow: In the Name of the Father, and of the Son, and other Holy Ghost. Amen." Jack pushed the small ring onto Claire's finger properly.

Together, they then both knelt down before the vicar as the parish began to pray.

"Let us pray. O Eternal God, Creator and Preserver of all mankind, Giver of all spiritual grace, the Author of everlasting life; send thy blessing upon these thy servants, this man and this woman, whom we bless in thy Name; that, as Isaac and Rebecca lived faithfully together, so these persons may surely perform and keep the vow and covenant betwixt them made, whereof this ring given and received is a token and pledge, and may ever remain in perfect love and peace together, and live according to thy laws; through Jesus Christ our Lord. Amen."

An amen echoed throughout the church.

The vicar joined their hands once more, and proclaimed, "Those whom God hath joined together, let no man put asunder. For as much as John Anthony Edward Beresford and Claire Frances Denham have consented together in holy wedlock, and have witnessed the same before God and this company, and thereto have given and pledged their troth, and have declared the same by giving and receiving a ring, and by joining of hands; I pronounce that they be Man and Wife together, in the Name of the Father, and of the Son, and of the Holy Ghost. Amen."

Man and Wife. The words sent a shiver down Jack's spine as it became official, legal. He had a wife. Together with the vicar and their witnessed, the register was signed, and it could not be undone. Jack and Claire were married.

CHAPTER 9

Though the gathering may have been small, the dinner given at Ashwood House was as grand as there ever was. No expense seemed to have been spared, and Claire could not help but worry about such matters being a ruse to fool gossiping servants who may have relayed any other oddities to their neighbours and friends in the parish.

If the younger Lord Beresford and his bride were not celebrated properly, ought that be something to be suspicious about? As it was, the vicar's wife was in attendance, and Claire knew that if she were not anything but a perfect bride, the whole village would be whispering.

Jack played his part brilliantly, effortlessly so. He kept a guiding hand on the small of her back when they were standing for conversation and positioned their chairs towards each other ever so slightly when they were seated. Claire could not help but feel as though things were under control when she was near Jack.

"It will not be long until we can retire," murmured Jack quietly as the servants took their dessert dishes away.

This comment, having meant to put her at ease, did quite the opposite, in reminding Claire of what was expected of her.

She did not have more than twenty seconds to compose herself before she felt a touch on her forearm. Claire twisted to look to Grace. She was seated beside Claire as her matron of honour, though Claire had barely spoken three words to Grace since the whole engagement was announced. Grace was too inquisitive, and Claire was far too fragile to keep up her charade.

Her sister was paler, upon closer inspection by Claire. Grace's usual perfect complexion seemed to have bene marred by interruptions to her sleep. Perrie, Claire thought, was quite independent in the nursery, so Claire attributed it to her own folly.

"Are you happy?" Grace whispered, so quietly so only Claire could hear her.

"Why do people keep asking me that?" Claire retorted thoughtlessly.

"Because you ... you don't look ..." Grace pursed her lips. "I had only hoped to see a different expression upon your face on your wedding day is all."

Claire wasn't cross. How could she be? Grace only cared. Claire cared about Grace's opinion perhaps more than anyone. "Jack is a good man," she promised, only wishing Grace knew just how decent he was.

Grace mulled over Claire's words for a moment before she nodded, accepting them. "Perhaps, one day, you might tell me about the Jack that you know," she probed. "I should like to know the sort of man who could win your heart."

Claire prayed her smile was still firmly in place and convincing. Oh, how Grace already knew and disapproved of the man who had first won her heart.

"It will be announced while you are on your honeymoon trip, but I wanted to tell you quietly now ... I am with child." All apprehension and exhaustion seemed to vanish from Grace's eyes as she revealed the happy news.

Claire did her best to retain her composure as she beamed at her sister. "Oh, what happy news!" she whispered excitedly. "Does Adam know?"

Grace nodded. "Yes, we were to announce at Perrie's birthday, but ..."

Claire bit down on her lip. She could not imagine returning her sister's news and receiving the same warm reaction. If Grace's news was announced at the table now, there would be a champagne toast. If Claire's news was announced ...? Not even Jack could save her then. The dates would simply not add up.

"No matter, no matter," Grace assured her. "The longer we delay in telling anyone, the longer I avoid Cecily telling me all the tricks to ensure the child is a boy." Grace winked. "They worked wonders with Perrie, now, didn't they? Though I know both Cecily and Adam would never trade Perrie for a son."

"What are you two whispering about?" Cecily called across the table to Grace and Claire. "There seems to have been something jovial we have all missed out on."

Claire lost her tongue, realising now that her mother-in-law had just addressed her for the first time. Grace was much more practised in how to navigate the waters with Cecily Beresford. But it was Jack who spoke first.

"What is more jovial than a wedding, Mother?" he offered firmly. There was a sudden tension about Jack, and it put Claire on edge. "Well, what a terrific offering. You shall have to give our compliments to Mrs Reynolds, Cole," Jack spoke to the butler coordinating the footmen by the servants' door.

"Certainly, milord," Cole replied, bowing his head.

"If it pleases everyone, I should think my bride and I would like to retire." Jack stood up from his place setting and held his arm out for Claire. She followed suit, nervously placing her arm in his as he began to lead her away to the choruses of well-wishes.

Jack silently led Claire upstairs to the family bedrooms. On the odd occasion she stayed at Ashwood, Claire always slept in the opposite wing. They passed the bedrooms she knew, before stopping at a door she didn't, and could only assume belonged to Jack.

The minute the door was closed behind them, Claire's heart began to race as she noticed the trunk of her things that had been brought over from her house in the village. All of a sudden, her life was combined with another's, her husband's.

Her husband, who was already unbuttoning his wedding coat and discarding it on the back of an armchair.

"You can change behind the screen if you like," Jack offered, motioning to the privacy screen which stood in the corner of the room.

Claire didn't need to be told twice. She flitted to her trunk and seized a nightgown, before racing behind the screen. No sooner had she got there, she realised that there were about twelve buttons fasting the bodice of her dress, and they were quite out of reach. She silently gasped, feeling a panic set in. She could not well ring the bell for a servant. This was supposed to be her wedding night, and surely any dexterous male was capable of unfastening buttons. But then her only option was to seek assistance from Jack, and that would not do well on her nerves, which were already wreaking havoc on her poor heart.

"Jack!" she all but squeaked.

"Are you alright?" he called out.

"Would ... would you ... could you ..." Claire huffed with em-barrassment. "My buttons ... I ..."

Claire clamped her eyes shut she moment she heard Jack come behind the screen. His hands moved with perfect ease and expertise as he unfastened her buttons from their loops, as though he had done such a thing many times before. He said nothing when he finished, merely leaving her alone.

Claire opened her eyes and quickly undressed, freeing herself from her gown and undergarments, before dressing in a clean nightgown. She pulled all the pins that she could feel within her hair and held them in the palm of her hand as she took a deep breath.

Claire could do this. She told herself it would be alright. It was expected. It was part of being married. She was the one who had gotten herself into this mess in the first place. Jack was her husband and he could demand certain things –

Claire froze when she re-entered the room. Jack stood over the settee, dressed in his own nightshirt, pulling cushions away so that he could neatly tuck in a sheet that he had taken from the recently disturbed bed linens.

"What are you doing?" The question escaped her lips before she knew what she was saying.

Jack stopped to frown at her, an expression of confusion on his face. "I thought I'd bake a pie," he said facetiously. "What does it look like?" he chuckled to himself. "It was either the settee or the floor, and I'd wager this old sofa is a lot more comfortable than a fifty-year-old rug." When Jack saw that Claire was not laughing, he took the time to inspect her frightened and dazed appearance more seriously. That was when his own face fell. "Oh, did you think ...? Claire, I am not an ogre about to impose myself upon you."

Claire could have cried with relief as an enormous amount of anxiety melted away. "I would not have blamed you ..."

"Despite what you may hear about me, especially in London, know I am not a brute, especially when it comes to women." He spoke seriously, his voice low, as though he wanted Claire to believe him, to comprehend his words.

And Claire did believe him. In witnessing his kindness, she suddenly felt foolish to have thought he would take advantage of any marital rights one might have deemed he had. "Well, I ought to sleep there," Claire protested. "This is your bedroom after all."

Jack laughed again. "You will sleep in the bed and I will not hear of any arguments. Go on," he urged. "We are away in the morning. You need your rest."

"Thank you," whispered Claire, not knowing if Jack could truly appreciate the meaning behind her words. She darted across the room and climbed underneath the bed clothes.

"Oh, there is one thing we need to do," Jack said, as though he suddenly remembered something.

Claire watched him curiously as he opened and fished through the drawer beside his bed, before he produced a dagger. Of all the objects he might have presented her with, that surprised her the most. She gasped as Jack pulled back the bed clothes with one swoop, forcing Claire to quickly cover her legs with the skirt of her night dress.

Jack sat down on the edge of the bed and rolled up his sleeve. He concentrated as he suddenly pressed the blade to the edge of his wrist, and Claire nearly turned green as a steady stream of bloody began to pulse outwards. Jack did not bind the wound immediately, but he held it over the clean, white linen.

The blood dropped, one, two, three, four times, before it collected in a small stain. It was then that Jack wound a fresh handkerchief around his wrist to stop the bleeding.

"These sheets will be changed tomorrow ... the maids will see the blood," Jack explained. "When we announce that there is to be a child ... well, now there will be no suspicion."

Jack turned his back on her and went back to the settee to lie down. Immediately Claire noticed that he was too tall for the small sofa, and his feet hung off the end of it.

Claire pulled back the bedclothes, covering Jack's little bright spark on ingenuity. Lord, she hoped his plan worked.

"By the way," Jack uttered, "you were a beautiful bride. I just wanted you to know that."

CHAPTER 10

Jack's back was throbbing, and he was fairly certain his neck was twisted in some sort of unnatural way. He had to resist groaning with fatigued pain so as not to wake his sleeping wife.

Wife.

That, perhaps, was the first time Jack had ever thought the word in its now correct context. The sleeping woman in his bed was his wife. He had a wife. He was married.

Claire had cried herself to sleep. She had thought she was being quiet, soundless even, but Jack could still hear her staggered breaths. He did not know what to do or say for fear he would make everything worse.

Jack had felt helpless, which was an entirely horrid experience. This whole arrangement was meant to help, and in hearing his new bride sob into the darkness, Jack felt like a cad. But why, when his only sin was that he was not the impudent blackguard who had compromised her so dishonourably in the first place. How could such a man have so blindly fooled Claire? Jack knew that were he ever to have a daughter, she would be so fiercely under his protection that she would never be so naïve.

Eventually she had stopped crying, and Jack had learned something he hadn't known about his wife. Claire snored. Jack wondered if she knew this. When she fell into a deep sleep sometime after midnight, soft, breathy snores reached him across the room.

In lying awake on the sofa, listening to Claire's attempts to soothe herself, Jack naturally began to have second thoughts about what had transpired. Perhaps this wasn't the solution. Perhaps Claire ought to have been sent abroad to a school somewhere for ladies to become accomplished debs. The sorts of places which discreetly covered themselves as institutions for girls in Claire's position. The child could be taken in by a couple in the country, and no-one need ever know. Ought that not better than to be miserable with a husband she clearly had absolutely no regard for.

Jack had very quickly learned during his sleepless night that such a union would not satisfy him. He would give her time, of course, but he wanted affection and regard. Claire was the woman he had married, and of course he would do right by her and the child, his child, now. But if she couldn't love him ... well, he'd endured enough in his life to know that he would go out and seek regard.

As so often he had done in the past as his reputation proceeded him.

Jack rose up off of the settee and stretched his arms, before twisting his torso back and forth, determined to try and click his back into place. He heard a few satisfying pops in his bones, before he yawned with exhaustion.

Jack quickly pulled on his breeches that he had discarded the night before and changed into a fresh linen shirt from the wardrobe. He walked quietly toward the bed, intending to wake Claire, but he found himself pausing at the foot of the bed.

Gone was the look of apprehension and worry from her face. Her pale skin was flawless. Her dark hair had come loose from the plait she had fixed, and it was now in disarray across the pillow. It was natural and beautiful, and Jack quietly acknowledged that he enjoyed Claire's hair down. Her pink lips were parted in thanks to her snoring, and her small hands were supporting the underside of her cheek.

Lord, Jack knew that he could love her well in time. Perhaps he had known it from the first time he saw her at the ball. What luck it had been that the first woman he had seen in an effort to spite his mother had been Claire Denham. She had been there, safely tucked away in the back of his mind, for all this time.

To be worthy of her, Jack knew that he had to improve himself. He was not a saint and had little to show for his excellent education and incomparable connections. But if he tried, would she notice? Or would it all be for nought? Would her heart always be lost to Slickson?

His thoughts were interrupted by a sudden knock at the door, one which woke Claire up with a start. She sat upright in the bed with a gasp, peering questioningly as Jack for a second, before her startled gaze went to the door.

"Get in!" hissed Claire, throwing back the bedclothes on the other side of the bed.

But Jack immediately ran to the settee, seizing the linens and pillow he had taken the night before and raced with them back to the bed. He threw the sheet across the foot of the bed before tossing the pillow at the head, diving underneath the covers to sit beside Claire.

Claire surprised him as she moved closer to him, almost resting her head on his chest as she did. Jack hoped she could not hear his thundering heart.

"Yes?" Jack called out.

The door was opened, and a housemaid entered, curtseying, before she was followed in by Mrs Hayes carrying a large breakfast tray. The housemaid began to open the drapes as Mrs Hayes brought the tray over to the bed, setting down at the foot.

"Good morning, milord, milady," greeted Mrs Hayes, as she curtseyed before them.

Jack immediately knew something was not right. Never in his six and twenty years had Mrs Hayes called him 'milord'. He has been John for the briefest of moments before Miss Hayes, when she was his nanny, had decided that such a name was far too formal for a one-year-old. She had been the one to call him Jack, and the name had become his far more than John had ever been.

"Good morning, Mrs Hayes," replied Claire with a nervous smile. "What a treat. I have never had breakfast served to me thus before."

Mrs Hayes offered Claire a genuine smile. "You ought to get used to it, my dear. You are married now. You will have a maid, and your breakfast will be brought to you each morning upon your return from your honeymoon journey."

"But surely it is not your responsibility to serve breakfast, Mrs Hayes," said Jack reservedly, eyeing the housemaid who was now tending to the fire. "I am certain you have far better things to be tending to."

Mrs Hayes smiled sweetly, her eyes crinkling. "Oh, no, I thought this my only opportunity to see the newlyweds," she replied, "owing the fact I was not invited to the ceremony, of course."

There it was, and what an oversight indeed. For a lot of his childhood, Miss Hayes, as she was then, would often have been the only one to offer Jack a kind word in a day. Any affection he received was from her, and such was the case for Adam and Susanna both. They all loved Mrs Hayes, and in the haste of the occasion, Jack had neglected her.

Claire looked between Mrs Hayes and Jack with an expression of admonishment. "Oh, dear, Mrs Hayes, please understand there was no offense meant," she apologised on Jack's behalf. "Everything was so quick, and Jack –"

"I'm sorry," Jack interrupted, apologising sincerely. "You know I would never neglect you on purpose."

Mrs Hayes seemed to accept his apology, and smiled, though this time, she did not appear as though she were about to scold him as though he were five. "No matter," she replied. "I wanted to offer you both my heartiest congratulations. No one is more deserving of a sweet match than Jack. You will take care of my boy, won't you, milady?"

"My boy?" Jack repeated with a groan. "Mrs Hayes, I could scold you, you know."

"And I could tell your new wife that I used to wipe your bottom now, young man," retorted Mrs Hayes.

Claire giggled her musical laugh. "I will do my best, Mrs Hayes," she assured her, placing her hand on top of Jack's.

Jack had not been expecting her touch and had so reacted as Claire did whenever he touched her. Mrs Hayes frowned momentarily before dismissing whatever thought crossed her mind.

"Everything is ready for you both to depart later this morning. But for now, enjoy your breakfast. Come, Martha," Mrs Hayes beckoned, before they both curtseyed and left them alone in the bedroom.

As soon as the door was closed, both Jack and Claire burst out into an uncontrollable fit of laughter. They were turned to one another, thoroughly enjoying the expression of pure amusement on the other's face for a moment.

When Claire laughed as hard as she was, her blue eyes squinted, and her nose crinkled in a truly adorable way. Jack rested his head back on the pillows hugging an arm across his now aching stomach. Claire did the same thing.

"Grace told me Mrs Hayes was once nanny to you and your siblings." Claire's voice was almost a wheeze.

"Yes, she was," confirmed Jack. "She was so indispensable that once Susanna was grown, my parents kept her on as our housekeeper. Truly, we three are grateful, as it would have been terrible to lose her. She ... well, she loves us."

"She loves you well indeed," agreed Claire. "I do feel awful now that no one thought to invite her, even if it was not a true wedding."

"It was a true wedding, Claire," Jack replied quietly. His tone silenced Claire, and that was not his intention. He had been enjoying their momentary ease in conversation. He needed to change the subject. "Did you know that Mrs Hayes was the one to call me 'Jack' in the first place?" he asked.

"No," replied Claire. "Though I am sorry for muddling your names. I think the name 'Edward' startled me. It was my father's name, did you know?"

Jack chuckled. "What does it matter? I have too many names anyway. Susanna has three middle names. I pity her husband one day having to stumble over Susanna Augusta Theodosia Euphemia before finally reaching her surname."

Claire laughed, and Jack smiled at his triumph. "My!" she exclaimed. "I feel awfully boring now with plain, old Frances."

"I think the mamas that my mother associates with have a competition of who can gift their children the most ridiculous of names. The longer, the grander, the more syllables, the more splendid."

He watched as Claire momentarily placed her hand on her stomach and uttered, "I wonder what ..." before she stopped herself.

Jack didn't want Claire to be reluctant to discuss such matters with him for fear it would offend him. So, he finished her sentence. "What we might name the child?" he surmised.

Claire's blue eyes flashed to his as she nodded. "Would ... would he or she need such a name?" she asked tentatively.

Claire's face had fallen again, and Jack knew it would take a great deal of time for her to stop feeling unease in his presence.

"No," replied Jack simply. "We may choose whatever we like. Do you have something in mind?"

Claire shook her head, though Jack could see the falsehood in her eyes.

"I thought we agreed never to lie," he murmured.

Claire bit down on her lip. "Oh, but this one will make you hate me," she worried under her breath.

Jack surprised Claire, catching the underside of her chin gently and pulling her gaze to his. "I could never hate you," he promised her. "Tell me."

Claire frowned sadly. "Well, I suppose my first thought would be to name him after his father," she whispered shamefully. "It was my only thought, and I haven't considered it since, of course. But that is the truth."

Jack did his best to control his expression for fear his facial muscles would contort into a sneer. The very idea of that innocent child being called Arthur made his skin crawl. It also made him uneasy to wonder if Claire still thought of that man as her child's father.

Unwillingly, his mind went back to the cold, cruel words Arthur Slickson had shouted upon their meeting in the woods. Arthur had taunted Jack, telling him that he would always know the child was not his. God, he prayed that would not be the case.

"We shall choose something we both like," Jack said conclusively.

Claire scrambled out from under the covers and crawled over to the breakfast tray, turning up the two teacups. "How do you take your tea?" she asked, changing the subject. "I suppose I ought to know."

Though he doubted Claire would ever have to steep a pot of tea again, it pleased him that she wanted to know. "Milk," he replied, "and one and one half of a sugar cube."

Claire looked back at him in confusion. "One and one half?"

"I make a mess every time, but I am very particular," Jack mused with a smirk, abandoning the bedclothes as well to show her. Claire poured the tea into both cups and Jack added his own milk.

"Do you take milk?" he wondered.

"Just a splash." She nodded.

Once the teas were both milky, Jack added one sugar cube to his cup, before crushing a second in his fingers and sprinkling in half, dusting the rest onto the tea plate.

"Do you know, if you had ever had to wash a dish, I'd wager you would have learned to enjoy two sugar cubes," mused Claire with a sly grin as she brought her cup to her lips.

Jack grinned back at her. She had teased him. It was familiar. And for a moment, it was easy. He knew the mood might change in mere minutes, but it could be familiar, and that gave him hope. Perhaps all was not lost after all.

CHAPTER 11

Claire had not expected to cry as she farewelled her family. It was not as though she would never see them again. After all, the plan for the honeymoon journey was merely a fortnight. But it was the first time she had ever left her family. Perhaps that very thought was why Mrs Denham kept dabbing her eyes with her handkerchief as well.

Ashwood's most stately coach had been ordered for their use, and Claire had never been inside something so grand. Really, there was room enough for Jack and Claire to have their own wide bench, but for the purpose of appearing as blissful newly-weds, they were seated beside each other. The bench opposite was occupied by a brown leather bag dutifully packed by Mrs Hayes, filled with anything they might need on their journey.

"We are to stay at Ashwood Place," murmured Jack once they were away.

Claire had not given much thought as to where they would stay. But, of course, the Ashwood Estate reached further than their Hertfordshire village. All society families had homes in London. She then recalled that the Beresfords had spent over a decade living in London, so they most certainly had a fine home. Claire could not envision Cecily living in anything less.

"Where is it?" she asked, as though she had any idea at all of the geography of London. He might have told her the Moon and she would have been none the wiser.

"Mayfair," replied Jack.

Claire had never heard of Mayfair, but she would have wagered it was terribly fashionable. "Do you live there always?" she continued to inquire.

Jack shook his head. "No. I have not lived there since ... well, ever really. When my family moved to London, my brother was sent to Eton, and I away to a formative boarding school before I could join him there. We had school holidays and Christmases at Ashwood Place, but it was never home. No, I live ... well, I keep an apartment for myself nearby."

Claire noticed Jack's tone change as he mentioned his apartment, as though it was something shameful to mention. She could not think of anything shameful about one's dwelling ... unless ... perhaps he was not the apartment's only resident.

"It must have been difficult being sent away to school so young," Claire decided to say, leaving that topic of conversation be.

"It is what's expected, I suppose," said Jack simply.

Claire felt her arm snake discreetly over her belly as the thought of her own child leaving home so young to go away to school filled her head. Surely, they didn't have to. Her brothers were educated at the church school. Peter ... well, Peter was terribly good with numbers, and he might have liked to study further, but Jem was just as clever as any other young boy.

Jack surprised her by chuckling. "Claire, if our child wished to be educated at home, I would take that as a personal compliment. It would mean that we have created an environment so positive and enriching that he or she would not want to leave. Trust me, that is the sort of home I would want to raise a child in."

"You seem to have mastered the talent of reading my thoughts ever so quickly," observed Claire.

"I am glad of it," replied Jack. "It saves me time when you will not share them with me freely ... yet."

The carriage travelled up the main street of the village purposely, at the behest of the vicar. Many parishioners had gathered to wave the newlyweds off on their honeymoon, just as they had gathered after the wedding of Adam and Grace. Claire found herself smiling, looking out the window, and waving to the people who had known her all her life. As they passed what was her home, Claire noticed a tall, blond man standing outside of it, leaning against the stone wall in wait.

Arthur's stare was cold and piercing, and it was enough to frighten her away from the window. Her reaction drew Jack's attention, and he noticed Arthur's presence just before they were too far away. Claire watched Jack's jaw clench, much the way it had this morning when she had confessed her original thought to name her child after his or her blood father.

"I didn't know he would be there," Claire whispered. "I promise."

Jack surprised Claire by putting his arm around her shoulder, almost cuddling her into his side. Such an action surprisingly settled her. "I know, Claire," he uttered. "Listen, I must confess something to you."

Confess? Claire wasn't sure she liked that word.

"My life is in London," Jack told her firmly. "Well, how I live my life is in London. My residence, the clubs I frequent, the people I socialise with ..." He sighed. "London can seem like a very small city at times, and the news that I am wed will, I am certain, spread quickly. I imagine it will draw much surprise and commentary ... given how I," he paused, trying to find the right words, "spent much of my time."

Claire nodded slowly, understanding his meaning, and not exactly knowing how to feel.

"I have already asked you this, but I will say it again. Please, don't believe everything you hear," he implored. "I hope I have shown you much of my character. It is very easy to fall into a pattern in London, when everything is at one's fingertips. I often seek ... well, what I seek, I look for in all the wrong places." He shook his head shamefully. "Underneath, my intentions are good, but ... my behaviour ... I am not proud of myself. I know I am capable of more ..." Jack seemed to be getting tongue tied, unable to finish a sentence coherently.

Claire surmised that Jack's reputation was, perhaps, more sordid than she was aware of. She did not doubt that he indulged in drinking, gambling, and women. He was an aristocrat, and that seemed to be normal. The fact that he felt guilt, however, was not.

Claire knew there was much more to Jack Beresford than his reputation, and she believed that she only knew the surface of his true character.

"It would injure me greatly, indeed, if you become embarrassed ... of if I embarrass you –"

Such a notion astonished Claire so much that she interrupted Jack. "Embarrass me?" she gasped. "Jack, if you are under the impression that I am some sort of saint, then you are most sorely mistaken. Or have you forgotten that I am ... sullied?"

"Sullied?" repeated Jack angrily. "What a foul word, and not one I would ever choose to describe you, Claire. You are my wife, and you are under my protection, and no such word shall ever be used to describe you."

His defensive tone would have been startling were it not so flattering. Claire had never heard any man speak so firmly, yet so tenderly before. "Well," she murmured quietly. "I might say the same thing to you. Are you not under my protection now, too? The man who was willing to become my husband is not deserving of the character you have just painted for him."

Jack smiled at her response, proudly so. "I like that you think well of me."

"Trust me," said Claire vehemently. "The feeling is mutual."

A sudden jolt shook Claire awake, and she straightened with a start. She had not realised that she had fallen asleep, and on so short a journey, too! It took a moment to realise that her hand was resting on Jack's thigh, and her head had been on his chest. She quickly removed her hand and Jack smirked.

"Considering the price of these bloody boxes, you would think they'd absorb the road bumps a little more," Jack tsked.

Claire put a slight space between them, but not enough to cause offense. "I did not mean to fall asleep," she said. "I have never been in a carriage this long before. I think the movement lulled me."

"I did not mind. Your back proved to be a fine armrest," Jack mused, motioning to her how he had been resting his arm. In his hand was a book. Jack looked to be nearly a third of the way through.

Claire smiled. "Are you a good reader?"

"Perhaps too good," he replied sheepishly. "I often take myself off to read when I really ought to be occupied on other things."

Claire could not remember the last time she had read a book. She could read just fine, and she had enjoyed varying forms of literature during her schooling, but there never seemed to be any time to read, especially after the death of her father. If she did not keep up the house, then no one else could.

"I wish I read more," Claire stated.

"I believe Ashwood's library is one of the more convincing reasons for me to make our home in Hertfordshire," replied Jack. "I have never encountered another like it. You shall have free reign."

Claire enjoyed that little titbit of information. "What are you reading?" she queried curiously, peering at the page he was on.

Jack closed the novel and showed Claire the cover. "Robinson Crusoe. I found it in the bag." He nodded to the open brown leather bag opposite them. "Mrs Hayes knows this was my favourite as a boy. I haven't read it since I was but ten. I find it enthralling still."

"What is it about?"

"It is an autobiography, I believe, or at least a true account of a man's survival," explained Jack. "This man, Crusoe, survives the perils of land and sea, and being stranded on an island for twenty-eight years, before he is finally rescued."

"Oh, my." Claire was only twenty herself. "What an awful long time to be lost."

"I thought nothing would be more incredible than being cast away when I was a boy," recalled Jack, chuckling. "Now, however, I do not find the draw of battling a cannibal so exciting."

"What on earth is a cannibal?" exclaimed Claire. "And why on earth would one need to battle it?"

Jack tensed slightly. "Oh, you know, they are a People with a rather unusual diet," he explained coyly.

"What could they possibly eat that is so unusual?" Claire thought for a moment, trying to guess at the oddest thing a person could consume. "Do they eat grass?"

At that, Jack burst into a fit of laughter, and Claire frowned deeply. She did not like not being privy to whatever this joke was.

But her displeasure soon cleared when she realised what was suddenly outside of her window. London. Buildings, houses, carriages and people, as far as the eye could see! Oh, how had Jack ever described London as small? Claire had never seen something so splendid and grand!

"I wish I remembered what I thought of London the first time I saw it," muttered Jack, smiling at Claire and her wonder.

"It is truly the most magnificent place I have ever seen!" Claire gushed, though not a hard feat seeing as her travel experience extended only to the Ashwood parish.

Claire all but pressed her face against the glass of the window to take in as much of the sights as she possibly could before the carriage passed them.

Without turning to look at him, Claire added, "You are going to tell me what a cannibal eats later, I hope you realise."

To which Jack laughed again.

CHAPTER 12

In the heart of Grosvenor Square sat one of the finest homes in London, and it just so happened to belong to the Beresford family. As the carriage pulled in through the black, wrought iron gates, Jack observed the household staff assembled to welcome them.

Jack did not recognise many of them, save for the under butler, Warwick. Of course, whenever Cole was taking care of Ashwood House, Warwick served as butler. Jack quickly realised that he had not been inside this house since ... well, perhaps his Cambridge days. He would have returned here for Christmas to be chastised about his reports from tutors, lectured about bills for damage after a night spent irresponsibly, and admonished about the company he kept. His mother would do the shaming, and then his father would pour him a port and privately congratulate him for sowing his wild oats.

Jack shook off thoughts of his father. He did not like his thoughts to linger on the late duke. It was too painful. "Welcome to one of your new homes, Lady Claire," murmured Jack with a wry smile, enjoying the look of astonishment and excitement on her face.

Footmen dressed in black livery came to attend the carriage as soon as it pulled to a stop. The door was opened, and the step let down, and a hand was offered to Claire as she exited first. Claire stepped out of the carriage with her neck craned upwards, taking in the full view of the grand house. Jack suddenly thought it a pity they were in deep autumn. He would have liked Claire to have seen the wisteria vines in full bloom.

Jack jumped down after Claire, and quickly claimed her arm, leading her up to the waiting butler, who promptly bowed.

"It has been quite a while, Warwick," commented Jack, smiling at the portly, but proud butler.

"Too long, milord," replied Warwick. "Welcome back."

"I thank you," replied Jack. "May I present my wife, Lady Claire Beresford." Another first. Using Claire's new name. He could see in the look of surprise on Claire's face that she, too, was experiencing a similar shock at hearing it.

"Welcome to Ashwood Place, milady," greeted Warwick, bowing again.

Jack nearly laughed when he saw Claire go to curtsey herself, before she quickly stopped herself, and disguised the movement poorly as stretching. Her cheeks flushed. She had no idea of her new rank.

"Thank you," huffed Claire bashfully.

"We were all so delighted to receive word from the duke of your nuptials, milord," continued Warwick, his round cheeks swelling. "He made sure the house was properly opened for you, and there is a delicious menu for your supper this evening."

Bless his generous brother. Jack knew Adam's intentions exactly. Jack did not doubt that Grace had shared her reservations about the match with her husband. Whether or not Adam believed them, Jack did not know. Adam had certainly not breathed a word. But Adam's idea of fixing Jack did start with a wife, and so his brother was positively elated with Jack's marriage, and only too happy to ensure that their honeymoon journey was as comfortable and luxurious as it possibly could be.

"The duke has also secured his box for you and Milady this evening at the theatre," added Warwick, only too pleased to report his master's generosity.

"Oh!" cried Claire. "I have never been to the theatre!"

Jack was well familiar with the duke's box. He frequented it often. The last time being not a fortnight ago ... when he had farewelled a certain acquaintance, promising to return shortly.

Damn Adam.

"Splendid," muttered Jack.

"Milady, allow me to introduce you to the household, and the maid who will be looking after you, as I see you have not brought one of your own."

Jack watched as Claire informally greeted each one of the maids and footmen, repeating their names as though she were committing them to memory. She was friendly and accommodating, and had smiles for everyone, and for a moment she looked completely natural.

Until Jack would inevitably say or do something that would cause her to retreat right back inside herself.

The house was exactly as he remembered it, with one significant change. The grand staircase, which was situated directly opposite the front door, now featured a new portrait. Jack supposed it wasn't new. His father looked ten years younger and two stone lighter in the portrait that now hung in the place that was once occupied but his great-grandfather. The painting had been moved from the drawing room to a rightful place of honour, and Jack found it suddenly confronting to be looking into the eyes of his father. He had to look away.

"The duke arranged for you to have his chambers for the duration of your stay, milord," Warwick announced as he directed the footmen who were carrying their trunks inside.

Jack wondered if the only rooms in the entire house which were not open were the duchess'. If this was the case, Adam was a sly man indeed, and he had certainly been speaking with his wife.

"Come on," Jack urged, "I will give you a tour."

Jack showed Claire the drawing, dining, parlour, sitting, and sunrooms, all of which made up the ground floor. Claire was amazed at every turn and kept making comments about whether or not they were allowed to be in the rooms. It made him laugh each time.

She did not remove her arm from his for the entire tour, something that Jack particularly enjoyed. If one were not privy to their circumstances, they looked like proper newlyweds, exploring their new home.

Jack saved the library for last. The double oak doors were enormous, and thick enough to block sound. Almost. That was the excuse that he had used as a boy to pretend he had not heard his mother shouting for him.

Though not as large as the library at Ashwood House, it was a great, rectangular room lined entirely with bookcases, save for large window which gave a view of the small front garden and the road.

"I suppose you spent much of your time while in residence in this room?" Claire guessed, letting go of Jack's arm for the first time to step properly into the room. She did an adorable sort of twirl as she peered up at the ornate coffered ceiling before her blue eyes settled back on him.

"If you shut your eyes, and concentrate really hard, you can hear the faint screams of a duchess, shouting after her trouble-some son," murmured Jack. To his delight, Claire smiled and shut her eyes. He took a few steps towards her, and gently turned her head towards the wingback chair situated by the window. He used but the softest touch, and his breath caught in his throat at the sight of the goosepimples suddenly appearing at Claire's throat. Could ... could he have affected her so? "And if you squint your eyes and look over there," he whispered, "you can see an eleven-year-old Jack Beresford, nose buried in a book, pretending not to have heard her."

Claire's eyes fluttered open and she looked over at the chair. She played along, squinting. "Why," she breathed, before her eyes met his, "what do you know? There you are." Her cheeks flushed a pleasing pink colour.

It was the very first time he had seen Claire flustered. Could he hope that he was, again, the cause of this?

"When I was a boy, my father told me that there was a secret compartment in one of these bookshelves," Jack uttered, his voice almost husky. "My grandfather smoked tobacco and my grandmother hated the smell, and whenever she found his stash, she would throw it away. So, he had a compartment fitted in the library, a room which my grandmother never entered. I asked my father where it was, but he never knew. I found it on one of my summer holidays when I was a boy." Jack walked over to the bookshelf in question, and Claire followed him, almost stumbling behind him. "In it, I found an ancient collection of my grandfather's. But I claimed the box as my own. I used it to keep my treasures hidden."

Jack felt underneath the shelf for the latch, having to feel along a foot of shelf before he found it. When he released it, the compartment dropped down, and a box was revealed. Jack removed it and brought it over to a nearby table. He had not opened it in years.

Opening the box, Jack chuckled when he saw that some of the flowers, he had saved had all but turned to dust.

"Robinson Crusoe," Claire realised, gesturing to the aging book Jack had kept.

"My second copy," Jack recalled. "Susanna drew in my original. I could have throttled her."

"On purpose?"

"Oh, yes. Susanna never used to like being ignored or excluded. I was her closest sibling in age, and I remember her always wanting to play tea parties. I refused one too many times and she trashed my book." Jack tsked. "As you can see, I am clearly over it."

Claire giggled. "Oh, dear. I can understand poor Susanna's frustrations. My sisters were always so much older than me. They had secrets I wasn't privy to, games I wasn't allowed to join because I was too young, and I was never allowed to bother them. It can make a child want to destroy something precious out of revenge."

Jack would have laughed, but he wanted to tease Claire. "You dare take such a villain's side over your husband's?" he playfully mocked.

Much to his delight, Claire's jovial mood allowed her to play along. Her eyes flared as a wicked grin settled on her adorable face. "I wouldn't dream of it, my lord," she admonished.

"Good." Jack chuckled, as he continued to fish through his treasures. He had saved clippings from newspapers for reasons he could not remember. There were tin soldiers and ancient sweets and a school report from Eton that he had managed to conceal from his parents. "Another little titbit about my family ..." Jack said when he spotted a small, leather jewellery box. "My grandmother, Susan, never liked my mother. I can imagine why, but I don't remember her. My mother merely described her as an old witch." Pot calling the kettle black, in Jack's opinion. "She died before Susanna was born, and my father insisted that she be named after his mother. My grandmother, apparently, liked me. She left these to me in her will, but my mother said it was simply to spite her as she had always wanted them." Jack flipped open the jewellery box to reveal two sparkling earbobs. They featured a flawless pink pearl in the centre, and a cluster of diamonds surrounding them.

Claire gasped as she looked at the jewellery. "Beautiful," she admired.

Jack snapped the lid shut, before holding the box out to Claire. "And now, they're yours," he decided.

Claire looked taken aback and seemed to instinctively step away from his offering. "What? Those are precious to you ... I couldn't possibly. It shouldn't be me ..."

"Just for whom should it be then if not my wife?" Jack posed the question. He realised then that they had once again reached the moment when he inevitably spooked her, and she lost all confidence with him.

Jack knew that the only reason Claire believed she should not have the heirlooms was because it was not a "real" marriage. She did not need to say it again.

"Claire," he sighed. "I want you to feel comfortable around me. I understand it will take time, but I am trying to tell you a little about what my childhood was like here ... I want you to know me, just as I would like to know you."

"Wouldn't you much rather give them to your daughter?" whispered Claire.

"Well, if she," Jack nodded down toward her belly, "is a girl, and they are to her taste, then she may have them if her mother no longer desires to wear them."

Perhaps expecting Claire to reach out and take the jewellery box was a bit too high of an aim. Instead, she stood before him, lip trembling, and she burst into tears.

Chapter 13

"If you hate them so very much, they can just go back in the box, it is quite alright," Jack uttered soothingly.

How Claire wished she was not hysterically crying right at that moment. Everything had just suddenly overwhelmed her. Jack was being so very kind and honest with her. She had loved walking about the house with him, and she truly was interested in the stories that he had been sharing about his time spent in this house.

But she still very much felt as though she was playing a role, the role of wife. To be offered such an expensive and precious heirloom was one thing, but to hear Jack refer to her child as their daughter, to hear him so casually discuss the possibility of her inheriting things from him, was another experience altogether.

It was so normal. Something that a father would do if he possessed fabulous things to pass onto his children. It was right. It was what a father should do. Perhaps it had not occurred to Claire until that very moment that Jack was going to be the father of her child. Perhaps, until that moment, she still somehow pictured Arthur in that role.

But Arthur would not be her child's father. Arthur had abandoned her, abandoned them. Jack had not. He had stepped up into this role when he had absolutely no need to. He could have returned to his life in London after Perrie's birthday and lived the exact same life had been living. He did not need to burden himself with a wife and a child so young. And yet he had. And he did not seem at all resentful.

Even now, he was looking upon her ridiculous state with sincerity and concern. For how long had she been looking into Arthur's beautiful green eyes and believing she saw sincerity there? Now she knew what sincerity was, and she much preferred Jack's dark shade of hazel.

The betrayal was still there. The pain she had felt, she still suffered from keenly. As much as she did not want to, Claire did grieve for the happiness, the innocent happiness she had once felt.

But she knew that if she did not try, not only would she be making herself miserable, but she would be making Jack miserable as well, and he did not deserve that. Perhaps she would never experience love again, but happiness and contentment could surely be found.

"I love them," Claire stammered, finding her shaky voice. "I am terribly sorry for crying at you."

Jack hesitantly held out the jewellery box once more and this time, Claire accepted it. "Claire, are you alright?"

Claire nodded helplessly. "Yes," she said breathlessly. "I just want to tell you that I am sorry ... for flinching away, for curt words, bad moods, any ounce of ungratefulness that you have perceived from me. I promise my mother did not raise me to be rude."

Mrs Denham did not raise Claire to fall victim to a rake and become with child out of wedlock, either, but that was an entirely different issue.

Jack smiled, and Claire observed that he had a very sweet, a very genuine sort of smile. Of course, he could display devilish grins, but his normal smile was very nice indeed. Claire suddenly had a memory flash to the front of her mind of the first time she had made such an observation about Jack. It was while they were dancing at the winter assembly that first night they had met.

For a brief moment, Claire wondered what her life might have been like now had she accepted Jack's offer for a second dance, rather than leaving him to dance with Arthur.

"You are not rude," assured Jack. "You are nervous, and rightly so. I am really a stranger to you, just as you are to me. But I appreciate your apology all the same. As I was saying before, I want you to be comfortable around me, and I want us to use this time to get to know one another."

Claire and Jack enjoyed a delicious dinner early that evening. They managed to stay quite happily in each other's company, and Claire found that she did not seize up or retreat within herself. Though not always perfectly at ease, she did find it quite simple to relax into familiar topics of conversation.

They found themselves chatting about their siblings, as Jack found it absolutely fascinating that Claire grew up with five siblings in a small home.

"And all three of you shared a bed?" Jack exclaimed in disbelief.

Claire nodded. "We could not very well fit three beds in the one bedroom," she countered. "When I was very small, I slept in a drawer and my sisters shared the bed, but I outgrew it quite quickly. Of course, when I entered my teenage years, my sisters and I did quarrel some about who was taking more than their fair share of room. Thankfully Kate got married when I was sixteen, so that allowed Grace and I a little more room. And, of course, when Grace went to work at Ashwood House, it was heaven." Claire popped a small piece of the sirloin into her mouth. "I suppose either Peter or Jemmy will take my bedroom now that I am no longer occupying it."

She watched in amusement as Jack enjoyed her story. Really, it was not a very odd phenomenon. She would wager most families in the Ashwood village had similar sleeping arrangements, but Jack would not be used to such things with such a luxurious sleeping chamber as his norm.

After dinner, they both needed to change for the theatre, and Claire realised this would be her first foray, for want of a better word, into society. Thankfully the season was long over, but it was still highly likely that the people in attendance that evening would be important men and women of influence.

Claire did not own a formal ballgown. Even her wedding gown had been a simple one that she had worn before. But it seemed that both Adam and Grace were on the same page, as hanging in the dressing room of the duke's chambers were five different, yet beautiful, ballgowns.

Claire had remembered to ring for her maid, which was something that she had never imagined she would need to do. Jack was readying himself in the bedroom, and Claire was privately closed away in the dressing room, one of two in the duke and duchess' suite.

The door from the duchess' room opened and Aisling Kelly, the maid she had been introduced to earlier, entered with a curtsey. Claire was certainly not used to being curtseyed to. Perhaps this would be a line of questioning for Grace. She had gone from being a housemaid to the mistress.

"Have you chosen what you'd like to wear, milady?" asked Aisling in her thick Irish accent. She was a sprite young lady, though Claire was not much taller than her. Her hair was more auburn than red, and she had dark brown eyes.

Claire had not even thought to choose. She was far to fixed on the fact that she had just pulled a cord for a servant to attend to her. "Oh, no, I haven't." The gowns were Grace's. She never wore such things often, save for when she attended balls or assemblies.

Aisling inspected the dresses, looking back at Claire as she deliberated between each one, before settling on a lovely blue gown. Claire remembered this gown as being one of Adam's Christmas gifts to her. It was in his favourite colour. "I think this will look just grand on you, milady."

Claire felt like quite the doll as Aisling helped her into the beautiful dress, holding the sleeves for her arms and buttoning up the back with care. She held the white gloves as Claire popped in her arms passed the elbow, before she stepped into the matching slippers. Claire and Grace were quite similar in their measurements, however, if this gown had been made for her, it might have needed to be half an inch tighter at the bust. She supposed in a few weeks she would not have the same issue.

"Have you ever worn rouge before, milady?" asked Aisling curiously as Claire sat down at the dressing table.

Claire shook her head before looking at her own pale reflection.

"The duchess has packed some for you. Perfect for a special occasion, no?" Aisling picked up a little porcelain pot and dipped into it with her finger. She then gently blended it into the apples of Claire's cheeks. Claire was amazed how she suddenly had the look of a healthy flush, without having to aggressively pinch her cheeks. Aisling added the smallest amount to Claire's lips, reddening them slightly, before setting the pot down. "You must have a similar complexion to the duchess, milady," Aisling noted. "That colour suits you beautifully, if I may say so."

Claire blushed, and there was suddenly no reason for rouge. Aisling must not have ever met Grace before. "The duchess is actually my elder sister. We are actually three sisters, and we all do look quite similar."

"I'm envious, ma'am," replied Aisling as she began to take out the pins of Claire's hair in order to style it for her for the evening. "I have seven brothers.

Claire merely chuckled, remembering what she had told Jack about her quarrels with her sisters about their sleeping arrangements.

Half an hour later, Claire would not have recognised herself. Gone was the pale, thin, dowdy village girl, and in her place was a lady, one who looked like she might even belong on the arm of a man like Jack. She had never felt so glamorous in all her life, and her excitement for that evening's festivities began to build.

Claire could forget everything tonight and enjoy herself.

Once Aisling had left, Claire wrapped a silk shawl around herself and walked back into the duke's bedroom. Jack was ready, sitting on the bed, dressed in a formal black coat, an ivory waist jacket, with shining brass buttons. His breeches were the same pale shade, and his ankles were crossed. His boots were beside the bed.

Claire realised this would be a regular occurrence that she would walk into a room and find Jack reading. He was leaning up against the bedhead, nearly all the way through Robinson Crusoe. My, he read quickly.

His eyes flicked to her momentarily before settling back on the book, before he stopped himself, snapped the book shut, and looked up again, staring this time.

Claire smiled, though she could not keep his eye, and found herself bashfully looking down.

"Don't tell Adam, but I think cornflower blue suits you more than it does Grace," Jack said in a hushed voice, as though Adam might overhear them.

Instead of feeling embarrassed, Claire laughed, and felt at ease. "Oh, you mustn't tell Adam that! I would be near blasphemy!"

Jack swung his legs out over the edge of the bed and pulled on his boots while laughing to himself. Once they were on, he joined Claire's side, before cocking his head a little. He lifted one of his hands, and lightly touched one of the earbobs that were clipped onto Claire's lobes. A smile of satisfaction spread across his face before he offered Claire his arm.

"Shall we?"

CHAPTER 14

The King's Theatre was quite busy for an October evening, and before they even stepped out of the carriage, Jack recognised several of the gentlemen, and the not-so-gentle men, of whom he regularly socialised with. They were not his friends, per se, but they were gentlemen in the same circle, who frequented the same clubs and parties. These were men he drank with, gambled with, and who knew every unmentionable detail about him. His mother already thought him about as well as rat poison. He could not bear to change the mind of someone who seemed to think well of him.

Jack felt the need to warn Claire, to remind her of his plea that she not believe everything she might hear, but he could not take away any of her excitement. When he looked to her, sitting beside him in the carriage, her blue eyes were wider than he had ever seen them, and she was terribly excited for her first theatre experience. Jack knew that he needed to get her from the front of the theatre to the duke's box as swiftly as humanly possible.

When the carriage stopped outside of the theatre, Jack heard the footman jump down onto the road before racing around to open the door for them. He let the step down and Claire was the first to eagerly climb out. Jack quickly followed her and watched as she smoothed out the skirt of her dress from the journey.

"Come along, let us take out seats," urged Jack, holding his arm out to Claire while keeping a keen eye on the gentlemen by the door.

"Are they ready for us?" asked Claire. "Everyone seems to be gathered at the door, or in the foyer."

"They will be ready for us," Jack assured her. "The estate pays enough for the bloody box," he added under his breath. Jack pulled the brim of his hat as low as he could without it looking ridiculous and walked with Claire on his other side so that his body was between her and the laughing men. They made their way through the crowd towards the doors, which were being manned by attendants in an emerald green uniform. No sooner had they taken a step over the threshold Jack froze.

"Beresford?" shouted one of them in question. "Beresford!"

"Wait for me inside," Jack instructed, and quite firmly indeed, enough to alarm Claire. "Go." He knew it was not terribly appropriate to leave Claire unescorted, but he would only be a moment.

Claire appeared a little startled, but she obeyed him, stepping through the doors and looking back at Jack over her shoulder. Much to Jack's chagrin, Claire did not go into the theatre properly, but she turned left, waiting for him by a closed door that was entirely made of glass. She was fully visible through the door to him and was watching him with a frown.

"God help me," Jack breathed as he turned back around and painted on a smile. "Gentlemen!" he called, taking confident strides toward their gathering. As soon as he reached the four men, he was met with jovial greetings and shakes of the hand. "Fancy seeing you here."

Lord Henry Tourney, a long-time acquaintance of Jack's, grinned wickedly. "Well, we imagined you were still out of town, Beresford," he chuckled. "Thought one of us might have a chance at the signorina without having to compete with her favourite."

Jack suddenly knew that here was indeed a God, as Claire could not hear this conversation. He could feel her eyes, but thankfully not her ears. The signorina in question was Giulia Panetta, the famed soprano, and the lady who would indeed be performing tonight. Jack was well acquainted with her.

"I will not be visiting the signorina this evening, gentlemen, fear not," murmured Jack uncomfortably.

"Whenever did you get back? We must have you at White's tomorrow evening," exclaimed Frederick Chamberlain. "You all but cleaned me out a fortnight ago and I have not yet had my chance at revenge."

"Tourney," said Charles Hastings, ignoring Chamberlain's question, "all is not lost. It seems that Beresford is already spoken for this evening."

He motioned for the men to look behind them at the window where Claire was waiting. The moment the men looked at her, Claire averted her eyes nervously, wrapping her shawl a little tighter around her shoulders.

Philip Yeardley slapped Jack on the back in congratulations. "Oh, well done, Beresford!" he exclaimed. "I thought I saw her on your arm just before. Wherever did you find her?"

"And why did you bother dressing her up when you know you are just going to un –"

"Finish that sentence and I might just cut out your tongue, Hastings," snapped Jack icily, shooting the man a warning glare. His warning did not seem to affect them one bit. The noises of appreciation they were making were vulgar, and Jack felt as though his skin were crawling.

"What a beauty! She looks French. Is she French?" appreciated Tourney as Jack stepped in front of their view. "You know what they say about French girls." He chuckled.

"She is not French. She is my wife," growled Jack. "You had all better avert your thoughts and your eyes this minute, or I will consider it a personal offence."

Gone were the sly, vulgar smiles and comments, and in their place were four very surprised looking men.

"Wife?" all four of them managed to exclaim at the same time.

"When did you have time to go and find a wife?" cried Yeardley. "Did you not return to Hertfordshire to attend a child's birthday?"

"And not even a fortnight ago!" added Hastings.

"I am pleased you are so current with my schedule," murmured Jack facetiously. "Yes, it was a bit swift but –"

"Oh!" realised Tourney. "Say no more. Though how you could be so foolish with a lady is beyond me. Utter moron." He tsked. "You had a bounty of women waiting for you and you could not wait?"

Jack realised that Tourney believed that he had compromised Claire. For a moment, for a brief moment, he considered this to be of benefit. When the pregnancy was announced, there would be no doubt that he was the father of Claire's child. But he quickly decided it against it. He would not have rumours floating around London about Claire when she had only just arrived. This marriage had been orchestrated to prevent rumours.

"I have known the lady, now my wife, for several years," Jack said firmly. It was not entirely a lie. "And when I saw her again, I knew I had to marry her. I am sure I will find my way to White's soon, but until then, good evening."

Jack bowed his head, offered a stiff smile, before leaving them dumbfounded. He turned back around and walked through the doors. Claire stood waiting for him; her hands knitted together in front of her. Her expression was curious yet reserved.

"I am sorry," apologised Jack immediately as he reached her.

Claire managed a small smile, before shaking her head dismissively. "Friends of yours?"

Jack nodded regretfully as he claimed Claire's arm. "Acquaintances," he clarified. "Come along," he urged. "Let us take our seats."

As Jack led Claire away from the door, and into the foyer filled with people who looked every so glamorous, Claire wondered why Jack did not introduce her to his friends. They seemed to have been having a nice laugh outside and they had asked about her. She had deduced that from the looking and the pointing.

But Jack had not fetched her, nor made any mention of making the introductions, and Claire did not know how to feel about that. It was quite plain to see on his face that he was embarrassed, but certainly she did not look like a country village girl in such a gown. She could pass for a gently bred lady, could she not?

Even now, as he ushered her away from the crowd, it was not difficult to guess at the fact that Jack did not want to be seen with her. She suddenly shared in Jack's embarrassment and felt like quite the pretender in Grace's dress.

They climbed what felt like a thousand stairs, more quickly than one human ought to climb stairs, before reaching the top floor. It was quieter, Claire observed, and there were several servants in black and white livery carrying silver trays of champagne. A buffet table was laid out spectacularly with divine smelling tarts and pastries, as well as tureens filled with fresh fruit. On the opposite wall were luxuriously thick red sets of curtains.

Jack let go of her arm to collect two glasses of champagne, before leading them into the furthermost set of curtains. They could not be farther away if he tried.

Claire was determined to not let this spoil her experience. What was she expecting, to be proudly shown off by her new husband? Theirs was not a society match, nor a love match. It was a patched-up scandal hidden by Jack's generosity. He had a right to be embarrassed when he could have married someone ten times finer. Claire needed to lose her wounded pride.

When they entered the box, Claire observed there were six chairs, all adorned with rich, velvet seat cushions, and decorated with gold filigree. On each of the chairs was a golden telescope, though it looked quite small. Huge vases filled with flowers sat atop the balcony, giving the area a very pleasant perfume. As Claire stepped into the box to see their view of the stage, she saw that they were terribly high up, and very close to the edge of the stage.

Jack set their glasses down on the edge of the balcony and removed their telescopes from their chairs. "Here we are." He smiled at her, motioning for her to sit down. When she did, Jack sat down beside her, before reaching out and collecting their glasses, handing one to her.

Claire had never tasted champagne before. Her mother had never let her. She took a small sip and her eyebrows rose as the bubble tingled on her tongue. It was not an entirely unpleasant experience.

Jack downed his glass in one go. "My mother, she ..." he trailed off, before laughing with what seemed like annoyance. "Whenever we would sit down in here, she would always declare that we were the best view in the House."

Claire frowned before peering over the balcony. Certainly, they were close to the stage, but the best view? They were at quite an angle. For an optimal view, she would wager the best seat would be down on the floor.

"Surely ... surely not those seats would give a far better view, would they not?" Claire pointed to the floor down below. "We are at quite an angle here."

Jack chuckled. "No, you misheard me, Claire. I said we are the best view in the House. Aristocrats do not pay for these boxes for their enjoyment of the stage. They pay to be seen. Everyone in this theatre can see us, and they know exactly how important we are because we are in a scandalously overpriced box."

"Are you sure that you really want to be seen with me?"

The question had escaped Claire's lips before she had even realised what she had said. She quickly gasped before slapping her gloved hand over her mouth.

"What was that?" Jack demanded to know, pulled her hand away. "Am I sure that I want to be seen with you?" he repeated questioningly. "What on earth sort of question is that?"

Claire flushed red with embarrassment, and with her rouge, she was certain that she looked like the colour of the crimson curtains. "Never mind," she muttered.

"No, I mind," retorted Jack firmly. "What you said was absurd!"

The theatre was filling now, and the hum of the crowds both below and in the boxes was beginning to grow.

Claire did not have a chance to justify herself as their box was entered by a servant ... who honestly looked quite embarrassed all of a sudden as he looked at Claire.

Lord, another one?

"Pardon me, milord," he said tentatively.

"What?" Jack cried exasperatedly, his hand still on Claire's wrist. He turned his head to look back at the servant.

"I am very sorry to interrupt, but I bring you a message." He looked very awkward indeed.

"What is it?" Jack snapped. "Tell me and get out. We are in the middle of a conversation."

"Oh, uh, Signorina Panetta heard you were in attendance this evening, and asked that you join her in her rooms after the performance." He spoke quickly and bashfully. "I am sorry, she did not write this down or else I would have given you a note. I do not think she was aware that you had company this evening."

CHAPTER 15

Jack's head about exploded as the servant rather awkwardly departed their box. He was already annoyed. Claire had said something utterly ridiculous, and Jack was certain that he had heard it correctly.

Where on earth she had got the idea that he didn't want to be seen with her, he had no idea. Were they not in the most visible box in the whole bloody theatre? The whole idea was to be seen!

But to have that incompetent servant interrupt them to pass on such a sensitive message without at least asking for a private word ... oh, Jack needed another drink. Claire had only sipped her champagne, and Jack had half a mind to take it from her.

Claire had been so excited to come to the theatre and Jack had been enjoying being able to give her such an experience. What had changed? She had appeared rather ashamed and embarrassed after she had told him to dismiss her comment, but now, after the servant's message, she looked completely humiliated.

While not a worldly woman by any stretch of the imagination, Claire could deduce what that message meant, and Jack was not being invited back to the actress' rooms to congratulate her on her performance. Claire's cheeks were bright red and she had turned away from him, keeping her eyes focussed on the stage.

Claire minded. If he could deduce anything from her reaction, it would be that much. Jack had no intention of visiting with Giulia, but the knowledge that Claire cared did help him a little.

"Claire," Jack began softly, trying to steer away from the outraged tone he had just been using with her.

"Hush," she replied quickly, not turning to look at him. "It's starting."

Jack uttered an expletive under his breath as the orchestra began to play and the curtain was lifted, revealing a beautiful set, and the performers ready to sing the opening aria. No sooner had the first tenor began to sing, Claire gripped her chair from underneath and began to shuffle.

Jack was about to ask her why she was moving away from him when he saw that she was pulling it closer to the edge of the balcony. Perhaps she couldn't see over, he surmised. She was not very tall. Claire further surprised him by forgoing the perfect posture of a lady and resting her arms on the balcony edge, knitting her fingers together before she leaned forward and rested her chin on her hands. She looked as though she were in a dream-like trance as she watched the performance.

Claire wanted to enjoy herself, and Jack did not want to spoil one minute of her first theatre experience by talking about Giulia Panetta. There would be plenty of time after the performance to explain that, as well as to find out whatever had made her believe that she was embarrassed to be seen with –

It suddenly dawned on Jack. Oh, of course. It was plainly obvious. He had sent her inside when he had gone to greet

Tourney, Chamberlain, Hastings and Yeardley. She had inquired after them casually when he entered the theatre to meet her and he had been dismissive.

The very idea that Claire could believe that his shame was directed on her. Jack stared at Claire, wishing that she would turn around so that he could see the happiness in her eyes. Certainly, she would believe him now that his shame was his own after the servant's damning message.

Jack found watching Claire far more amusing than watching the performance. Her shoulders tensed during moments of suspense and she tapped her feet excitedly when she was enjoying a song. But as much as he liked seeing her enjoy herself, Jack felt as though he was missing out on her company. He knew all was not well.

During the intermission, Claire excused herself to the ladies parlour, and passively refused his offer to show her the way, electing to ask a servant. She did not return until the curtain was being lifted for the second act, and she resumed her seat right by the edge of the balcony.

Jack wanted nothing more than to shout an apology at her, but he was determined in his conviction to allow Claire to enjoy the opera.

Giulia performed the opening aria of the second act, and it occurred to Jack that he had not been paying attention to the show one bit. What made him greatly uncomfortable was the fact that Giulia was looking up at his box quite frequently with a smile on her face, before she put on her dramatic mask once again. Jack prayed Claire did not notice. She did not know who Signorina Panetta was.

When the final note was sung, the curtain finally closed, and the final applause was heard, the show was over. Claire clapped animatedly, before finally sitting back in her chair.

"Did you enjoy yourself?" asked Jack quietly.

Claire turned back to look at him with tears in her eyes, making the blue of her irises appear like oceans. "Oh, it was wonderful!" she gasped. "I ... I did not understand a thing, and yet I felt every word."

Jack could not help but smile, and truly wish that he had but an ounce of Claire's appreciation and wonder.

But as the hum of the audience returned, and people began to leave their seats for the foyer, Jack noticed Claire's expression fade. Now was the time.

"Claire." Jack stepped towards her, standing not a foot from her. "I could never be ashamed to be seen with you. You must understand that," he told her vehemently.

Claire's eyes fell as she spoke. "I would understand," she replied softly. "I know I am not the sort of woman who would –"

"Stop," he instructed. "I won't hear you disparage yourself. Believe me, I was sparing you an introduction earlier this evening. If I were proud of such connections, you can be certain that I would have had you on my arm."

Claire exhaled and nodded, seeming to believe him. "Thank you for explaining," she uttered. "I ... I am glad to know that you are not embarrassed to be seen with me."

Her words spoke forgiveness, but her tone said otherwise. Before Jack could even explain or apologise, Claire continued.

"Now, don't you have an appointment to keep?"

Jack's mouth resembled a flytrap.

Claire took a step backward, clasping her hands together in front of her as she looked upon him expectantly. Raising her eyebrows, she added, "It is not polite to keep a lady waiting."

When Jack didn't respond, Claire's cheeks blushed deeply.

"Really, Jack. I know I am naïve, but I am not so ignorant as to how a man of your position conducts himself." Despite her red colour, Claire spoke remarkably plain. "Granted, I have heard my information from Ashwood House, but know I do not expect you to miraculously abandon your life. I understand gentlemen marry, not for love as we, and keep the women whom they prefer in comfort. I ... I once overheard your mother telling mine this. I was not supposed to hear but know I do not think ill of you for behaving normally." Her voice shook a little as she lost some of her confidence. "I hope you do not feel as though you need my permission, but if you do, you have it. Please, go to her. If she was the soprano with the golden hair, then you have ... very beautiful ... taste."

Jack could not quite believe what he was hearing. Claire was granting him permission, permission, to visit with a mistress, to have mistresses. She did seem to mean the plural. She didn't mind. She understood.

It was the first day of their honeymoon.

Love or not, what sort of man did she believe him to be?

But his thoughts could not translate to coherent sentences. Instead he became angry, bitter, annoyed, frustrated. She didn't care as he had previously thought in hope. No, she was practically lighting the way to Giulia's rooms for him.

Jack furiously knew there was a reason, one reason why Claire did not care. She preferred the man who abandoned her. He wanted to shake her. What hold did that man have over her? Jack was second, once again, and he always would be.

Second best, and the spare that nobody needed or wanted.

Jack was seeing red as he practically dragged Claire out of the theatre. Claire could barely keep up with him, and he knew that they appeared without a shred of decorum, but he could not have cared less in that moment. Claire did not protest, nor ask what he was doing.

Their carriage was waiting for them, and the footman was standing beside it with the door open. As soon as Claire was inside the carriage, Jack slammed the door shut behind her. He heard Claire gasp with surprise from within and she looked back at him through the window.

"Take her home," Jack barked at the driver, still absolutely furious, and using a tone he would never normally use when speaking to an Ashwood employee. Jack turned his back on the carriage when he heard it away, and stalked over towards a hired hack, one of many which were waiting to take theatre goers home. Before pulling on the door, he snapped. "Take me to White's, St James's Street."

Claire flew to the other window of the carriage, watching as Jack furiously stormed toward a small black carriage. She didn't know who it belonged to, but he climbed inside after saying something to the driver.

Why was he angry at her? Claire thought she had done the right thing, but by the look of pure shock and horror on his face, she clearly had not. He had returned from London not even two weeks ago! Claire was certain that he was living a life very similar to the one she had just assured him that he could still. Jack's family were well aware of his reputation. Why would he not see it as a good thing that Claire did not expect him to give up everything for her? He had already given up his chance of marrying a woman of his choosing. She thought that he would be pleased if she did not prevent him from spending time with a lady who was clearly known to him.

All she was trying to do was to make this strange situation a little easier for him. He had done so much for her already … going so far as to sleep on the settee on their wedding night and not demand things from her that she was not prepared to give. He was a man and, as her mother had explained to her the night before her wedding, they expected certain pleasures.

But what confused her further was that he was not inside this carriage yelling at her for offending him. He had sent her back to Ashwood Place alone while he went God knows where. Did he and Signorina Panetta have a secret rendezvous meeting place? Why would he be angry when he had gone off to do what she had just encouraged him to do?

Claire couldn't know. All she did know was that her husband was furious with her, and he was currently, if not now then soon, spending the first night of their honeymoon in the arms of the woman he preferred.

Claire felt an odd twisting sensation in the pit of her stomach. At the same time, her throat tightened, as though she was having a hard time swallowing that knowledge. Her eyes filled with tears as she realised that the very notion of adultery made her uncomfortable. She did not begrudge Jack, not one bit. He deserved to do what he liked, and she knew she would have to get used to it. But when she pictured her parents, their loving union that she had watched as a child, she felt cheated. Grace and Kate had both been similarly blessed with husbands who worshiped the ground they walked on. For the last three years, Claire had been certain she would join them with an equally joyous union. But now, she knew she had to accept that this was going to be normal.

By the time the carriage reached Ashwood Place, Claire had managed to stop herself from crying, and she had tried her eyes and face with her handkerchief.

Claire was helped out of the carriage by the stoically silent footman, and Warwick awaited her at the front door, curiously watching as she entered the house alone. He cleverly did not inquire after Jack.

"Might you like some warm milk, and perhaps some biscuits, up in your bedroom, milady?" he offered politely, a hint of sympathy behind his voice.

Claire looked out at the darkness behind her, and saw that Warwick was holding a candle to illuminate the foyer. The house was clearly abed, though the offer was extraordinarily tempting.

"Might you show me down to the kitchen?" Claire asked instead. "I can manage from there, I assure you. I do not want to wake anyone."

Warwick stared at her as though she had just asked him how to fly to the Moon. Claire did not want to have to reveal that she had spent the best part of her life up until her marriage cooking, cleaning, and maintaining her mother's house. She had warmed hundreds of saucepans of milk in her time.

"Nothing is too much trouble, I assure you, milady," Warwick replied.

Claire smiled, albeit sadly. "No, I am sure it isn't," she said gratefully, "but I am going to have to insist."

Claire had been right to assume that the house was closed for the evening. As Warwick led her downstairs into the kitchen and servants' dining room, Claire could see that everything was spotless and put away, ready to be done all again tomorrow. She spotted the saucepans immediately stacked neatly on a shelf near the stove. She stood up on her toes and reached to fetch the smallest one. When she turned around, Warwick had dutifully fetched her a pitcher of milk and a silver tray. She knew the kindly butler would not allow her to carry her own tray, even if she was to prepare her own drink.

"I don't suppose you know how to light a stove, milady?" murmured Warwick, in a tone that suggested to Claire that he did not concern himself with cooking matters.

"Do not worry. I know how." Claire checked the firebox for wood and kindling and saw that it was freshly prepared for tomorrow morning. Once she had the fire going, she shut the firebox and adjusted the vents to control the flame. She could feel the heat coming from the stove as she placed the saucepan down and poured in enough milk for the two of them.

Claire watched the milk like a hawk, stirring it with a spoon she found, and checking the head of the milk by pressing her knuckle to the back of the utensil. When it was heated, she suffocated the flame and put out the stove, bringing the saucepan of milk over to the bench where Warwick had placed a wine glass.

"And one for yourself," she urged.

"Oh, no, thank you." Warwick shook his head.

"Please," encouraged Claire.

"You are kind, milady." Warwick smiled as he fetched a glass for himself, though Claire noticed it was not as fine as the one he had laid out for her.

So she thought when she took any guilt of her husband's away in seeing –

Claire shook off the thought as she poured them both a glass. Warwick did carry her tray upstairs to the duke's bedroom, and dutifully handing it off to Aisling who had been waiting for Claire since she had arrived home. Claire immediately felt guilty in not bringing Aisling a glass. She was wholly unused to people waiting on her and attending to her needs.

Aisling set the tray down on the breakfast table and Claire picked up one of the butter biscuits, before offering the dish to Aisling. With the insistent look on Claire's face, Aisling gratefully accepted one.

"Did you enjoy the theatre, milady?"

"Oh, yes." The performance had been one of the most brilliant things Claire had ever seen. The rest of the night, however, was entirely a mess.

Like Warwick, Aisling did not ask after Jack, and she assisted Claire quickly and quietly with getting out of her gown, letting out her hair, before turning down the bed and leaving her to herself.

Claire sat back down at the breakfast table and sipped her milk, bringing her knees up to cuddle them to her chest, letting her heels rest on the edge of the chair. She could see Jack's abandoned copy of Robinson Crusoe on the bed where he had discarded it upon seeing her in her dress earlier that evening.

Save for the candle on the table, she sat alone in the dark, and she began to cry again. Fear rippled through her as she longed for comfort and security. Her mother, her siblings ... and Jack. How quickly he had become security for her. Claire didn't know what she had done wrong, but she hoped that something could be done. She needed Jack as her ally, as her friend, for she could not go through this alone.

When she was thoroughly exhausted, Claire pulled a blanket and a pillow off of the bed and relegated herself to the settee. She was far smaller and would certainly fit better ... and she hoped that whenever Jack returned, if Jack returned, he would be pleased.

CHAPTER 16

Claire awoke with a start when she heard a loud bang, one that made the walls, and the picture frames that hung on them, shake. The small crystal chandelier that hung above the sitting area of the duke's bedroom began to move, with the pieces making a light twinkling sound.

Were marauders in the house? Claire leapt off of the sofa, seizing hold of the candelabra from above the mantle as a weapon.

Only a moment later did the bedroom door open and a dark, stumbling figure practically fell over the threshold. He was being supported by another imposing figure.

"There you are, sir," mumbled a deep, almost frustrated voice.

No sooner had she heard the voice did Claire's nostrils fill with the stink of ale. Wherever Jack had been, and whomever he had been with, had been filled with hours on nonsensical drinking.

"I shank you muchly!" cried Jack, giggling at his slurs.

Claire abandoned the candelabra and seized the oil lamp that she had left on the side table, turning up the dimmed flame so that there was light in the room. Jack was in a total state on the floor, and the man accompanying him Claire did not recognise.

She was in her bedroom, in a nightgown, with her only means of protection inebriated beyond recognition. She dared not approach. Oh, God, why had she tossed away the candelabra? Claire felt her heart hammer in her chest and she filled her lungs with air ready to scream.

But the man, who wore a plain black coat, the coat of a tradesman, spoke first. He looked up at the hesitating Claire and asked, "He yours, miss?"

Claire nodded silently.

"White's, the club on St James's Street, had shut him out on the street. I only picked him up because he said he could pay me. I helped him inside because I didn't want him being sick in me hackney, miss. Pardon the intrusion." He politely tipped his hat, and Claire relaxed a little, feeling slightly guilty for judging the man so harshly.

Claire had never heard of White's before, but she hated to think what went on inside. Money. That was what she needed now. Money, money, where would Jack keep his money? Claire spied several of the drawers around the bedroom, but seeing as it was not Jack's usual bedroom, she doubted many of his things were inside. Instead, she stepped forward and knelt down beside her drunken husband and opened his coat to check his pockets.

"Claire!" he giggled.

Claire winced as she caught some of his breath, before she found his leather purse. She stowed the lamp on a table near the door and looked up at the hackney driver. "How much does he owe you, sir?"

"Five pennies, miss," replied the driver.

Claire nodded, before opening Jack's purse. However, she soon realised that he did not carry such small change. The smallest denomination she found was a shilling, and she handed the coin over to the driver. "Thank you for bringing him home," Claire said gratefully.

The driver's eyes widened at the coin before he clasped his fist around it. "Much obliged, miss." He tipped his hat to Claire. "I can see myself out. You enjoy that now," he said, nodding to Jack on the floor before he turned on his heel and headed back towards the stairs.

Claire shut the bedroom door when she heard the driver leave through the front door. She turned to look at Jack who had managed to sit up, though his head hung between his knees. She had never seen a man this way. She had never seen anyone this way. What on earth had happened to make him drink to such an excess?

Was Jack a drunkard? Was this something that she ought to have known? Mr Andrews, the senior Mr Andrews who used to be Ashwood's grocer, was well known to drink until he was unconscious. It was the drink that killed him, at least that was what everyone said, and the doctor declared his cause of death to be a bleeding ulcer.

"What did you do to yourself?" Claire wondered softly as she knelt down beside him.

"I don't feel well," Jack grumbled.

"No, I should imagine not. May I fetch a glass of water?"

Before he was able to get up of the floor, owing to the fact that Claire was far too small to lift him herself, Jack drank two tumblerfuls of water and promptly brought up his stomach contents into the wash basin. Claire blocked her nose as she tossed it out the window, before Jack was finally able to stumble his way towards the bed, groaning as he went. He stepped out of his boots and breeches and abandoned his coat and waistcoat on the floor, leaving only his shirt.

He climbed in the side that Aisling had turned down for Claire and threw his head back lethargically on the pillow. Claire didn't know what else to do. She wanted to send for a doctor, but she knew that was an overreaction, but then she had never cared for a drunk person before. What if he was sick in the night and she didn't hear him?

In the midst of her worries, Jack surprised Claire immensely. He began to sob. Sob. His face contorted as he wept, and he slapped his hands to his face to shield himself. "I'm sorry," he wailed. "I'm sorry. I'm sorry. I ruined everything. I always ruin everything. That's why ... that's why ..."

"Why what?" pressed Claire gently. She came to sit beside him on the bed and placed a hand on his forearm. It was cool and clammy.

"I wonder why, don't I!" Jack stammered and slurred, still covering his face. "Every time I wonder why but I don't give them any reason to ... any at all ... why would they? How could they? I certainly don't! And you certainly won't ever!"

"Jack, what are you talking about?" asked Claire, a little more firmly this time.

But as soon as the question had been asked, Jack's sobs ceased, and they were replaced with snores. His hands flopped to his sides and he was fast asleep. As much as she was worried, angry even, at Jack's state, she couldn't help but see that underneath the mask, the man, was someone who felt deeply. Those were honest fears, and though they did not make any sense, Claire felt her heart reach for him.

Claire dragged one of the armchairs from the sitting area over to beside the bed. She placed the wash basin on the floor beside the bed before she curled up in the chair with the blanket that she had taken from the bed earlier. She was not five feet from him. If he was sick, then she would awaken.

"Thank you. That will be all. Lady Claire and I are taking this morning to ourselves."

Claire's eyes fluttered open as she heard the bedroom door shut gently, before she heard the soft rattle of a silver breakfast tray. She was still curled up on the armchair, hugging her knees to her chest. Her eyes found Jack instantly as he was setting the breakfast tray down on the table beside the tray that she had the previous night.

He looked awful, though was decidedly more human that he had been the night before. His shirt was dreadfully creased and evidently slept in, and his only other clothing were his breeches, which were indeed pulled on quite lazily and were not buttoned. Claire could see fatigue on his face, and he had not regained his colour fully. His hair, which always had a lovely, natural curl to it, was sticking up and pointing in every possibly direction.

Claire watched as he made two cups of tea, adding in the one- and one-half sugar cube he liked, before adding a splash of milk to both cups. The moment he finished, he looked up at her, and appeared surprised to see her watching him. His surprise quickly changed to remorse and he crossed the room to her side in what seemed like two bounds.

"I am so sorry," he apologised sincerely, kneeling down before her. Claire saw fear in the hazel depths of his eyes. "My behaviour ... it was unacceptable. I was a boar last night, I know it."

Claire straightened her posture and stretched her stiff legs out to rest her feet on the floor. She looked down at Jack with a furrowed brow. The man he had shown her since he had learned of her situation had been one of good, kind character. Something had flipped in him last night, and he had become someone unrecognisable.

Of all that she could disapprove of, she had to share with him her worst fear. "You put me in danger last night, Jack," Claire whispered, her voice a little hoarse from sleep.

Jack's eyes widened.

"You sent me away unaccompanied," she continued softly, "with no explanation. And when you returned, at God knows what time, you were helped in this bedroom by a strange man. You were on the floor incapacitated and he was standing right there!" Claire gestured to the door of the bedroom. "I was in danger and you, my only protection, were voluntarily incapacitated."

Jack, who was already pale, went white as a sheet. Claire could see every one of his fears in his eyes. "Good God, you weren't –"

"No," Claire answered quickly. "Thankfully, the hackney driver who kindly brought you home was a decent man. But that did not change the fact that I felt afraid, Jack!"

Jack's head dropped until it was resting on her knees. He placed his hands either side of her on the arms of the chair.

"God forgive me," he seemed to utter in prayer. "Claire, I'm sorry. I'm so sorry." He repeated his apology twice more. "That is unforgivable ... I cannot believe I did that, I put you in such a situation. How could I be so foolish, so selfish?"

But Claire had forgiven him. She realised it as he apologised in a tone that reeked of self-hatred. She could feel it emanating from Jack, and slowly, his rambles from the night before became a little clearer. "What did I do to make you leave me to travel home alone?" Claire asked calmly, placing her hands on either side of Jack's head so that he might lift it to look at her. "If I did something to offend you, then I do not want to repeat it, and have you end up in such a state again."

Jack quickly captured Claire's hands in his before he looked up at her. Claire saw an entirely different man before her. A vulnerable, hurting man. "Claire, you did nothing wrong," he promised her quietly. "I wish I could tell you that was the first time I have behaved in such a way, but it isn't. Whenever ... whenever something happens ... something that angers me or frustrates me ... I choose to forget and I all but annihilate myself." He looked so regretful. "I cannot tell you how sorry I am."

Claire nodded slowly as she learned that alcohol was how Jack coped, what he turned to when he became overwhelmed by something. Whereas she might have talked to her sisters, about any subject other than Arthur, Jack talked to the bottle. "But something must have happened to upset you," Claire pressed. "If it is something I did, please tell me."

She watched as Jack hesitated, and Claire realised that she had done something.

"Please," she urged, "speak plainly."

Jack took a deep breath. "I never went to visit Signorina Panetta." He spoke very quietly, but Claire could still hear him. She heard him swallow as he battled to maintain some composure. "It angered me a great deal that you were so at ease with the idea of me visiting her. You were practically pushing me toward her."

Claire sat back in the chair as her eyes widened. Why, she thought she had done the right thing! Was that not what most husbands of his rank did anyway? But it had angered him, and Claire wanted to know why.

"I thought you would want to," whispered Claire. "I thought I would be taking away any guilty obligation you had towards me, and I did not want to prevent you from carrying on with your life as it was. I did not want you to think that I expected your faithfulness when it is not a true marriage."

"It's a true marriage to me." Jack spoke so forcefully, so firmly, that it made Claire jump. He immediately squeezed her hands soothingly. "Claire, what part of last night tells you that the life I was living is worth carrying on?" he asked helplessly. "I made vows and promises, and I intend to keep them. I will not see or keep other women, the same as you will not carry on with another ... man." He forced the last word. "I don't want to be the man I was, the man I was two weeks ago, the man I was last night. That man is not worthy ... no one could ever ..."

"Love you?" concluded Claire gently.

Jack's eyes bore into Claire's, and she knew she had chosen the right words. Jack didn't believe anyone could ever love him. Claire was quite certain that he did not love himself. But in that realisation, Claire learned exactly what Jack needed, and what he wanted from her.

Jack wanted Claire to love him.

Just like Claire, Jack was quite heartbroken in ways she did not yet understand. He was not a perfect rescuer, but a man who suffered keenly behind a mask of charm. She believed she had seen his heart in his kindness since their meeting in the library, but Claire now knew that his heart was hurting quite like hers.

Claire did not know if she was capable of falling in love again, and so soon after Arthur. One heart could only go so far, and hers had been ripped out, trampled on, and shoved back in her chest bleeding beyond repair.

"You asked me never to lie to you back in Ashwood," Claire reminded him. "The same goes for you. For us both. We need to talk to one another, to know each other properly. To go beyond how we each take our tea."

Jack nodded in solemn agreement.

Chapter 17

After the troubling and revealing first night of their honeymoon, Jack and Claire managed to find a middle ground for the remainder of their time in London.

Even conversations that seemed to be about nominal interests turned into revealing conversations. A week after their night at the theatre, Jack and Claire had taken a picnic lunch in one of Ashwood's curricles to sit in Hyde Park. The weather demanded it, and as sunny days in autumn were few and far between, an outing was necessary.

Claire enjoyed people watching in London. Everyone always looked as though they had places to be and people to see. They were always dressed in their very best clothing, and each woman seemed to be wearing a more brilliant bonnet than the last. Certainly, Claire had never seen so many people before in her life.

Her entire world had been the Ashwood parish, and it was fulfilling to learn that there was so much more to the world than just the little village main street.

She looked up at Jack when she heard him chuckling. He, indeed, looked just like the other gentlemen. Extraordinarily dapper in his form-fitting coat and matching top hat.

"What?"

"I like seeing this city through your eyes," he said with a smile. "What an extraordinary talent you have for seeing the good in anything ... and anyone."

After wandering through the beautiful park, or promenading, as Jack called it with a roll of his eyes, they found a nice area in which to sit and eat their delicious cut sandwiches. They both settled after eating, enjoying the privacy of some trees in order to lie back on the blanket and relax in the sunshine.

Claire watched as Jack pulled a book out of the picnic basket, and she wondered when he had snuck that in there. She spied the cover of the thick book and read Don Quixote. Jack seemed to tear through books, Claire noted. He never seemed to be able to sit. He preferred to read. He loved to read. It was evident on his face as he flipped open to wherever he had been last.

"Can I ask you something?" Claire wondered aloud.

Jack snapped the book shut immediately. "Of course," he said earnestly.

"What is it about reading that you enjoy so much?" she posed. Claire did want to become a better reader herself, only she'd never had the time to dedicate herself to finishing a novel.

Jack thought for a moment, before he smiled. "A book has the power to take you to a place far from where you are in reality. They are filled with adventure and conflict and romance, and anything is possible. Don Quixote, for example," Jack noted, holding up the book, "has gone mad, and believes himself a knight and endeavours to serve his country and put right all that is wrong. And while he may be mad, this book teaches me that be mad is to be right. Is a man who is dissatisfied with society, and empowered to do something about it, so wrong?"

Jack paused and sat up, twisting himself to face Claire, who in turn sat up as well.

"I have never been happy in my reality," he said quietly. "I would have gone quite mad myself without the solace of books. If I was reading, I was somewhere else, and not some place where I would let someone down."

As much as they had been talking this past week, Jack had not divulged his deepest demons to Claire. She didn't like to pry anything out of him, and they had been enjoying sharing what they had been comfortable to share.

Claire brought her knees up to her chest and wrapped her arms around them as she listened.

But instead of sharing, Jack laughed, albeit quite nervously before he looked away.

Not yet, Claire surmised. "Have you ever thought about writing yourself?" she wondered, softly changing the subject.

"Yes," replied Jack, "before I quickly discovered I was rubbish at it. Show me a career in reading and I shall be a successful man."

Claire laughed. "I'll think on it, shall I?"

Jack placed the book down beside him as he turned back to look at her. "Tell me a memory you have, a memory where you were truly happy beyond anything."

Claire was startled at the sudden question and frustrated when her mind immediately went to her liaisons with Arthur.

But Jack had asked for a time when she was truly happy. Though she might have thought it, she was not truly happy with Arthur.

"Nine years ago, this November," Claire decided, a smile teasing her lips.

"What happened nine years ago this November?" asked Jack.

"I was eleven," began Claire. "My sisters were fifteen and seventeen, and it was the first winter assembly my parents had allowed them to attend. I was furious. Always younger. Always left out. Always thrown together with my brothers as one of the little ones." Claire laughed. "I remember Grace being allowed to go, and Kate whining until she got her way. The same tactic did not work for me."

Jack listened intently.

"My mother did not have much sympathy for me, and rightly so. I was still a child. But my father –" Claire's breath caught in her throat as she remembered the utter kindness she always saw in her father's eyes, "– he danced with me, my very first dance, in our kitchen. I was on his toes as I did not know the steps. We laughed and he held me, and I felt like a princess. And I know I was truly happy. I never got to dance with him at my wedding, but we did dance together."

Claire didn't cry. She still did, of course, but not so much anymore. She could think of her beloved father and smile now and take comfort in the fact that he knew her last as an innocent, pure twelve-year-old girl.

"I wish I knew him," murmured Jack. "My brother practically lived with you when we were children. He could not speak more highly of him."

Claire nodded in agreement with a smile. "Same question. Your turn," she urged.

Jack chuckled. "I'll let you know," he replied simply.

Jack tried not to laugh as he watched Claire awkwardly stand for the dressmaker. It was clear that she had never been fit for a gown in her life. She was the third daughter, and so most of her clothes had come to her made to the size of someone else, and worn twice over by her elder sisters.

Jack knew it was very uncharacteristic of a gentleman to be seated on a chaise in front of a mirror while the dressmaker measured his wife, but he had no desire to be elsewhere. Besides, he found it quite hilarious when Claire would glare daggers at him as he sniggered whenever the dressmaker would accidently tickle her. She had blushed in the beginning to be seen in her undergarments, but she was properly covered and he had seen in her in nightgown each evening.

He'd ordered five day dresses and her own ball gown. Claire's mentioning of the winter assembly during their luncheon in Hyde Park five days earlier had reminded him that the annual dance was coming up, and so he intended to pay the dressmaker handsomely to ensure the dress arrived on time.

Claire had, of course, protested the expense. Jack was certain that Claire had never had a shilling of her own money before, and the idea that he was spending what she considered to be a small fortune on her was unsettling. Jack was quite certain that Claire had no idea the value of the Ashwood estate.

The dressmaker was discreetly advised of Claire's condition, but saw nothing more than two newlyweds who did seem to enjoy one another's company. She was to make the gowns suitable for when Claire was larger. Claire was helped to choose fabric that suited her colouring, and Jack enjoyed the excitement on her face when it came time to select the silk that would be used to make her very own ballgown.

He checked the watch in his pocket and noted that at this time tomorrow, they would be on their way back to Ashwood House. The very idea put a dampener on an otherwise glorious mood. He never liked setting foot in that house.

He hardly liked setting foot in Ashwood Place. But this trip had been different. Aside from their misunderstanding, and his wholly idiotic behaviour on their first night, Jack had never liked London better. He had told Claire that he would let her know his happiest memory, and Jack was quickly becoming certain that it would include her.

Perhaps, he hoped, venturing back to Ashwood with Claire by his side would make things easier. Through their unlikely union, Jack had found an ally, and indeed a friend, and he hoped, one day, a family.

When the measurements had been finalised, the fabrics chosen, and Claire was dressed properly once again, she returned to him with rather a giddy smile.

"I have never had anything new before," she whispered excitedly. "How terribly shallow does that make me to be excited about something new?"

Jack chuckled. "Not shallow at all. I am glad to play a role in this excitement."

"I saw you looking at you watch just before. Is there somewhere we ought to be? Or somewhere you need to be?"

Jack shook his head. "No. Not this evening. I was merely thinking that this honeymoon is nearly at an end. We are to return tomorrow."

Jack could have sworn he saw the same look of disappointment in Claire's eyes as he felt deep within him. It had been quite easy to be normal in London. When they returned to Ashwood, they would need to start playing pretend. Their ruse would well and truly be underway. That and the fact that he would be forced to live under the same roof as his mother, something that he had been actively avoiding since he was eleven years old.

"It bothers you deeply to be there, doesn't it?" Claire queried softly.

Sometimes Jack wished that he were not so transparent. "Let me settle our account and then we shall return to Ashwood Place for dinner."

CHAPTER 18

Jack watched as the familiar sights of London slowly started to disappear and their windows became greeted by a sea of countryside. Not even his book, which was sitting opposite him in the bag filled with essentials for the journey, would distract him. And that was indeed a first.

Never once had he been happy in that house save for these last two weeks with Claire. They truly were in their own little world, and Jack was entirely anxious for leaving it.

"When shall we announce the pregnancy?" Claire uttered quietly, breaking the silence with a question that she already knew the answer to.

They had discussed this a few days earlier, but Jack was grateful for the distraction.

"We agreed in a fortnight, yes? After the assembly. By your calculations, you will be nearing three months into your pregnancy. When the child is born, we will just say it is an eight-month baby, or perhaps we might even return to London for the birth and mask the date of birth."

"I should like to return to London," agreed Claire. "I ... I had such a marvellous time, Jack. I never thought I would be able to have such fun, but I did."

Her wording caused Jack to look down at her, and in her eyes, Jack saw the same anxiety. Claire was nervous, extremely so, and she had every right to be.

"They won't doubt," he promised her quietly. "We will ensure that they do not." Jack covered her hand with his and held it tightly. "I am glad you enjoyed yourself. Truth be told, I have never had a finer time in London, either."

"Do you think ..." Claire began, but then she stopped herself.

Jack frowned. "Do I think what?"

Claire looked down. "No, forget I said anything. It is really not my place."

Jack's curiosity was indeed intrigued, and anything was better than thinking about Ashwood House and its residents at that moment. "Tell me," he pressed. "It is your place as my wife to ask me whatever you like."

Claire took a breath. "Do you think, now that you are married, seemingly settled, your mother will be kinder to you?" Claire looked as though she regretted asking the question the minute it escaped her lips, and Jack couldn't help but let his shoulders roll forwards in disappointment as her question did not serve as a distraction.

"No," he replied simply.

"Because she does not approve of me?" Claire guessed.

"It is highly likely that she does not approve of you, but a wife is inconsequential to my mother's approval ... unless, of course, I wed a princess or something." Upon seeing Claire's disappointment, Jack clarified, "It would not be a personal slight, Claire, I assure you. I am certain, in time, my mother will like you very well. She certainly gets on with Grace, it appears. But I would still wager that if my brother felt inclined to wed an heiress with a dowry the size of Susanna's, she would be singing from the rooftop."

"She frightens me," confessed Claire. "I do not know how Grace manages her."

Jack chuckled. "Grace humours her, or at least from what I have seen. She listens to Cecily's lectures and advice before going behind her back and doing whatever she likes."

"You trivialise her, and yet I know she affects you," observed Claire. "I promised myself I wouldn't pry, but seeing as we are both going back into the lion's den, won't you tell me anything?"

Jack rested his head back against the glass of the back window. The movement of the carriage making his head tap against it lightly. "It's not prying," he assured her quietly. "Every great family, and I say great without the positive meaning, must preserve their legacy through siring sons. My father used to make it sound like a bloody stable, and I hate that I cannot think of it otherwise." He huffed. "There must be an heir, of course. The lack of an heir is tricky. Lawyers are brought in and heirs are located outside of the family. Once influential families can be ruined without an heir. But there must also be a spare. A second son must be produced, an insurance policy in case bloody lung fever or something gets the first. If a couple is so inclined, a third son would be classed as a bonus, but many couples, like my parents, well, they couldn't stand to copulate any further after the third attempt became Susanna.

"I suppose when I was younger, I was quite the hellion. I never received any attention, but then most children in our sort of family don't. My mother became obsessed with Susanna becoming a lady. My father invested all his time into Adam. And I was left behind. I misbehaved on purpose, I talked back, I was disrespectful, and ... really, quite unendearing.

"My father did, occasionally, spend time with me. He taught me to ride, fence and shoot. But my mother ... my mother severely disliked me. By the time that I realised my behaviour wouldn't do me any favours with her, it was too late. She had no use for me, and certainly no time. She would say things to me, things that a son would never forget from his mother."

Jack did not remember how old he was when he first started taking himself off to the library, or wherever he could find a quiet corner to read, but it was soon after Cecily Beresford declared that her second son was good for nothing.

"After a while my behaviour turned spiteful," Jack confessed, "and I assure you that I am not proud of it. I was afforded the very best of educations that money can buy, and I spent my years terrorising my teachers just so my mother would get a letter about me. I really don't know what I was trying to achieve, but I couldn't allow myself to conform. I wouldn't be what she wanted me to be after so many years of her putting me down.

"There are two, maybe three respectable vocations for a second son as he lies in wait ... waiting for his brother to drop dead of plague or waiting to be superfluous once he produces his own heir. The church or the military. My mother had always meant me for the church as she didn't trust that I was disciplined enough to serve in a regiment. To her credit, I probably wasn't.

But I knew from quite early on that I was not meant to waste my life away writing sermons. And when I gave it up, she might as well have done the same to me.

"She never spoke to me save to lecture me or to scold me. If my name was on her lips, it was being hissed. She never met my eye with anything but a glare.

"I'm a failure in her eyes. I have amounted to nothing, and she detests it. She sees nothing good in me, or about me, and she can't help but point it out every time she sees me. And I think the reason why I stay away, why I avoid my family, is because, deep down, I know she is right."

Jack had never relayed that tale to another before, and once he had begun, he couldn't stop. He had certainly never revealed that he believed his mother was right about him, and he hated that he had just said such things to Claire. Jack liked, no, he loved that Claire thought well of him, and he honestly didn't know what he would do if she ever saw him as his mother did.

"I know my mother has a heart. I've seen it. But she has never shown it to me. Before my father died, he told me ..." Jack's breath caught in his throat. Peregrine had told Jack that there was greatness in him if he only found his purpose. The peace it gave Jack to know that his father saw such potential was profound, but the subsequent shame in amounting to very little nearly three years later was great indeed. "Well, I am glad he can't see me."

Jack and Claire sat in silence for a few minutes, listening to the sounds of the carriage wheels turning over the stones scattered about the road. Jack stared directly ahead, unable to believe he had just confessed so much. It was a burden that had weighed heavily on him, but he dared not look down at Claire.

She surprised him, however, when she brought her other hand across to place it on top of the one that was already holding her left. "I wish my father could see you," she said quietly. "I wish he could have known you."

Jack felt a very unfamiliar feeling of swelling in his chest as his head and gaze snapped down to hers. Claire was smiling, sympathetically, warming, kindly, all at once.

"One does not need to have an extraordinarily successful career in order to be a person worthy of respect," Claire said vehemently. "My father was a country tailor and it was a good week if we were considered to be poor. Often, we were poorer than that. But that did not mean my father was not respectable. He was a good man who made the right choices about the people for whom he was responsible." She turned on the seat a little so that she could properly face him. "I do not think you realise just what you have done for me, Jack. Me, someone you barely knew before our wedding. Do you know how many men would have heard my situation and then offered me their hand? You are respectable as a minimum. I could think of far better descriptors for you. Which is why I wish my father could have known you, because I am certain he would be glad that I married someone so incredibly kind and decent."

Jack had never heard such words from anyone before. He had never heard anyone defend him thus before with evidence of his merits. Did it matter what his mother thought if Claire thought this well of him?

"I am on your side," promised Claire, "and as much as the duchess frightens me," she shuddered, "should I hear anything about you that does not align with your true character, then I will protect you. Just as you are protecting me."

Jack had to smile as he imagined Claire, as little as she was, standing up and shouting at his mother across a dinner table. He would pay to see that. But then, he realised, Claire was willing to set aside her fears to stand up for him.

They might have journeyed to London as strangers, but they were returning as a team.

Chapter 19

"Do you suppose we can sneak in through the kitchen?" Jack whispered to Claire as their carriage pulled through the gates of Ashwood House.

But they both knew any hope for a quiet entrance was too late as the front door opened and a parade of footmen, led by Cole, spilled down the stairs.

"We don't need to lie when they ask us questions about the honeymoon trip," Jack continued quietly. "Though ... you are welcome to tell anyone about my ... er ..." he trailed off awkwardly.

"I won't tell anyone about the aftermath of our trip to the theatre," Claire assured him. "If they ask, we have plenty of anecdotes to share. It was a wonderful trip."

Jack chuckled, though clearly relieved. Claire could see how anxious he was, still, and it did anger her that a man with so much good in him could be perceived so incorrectly by one who should love him unconditionally. Though he claimed it a lost cause, winning his mother's approval did mean a lot to Jack, Claire observed.

When the carriage pulled to a stop, the door was promptly opened and Claire was assisted out, closely followed by Jack.

"Good afternoon, milord, milady," the butler greeted formally, with a bow of his head.

"Good afternoon, Cole," replied Jack. "I suppose all of this will need to go up to my old room, then." He motioned to the trunks, and the shopping boxes that they had accumulated while in London.

"The duke took it upon himself to have your things moved to the south wing, milord," reported Cole. "A belated wedding gift. Privacy. There is a proper suite of rooms waiting for you and Lady Claire."

Jack frowned. "Are you speaking of the Rose Room?" he clarified.

"Yes, milord." Cole nodded.

"Great, just when my mother didn't already want to kill me," he hissed under his breath. "Brilliant. Thank you, Cole." Jack took Claire's arm and swiftly led her away from the carriage and up the stairs.

"Is there something wrong with the Rose Room?" Claire asked as she practically ran up the stairs alongside Jack. Personally, she liked the idea of privacy. She was worried that Grace might enter into Jack's bedroom unannounced and notice their odd sleeping arrangement.

"Oh, no, it is palatial and perfectly luxurious, or so I'm told," replied Jack. "My mother loves those rooms. Personally, I have never been inside. No one has. We were told as children never to snoop in there as they were reserved for royal guests."

"So, Adam has gifted us rooms fit for royalty?"

"Yes. I don't know what he's playing at."

Claire couldn't believe that Adam was playing at anything. Surely, he was merely being kind and offering Jack rooms fit for a married man, and not a bachelor. Considering Claire had spent the best part of her life sharing a bedroom, and a bed, with her two sisters, she was quite excited to see the room that was supposedly fit for a queen.

As they walked across the marble foyer, Jack suddenly stopped and turned to Claire. "Are you alright?" he suddenly asked, his brows furrowing.

Claire was nervous, certainly, but she knew that everything would be alright. She trusted Jack. Claire nodded.

Jack checked the time on his pocket watch briefly. "I am going to go and see my brother in his study. Why don't you go into the drawing room and ring the bell for some tea and get the servants to tell Grace and Susanna that you are there."

Jack quickly left her and climbed the stairs out of sight. Claire stood in the middle of the foyer as the footmen began to bring their trunks inside. She quickly moved out of the way and thought about what Jack had said. He wanted her to summon a servant. She had never summoned a servant before. Not even while they were in London. Aisling had always been there to service her needs. Claire did not even have to ask. She was entirely unused to being waited on.

Cole saved her the job of finding the bellpull in the drawing room. "Might I see to some refreshment, milady?" he asked. "Perhaps a tray of sandwiches?"

As if on cue, her stomach grumbled, as it seemed to be doing more frequently. Claire had noticed an increase in her appetite, and she nodded. "Yes, please," she agreed. "And would it be any trouble to tell the duchess that I have returned? Or, if you tell me where she is, I might go and visit with her."

"It is no trouble. The duchess has become fond of tea and a light meal in the afternoon, owing to her condition, of course." Cole showed Claire to the drawing room and closed the door, leaving her inside.

It was impossible to believe that she was now a resident of this fine house. The last time Claire had been in this room, she had been wearing a gown that had been made by their mother for Grace nearly ten years earlier. Now, she was wearing yet another gown of Grace's, only its value was quintupled.

The drawing room had a beautiful view of the garden through its large window, which caught the last delights of the afternoon sun. A book had been left on one of the canary yellow settees, as though someone had been reading in here recently.

A portrait of the Beresford family hung above the fireplace. Peregrine, the late duke, sat in the centre, his wife beside him. It must have been painted some years ago, as Susanna appeared no more than eleven or twelve. She was seated in front of her parents, and behind them were their two sons. Adam stood proudly, but Jack ... somehow the artist had managed to capture Jack's genuine discomfort. Why could Cecily not see how wonderful Jack was?

Jack had mentioned that he knew his mother had a heart, and Claire believed him. She had seen it, too. Cecily was an odd, doting sort of friend to her mother. Mrs Denham entertained the duchess regularly for tea and received invitations from Cecily personally just as often. She was also a very proud grandmother, and Claire had watched these last two years as she fawned over Perrie. Why could she not bestow the same love on her own son?

If she could, if it were possible, Claire would have swallowed her fear and marched right up to Cecily to tell her what Jack had done for Claire.

"... I've heard that eating the eye of a lamb can ensure an unborn child is a boy, or is it the bladder ...?"

Claire spun around the moment she heard voices approaching the drawing room, and she recognised the loudest as the duchess'. The door was opened for them by Cole and Grace, Cecily, and Perrie were announced.

Perrie toddled in ahead of her mother and grandmother, and excitedly ran to Claire with her arms extended when she saw her aunt. Perrie was wearing white today, with a blue ribbon fixed in her dark hair. She giggled as Claire picked her up, and for the first time, Perrie's giggle thrilled Claire from deep within.

"I missed you, dear one," she said, kissing Perrie's temple.

Grace was quick to collect them both in a hug, squeezing Claire tightly. When she pulled back, Claire noticed how perfectly rosy Grace was. Claire could see, poking out from underneath her skirts, was a perfectly noticeable protrusion.

"I missed you more," insisted Grace. "How are you? How was your journey?"

"Let the girl breathe, Grace," tsked Cecily. "Besides, I need to finish telling you about these lamb's bladders. I've had it on good authority that –"

"Cecily!" cried Grace, in a tone that Claire would never be game to use, not for a hundred years. "I am not putting a lamb's bladder in my mouth!"

"It would not be raw!" protested Cecily. "I'll have Mrs Reynolds pop it in a stew. You would hardly notice it!"

Claire remembered Jack telling her that the reason Grace managed Cecily so well was because she humoured her. Consuming the bladder of an animal seemed one step too far for Grace. Personally, Claire could not imagine anything more foul.

"How are you, Your Grace?" Claire said politely, her voice a little shaky. She immediately chastised herself. How on earth did she ever believe herself capable of swallowing her own fear when it came to this woman?

Cecily sighed, arching an eyebrow as she looked over Claire was a sudden, intense, scrutiny. "Well, I would be better if my daughter-in-law would take on the advice of a woman who birthed not one, but two sons."

"If you swear to God and tell me that you consumed bladder while pregnant with either Adam or Jack, then pray, boil one for me!" declared Grace.

Cecily's eyes narrowed in her displeasure. "Well, at least we can be certain that any child your sister may have conceived while on the honeymoon journey will be a boy."

Claire's cheeks suddenly flamed crimson. In her embarrassment, she quickly put Perrie on the floor and turned toward the window. How could she possibly know that? Was ... was she carrying a son?

Grace, thankfully, read Claire's mind as asked the question. "How could you know that?" she asked.

"An autumn conception, dear!" Cecily exclaimed, as though it was obvious. "Everyone knows that a child conceived in autumn is likely to be a boy. Had you and my son only waited but a few weeks more, I might have saved the servants the trouble of sourcing a bladder for me."

Claire did quick arithmetic in her head as she calculated that she was about nine weeks into her own pregnancy. She paled when she realised that meant a summer conception. If ... if the child was a girl, would Cecily discover the truth?

"I have never heard anything more ridiculous," declared Grace.

Claire could have kissed her sister.

"You are awfully unamenable when you are expecting," Cecily observed in annoyance.

Cole returned then, flanked by two footmen, as they brought in the tea service, and a platter of delicious looking sandwiches. Claire was famished, and Grace, too, excitedly approached the food.

"Ah, Cole, just who I wanted to speak to," Cecily quipped. "I want you to find me a lamb's bladder."

The butler appeared utterly perplexed as Grace shouted, "No! Mr Cole, she is trying to poison me!"

"Your Grace?" Cole appeared very alarmed.

"Oh, Grace, stop being dramatic. When you are cuddling your very own son and heir, you will thank me," Cecily said dismissively.

Grace glowered at the back of Cecily's head. "I am not eating anything I cannot identify," she whispered to Claire as she accepted one of the sandwiches from a footman. "Tell me about your honeymoon," she insisted, now speaking in at a normal volume. "How is Jack?"

Now, something she could attest to confidently. "Jack is wonderful," Claire said firmly, but entirely sincerely.

As Jack approached the door of what was now Adam's study, he realised that he had not been inside it since he was perhaps ten or eleven years old, and then it had been Peregrine sitting behind the great desk.

Jack knocked once but did not both waiting for Adam to allow entry, pushing open the door immediately after. He stopped in the doorway for a moment, looking at his brother behind the desk. Adam had stacks of books around him, and a mess of papers in front of him with a quill in hand. A tea tray sat idly to his left.

When Adam looked up, he smiled. "Jack, you're returned!" He stood up from his chair and abandoned the quill, making his way around the desk to greet his brother. Adam hugged Jack, slapping him on the back twice. "How was it with Claire? How do you feel?"

"Do I ask you such questions about your wife?" Jack countered teasingly.

Adam rolled his eyes. "You know what I mean. How was London? Was the house to your liking?"

"Yes, the house was good. I appreciate ... Claire especially appreciated the house." Jack knew she still felt terribly awkward when servants waited on her, but as someone who had worked dawn until dusk nearly every day of her life, Jack was pleased to see her relax.

Adam smiled cheerfully, yet knowingly. "I wish I had known about you two, seen it or ... I don't know. I suppose romance by correspondence is the order of the day now anyway."

So, Adam, at least, bought their ruse. "I suppose it is," agreed Jack.

"I couldn't have chosen a more lovely girl for you. Claire is very sweet and ..." Adam paused.

Jack frowned. "And what?"

"Oh, no, it is nothing awful. Grace always used to worry, still worries, about how terribly naïve Claire is. Grace told me once that she was worried Claire would fall prey to someone she fancied herself besotted with." Adam shook off the thought. "But you obviously have nothing to worry about. This was, of course, some time ago."

Jack hated that his first thought was bitter. Why hadn't Grace and her mother kept better watch over Claire? How was such a naïve girl allowed to fall victim to that lout?

"I can't tell you how pleased I am to know that you have made a match for yourself, and not married someone that Mother would have chosen for you."

"Speaking of, arc you trying to have me skinned alive?" Jack asked. "The Rose Room?" he prompted, when Adam looked utterly confused.

"Oh," Adam realised. "Actually, that was Mother's idea," he informed Jack. "She insisted that you needed to have proper rooms now that you are returned from your honeymoon."

Oh, Jack realised. Rooms. Plural. As was society tradition. It wasn't normal for a husband and wife to share a single bedroom. He wondered if that meant that Claire would sleep in the lady's bedroom now? He had grown quite used to her snoring.

Still, he was quite shocked that Cecily would gift him those rooms. Jack couldn't help but suspect an agenda. "The rooms are not the only reason I wanted to speak with you."

"Oh?"

Chapter 20

J ack felt nervous, which he knew was entirely ridiculous seeing as his brother had never wanted anything more than for Jack to get his life together. Well, perhaps coveting Grace might have been first in his wants, but Jack was a close second.

"I know you have been generous," Jack began awkwardly. Behind Adam, Jack could see the responsibility that was the Ashwood estate. Jack did nothing to aid his brother in its up-keep, and now he was feeling the immense guilt of what he was to ask. "But I need to talk to you about my finances."

Adam took a step backward and nodded seriously. "Of course. You're married now. Do you want a bigger allowance?"

Jack shook his head. His allowance, gifted to him by Adam, allowed him to live in London as a gentleman. And it was suddenly occurring to Jack just how ridiculous that was. "I don't want an allowance. I want a legacy," Jack said simply. "I want to have something to pass on to my child ... if and when we are blessed with one.

"I haven't thought it over, and the idea has only just come to me. It was sparked from a conversation I was having with

Claire in Hyde Park the other day. Adam, I want to establish a publishing house."

Jack couldn't believe the words had escaped his mouth, or that he felt such conviction over a potential career. He was a hopeless writer, but there was a career for a seasoned reader. Jack knew nothing about publishing. He knew nothing about running a business, and he certainly didn't have the funds or collateral to establish one. But if he could but succeed at something, at this, then he would have made something of himself. He would be able to independently support his family. He would have something to leave his child.

Jack didn't want to be a failure anymore.

"Publishing?" repeated Adam, raising his brows, before remaining quiet for a minute, mulling over the idea. "What does Claire say to this?" he asked suddenly.

"She doesn't know," replied Jack honestly. He would tell her if Adam approved of his idea, and made it financially possible, but he had just a little too much pride to tell her such an idea before confessing it failed for lack of funds.

"Publishing?" Adam said again, turning around and heading back behind the desk. He opened one of the drawers in the desk and began to sift through papers, clearly searching for something.

"If you think it is an awful idea, please put me out of my misery," Jack insisted, his feet still glued to the spot. Oh, it was a stupid idea and Adam knew it. Jack didn't know the first thing about publishing, and it probably wasn't at all how he imagined it. He would no doubt fail at it as he did everything else. He would just cause embarrassment and it would be yet another thing for his mother to shame –

"For when Jack finds the greatness that I know is within him. Love, Father."

Adam's voice interrupted Jack's panic, and his eyes flashed to his brother. Adam was holding a card attached to another sheet of paper. Jack stared at Adam as he suddenly realised that he had read off a letter, something from their father.

"What did you say?"

"I found this in Father's desk not long after you left when he died," replied Adam, holding up the note. "It was in and amongst his things. You know, Mother's trust, Susanna's dowry ... and this. With it came a letter for me, telling me to hold onto it until you came to me, like you have today. I think Father knew you better than you thought." Adam walked back around the desk and brought Jack the note. He practically had to place it in Jack's frozen hands.

Sure enough, there was a note written in his father's hand. It was dated the 26th of November 1806, which would have been a month before he had died. The letter was attached to a promissory note, totalling –

"Oh my God!" exclaimed Jack as he laid his eyes on the amount.

Twenty thousand pounds. Peregrine had gifted Jack twenty thousand pounds.

"I had to go back in the ledgers a little," commented Adam. "I was curious as to where he'd found such a sum. Do you want to know when he put that away for you?"

Jack looked up at him in disbelief. "When?"

"1789," chuckled Adam. "When you were but six years old. Father sold off some land and property and tucked the sum away. Hid it from Mother, of course. His annotation in the ledger made me laugh. I shall have to find it for you. He wrote: £20 000 – JB is no clergyman, but he will be great." Adam laughed lightly. "Father knew even then what I've known all along."

Jack needed to sit down, and for lack of a chair in his immediate vicinity, he all but collapsed onto the floor, clutching the promissory note, and his father's missive, in his hands.

Adam knelt down beside him. "You don't need my permission, Jack. You don't need my help. Father ensured your future years ago and made it so that when you were ready to take it, you had everything you needed."

Jack knew that his brother was right, but he couldn't help but wish that his father had told him about this years ago. Peregrine knew he would amount to something when he was but six and terrorising the house? Had Jack known the faith his father had in him; he couldn't help but wonder if that might have changed things.

But it was no use wondering. In his hands was his ticket to a legacy. Jack would be able to support Claire, their child ... and he would have something to bequeath.

"I just can't believe that everything could work out like this," Jack remarked.

Adam grinned. "My brother, the publisher," he said proudly.

Pride. Jack heard it in his brother's voice. He had heard it before, of course, but often etched with sympathy or hope. This was complete with confidence, and Jack could feel his own pride building. He thanked God and his father that he would now have this opportunity to build a legacy.

Nothing, Jack mused, nothing could spoil his mood.

"Publishing?" cried Claire excitedly as they sat together on the bed in the Rose Room that evening.

Jack could see the genuine delight in Claire's eyes as she read over the note from his father.

"I couldn't think of anything more perfect for you! I know of no one with a better love of literature," declared Claire, before pausing. "Well, I suppose that is because most of the people in my acquaintance do not have the time to read, but if they did, I would still wager –"

Jack interrupted her with a laugh. "I know what you mean," he assured her. "Now, you must keep this to yourself. I've asked Adam to as well. This will take a lot of time and research ... and if it fails –"

"It will not fail," Claire said emphatically. "Jack, I cannot tell you how pleased I am for you."

And she was sincerely happy for him. Jack could see Claire's kindness as though she were wearing it on her sleeve. She genuinely cared about him, and that gave him a different sort of thrill.

"For us," he corrected. "This will be ours, and one day, our child's." He motioned to her belly, though it was still flat.

Claire's eyes became glassy and her lower lip trembled for a moment before she regained her composure. "I suppose we ought to go to sleep," she uttered.

They had long been left in their rooms by the servants who had prepared both bedrooms. The suite itself consisted of five rooms. Two enormous bedrooms, two dressing rooms, and a washroom containing a large bath and a privacy screen. All had interconnecting doors. Both Claire and Jack had enjoyed exploring their new quarters, and Claire had declared their rooms were larger than her house in the village.

But now begged the question of where would they sleep?

Claire had taken pity on Jack for the remainder of their honeymoon in London. She had allowed him to sleep beside her in the bed. It was large enough that they would have their own space without the stress of questions and whispers from the servants.

But now it was not expected. Married couples had separate bedrooms. There was a perfectly good room turned down waiting.

And yet, Jack didn't want to sleep apart from Claire. In just a few short weeks, she had become perhaps the closest friend he had. The trust between them was unlike anything he had previously experienced.

His attraction to her was obvious, but it was something that he kept at the very back of his mind. She was not ready. Though it was often quite difficult when she was staring at him with blue eyes as big as saucers and her dark hair down and cascading over her shoulders.

She was waiting for him to say something.

"It would be awfully strange for a couple to have married in our quick circumstances to be so suddenly sleeping separately, don't you think?"

"Yes! I quite agree!" Claire exclaimed, a little too loudly, a fact that made her cheeks flush.

Jack grinned. A legacy, and a bride.

The following fortnight flew by, and Claire found herself shadowing her sister quite closely. Claire watched how Grace behaved and how she occupied herself. Claire knew that she had a lot to learn.

Cecily still bothered Grace incessantly with tips and tricks on how to ensure a baby was male, and Claire watched as Grace expertly handled each one. Claire watched, learned, and wondered if she would ever have the gall to speak to her mother-in-law the way Grace did. Cecily did not pay much heed to Claire, but perhaps that was because she was often as quiet as a mouse in her presence.

As the day to announce her pregnancy approached, Claire found herself watching how Grace mothered Perrie quite closely. Once it was known, she would be able to seek advice from her own mother, but for now, she had a daily lesson, as though she was back in school.

Claire was just not expecting Grace to guess before the announcement was made. A few days before the winter assembly, they both were seated in Perrie's nursery alone. Grace sat with Perrie on her lap as she combed her hair into a ribbon. How she managed it with a pregnant belly, Claire didn't know.

Claire was starting to notice her own figure changing already.

"Are you with child, Claire?"

The question so shocked Claire that she nearly fell off of her stool. To make the answer completely obvious, Claire looked down at her stomach, checking to see if the tiny, rounded protrusion she had noticed underneath her chemise was visible through the fabric of her dress.

"I thought so," murmured Grace nonchalantly as she tied Perries ribbon into a bow.

"How did you know?" Claire asked anxiously.

"The servants," replied Grace. "I was once one of them, so I know the gossip that goes on downstairs. Ruby told me that the maids have been keeping an eye on your sheets."

Claire flushed a deep red. She remembered Jack leaving blood on the sheets on their wedding night to fool the servants. She felt terribly embarrassed to know that the servants were discussing whether or not she had bled.

"The housemaids from Ashwood Place work through winter at the house, and apparently they have reported that your sheets were clean throughout your honeymoon. It has been a month," Grace continued casually. She shifted Perrie off of her lap once her hair was fixed. Perrie darted over to her collection of dolls to play.

Claire was in a panic. Did Grace know? Was she about to ask her a question that would require a direct lie?

But Grace smiled. "Well?" she said expectantly. "Don't you want congratulations?" She laughed lately. "This is good news, isn't it? Does Jack know? Is he excited?" She stood up from her chair and made her way over to Claire, wrapping her arms around her sister once Claire had stood up as well.

Relief flooded through Claire as she received her sister's hug. If Ruby had relayed the message to Grace about the clean sheets, then she prayed Ruby had passed on the message of the sheets on the wedding night. Grace believed that Jack was her child's father. "Yes," confirmed Claire. "It is early," or eleven weeks along, "but he is excited. We were going to tell everyone on Sunday when Mama is here."

Grace cupped Claire's face. "I am pleased for you. I can't tell you how pleased I am. I won't lie, I was very worried about you. When I saw you at Perrie's birthday, I thought the worst." She sighed. "I can't tell you what I worried over ... and I did doubt Jack. I hate that I did, but I have been watching you two since you have returned. I suppose I owe you and Jack and apology."

"Whatever for?"

"I don't think I have seen two people who so clearly belong to one another before," Grace murmured peacefully.

CHAPTER 21

Claire's ballgown arrived early Saturday morning, and the timing could not have been more fortuitous seeing as the winter assembly was that evening. What was not fortuitous, however, was that her measurements were not what they had been a few weeks earlier. Even with the slight give of the fabric, Claire felt as though she had grown rather voluptuous for her small frame, and the neckline did nought but display it.

The fabric was a beautiful white silk, with the bodice and sleeves adorned with Chantilly lace and pearls. Claire would have wanted to wear the diamond ear bobs that Jack had gifted her, but on top of the gown, Claire would not have felt right wearing such riches in front of people she knew so well.

"I don't suppose you could lace me in a little tighter, Ruby?" Claire asked her sister's lady's maid. As Claire had no maid of her own yet, Ruby had been attending her as well. "I seem to have indulged a little at luncheon," she lied feebly.

After knowing what the servants discussed downstairs, Claire knew that Ruby was aware of the true reason her gown was a little snug. But she didn't say anything as she tightened Claire's corset. Claire prayed her chest did not appear inappropriate.

Ruby had fixed Claire's hair immaculately, and she had once again donned rouge. Claire felt the prettiest she had ever been. Once her gown was buttoned, and appearing semi-decent, her gloves were on, and she had stepped into her slippers, Claire departed her dressing room to find Jack waiting for her on the bed.

Reading, of course.

Jack hadn't noticed her for a brief moment, and Claire couldn't help but smile at him. He was slouched against the pillows, his head cocked to the side. His dark hair, which needed a trim, was curlier than ever as it fell across his forehead. He had an expression of deep concentration, though she could see the excitement in his hazel eyes as he read something gripping. It was though she was staring at innocent wonder, and there was great beauty in it.

Claire cleared her throat and Jack looked up, a wide, appreciative smile spreading across his face. It was the smile she liked, the one that touched his eyes, and the one that often seemed to vanish at times in this house.

As he stared, Claire quickly became self-conscious, and would have no need for the rouge. "It is a little tight," Claire uttered nervously, attempting to pull up her gown from the neckline. "I did not realise how quickly expectant women expanded."

Jack laughed quietly as he abandoned his book and climbed off of the bed. "You are beautiful. You are the standard of beauty all women aspire to, for true beauty shines from within."

Claire's lips parted in surprise as Jack reached her. She could feel that he meant every word with the utmost sincerity, and he was gazing upon her with what could only be described as desire. Claire was instantly reminded of what Jack wanted from her, and she felt a nervous flutter of apprehension in her stomach.

Claire forced it aside, hating that her natural reaction to affection had become suspicion. She wanted to enjoy their evening, their first as a married couple in the Ashwood parish.

Jack seemed to sense her hesitance and he smiled sympathetically. "Did you know it is three years tonight since we met?" he asked.

Claire's eyes widened. Indeed, it was. Three years since their first and only dance together.

It was also three years this evening since Claire had begun what she thought was a courtship between herself and Arthur. Would he be in attendance? For certain he would be.

She had managed to get out of attending church since returning to Ashwood by feigning fatigue, and Jack had been only too happy to stay home as well. Grace had sincerely been suffering with bouts of nausea and was often feeling poorly in the morning, and so the Beresfords had not been in regular attendance. But Claire's complaints were in effort to avoid the inevitable.

What would she do? What would she say? Claire knew she ought to do and say nothing, but what if he approached her? Jack had forbidden her from ever seeing him again, and Claire meant to keep that promise, but Arthur's cold words from whence they last spoke haunted her.

Claire wondered if she should tell Jack of her apprehension. "I suppose it is high time we danced a second, then," Claire managed to reply with a small smile.

"Well, if you recall, I did ask you, but –" Jack stopped himself, and Claire's eyes flashed to his.

She knew exactly what he was going to say. But she had spurned him for Arthur. And Jack couldn't say it. Wouldn't say it, more like. And she knew she couldn't say anything about what she might feel upon seeing Arthur again. She didn't want to upset Jack.

"The waltz, I think," decided Jack. "At the very least. I would love to dance a waltz with you."

"Mother, I am two and twenty. I can dance with whomever I please," Susanna insisted with a huff.

"You could be two and forty for all I care," Cecily replied, equally as displeased. "The last thing you want to do is dance with the sort that will start the whispers in this village. We are already returning to London next year for your third season," Cecily tsked. "You have two brothers ... and I suppose the eldest Denham boy. He is a sort of brother now."

Susanna scowled as Jack and Claire exchanged an awkward glance. They had been lucky enough to share a carriage with Cecily and Susanna while Adam and Grace travelled in the larger carriage to collect Mrs Denham, Peter, and Jem, the latter of whom would be attending his first assembly. Claire could not hide her annoyance at the fact that her mother was allowing Jem to attend a ball when he was a full two years younger than she had been her first time out.

Yet another of the many privileges that came along with being a part of the male species.

Nevertheless, it meant that Jack had been very quiet while they listened to Cecily lecture Susanna. To Cecily's credit, since they had returned from London, Claire had not heard her say anything particularly cruel to Jack. She did not say anything in particular to him at all. They were an odd pair really, who treated one another with indifference, and exchanged barely a word or two a day.

Claire supposed though that this was what culminated of an existence of lectures, and now Susanna bore the brunt of it. Claire felt bad, really, considering she was two years younger than Susanna, and yet because she was married, she was held in higher esteem.

"Mother, a dance is not some sort of devilish tryst," Susanna snapped. "I am not the sort of stupid girl who could be duped by a man with a few nice words for me. Really, should I be insulted at how thick you think me?"

Claire was thankful that the carriage was near dark, as her cheeks flamed red. Jack subtly reached for her hand and held it in his, saying nothing.

"Oh, Susanna, you know not of these things. Villages like these thrive on such scandals. Nothing ever happens and their lives are so dull that they live for a girl's stupidity," Cecily retorted. "And it is never the man who faces reprimand and ostracism. You dance with a sweet-looking butcher and the next thing you know you will have a rumour floating around about you and he, oh, I don't know, that he was ravishing you or something."

Jack squeezed Claire's hand.

"Ravishing," repeated Susanna slyly. "How marvellous."

Claire knew that Susanna was normally not so antagonistic, but she so wished that their line of conversation was not so close to Claire's own stupidity, as they so described it.

"Watch your tone," said Cecily tersely, "or I will have Mrs Hayes put you over her knee again like she did when you were a child."

"I never get to have any fun," complained Susanna. "The only men you allow me to dance with are the stuffy, boring ones in London out for a rich wife to put on their mantle. How lucky you are to have married for love, Jack."

Susanna's address startled Jack. "Oh … yes," he said awkwardly. "I know," he added, with a little more composure.

"I shall make it a personal goal of mine, I think, to one day dance with a man Mother deems so inappropriate, she will faint. How I will laugh," Susanna declared, and Cecily glared at her.

"Would you like me to send you home?" Cecily threatened, raising her eyebrows.

Susanna rolled her eyes subtly. "No," she sighed.

The carriage pulled to a stop outside the assembly hall, and they all got out into the brisk, chilly air. The other carriage arrived shortly after, and their party entered into the assembly together, with Claire hearing herself being announced to a ballroom as Jack's wife for the first time.

All eyes were on the Beresfords as they descended into the ballroom. Grace refused a dance card owing to her pregnancy, but Claire accepted one slipping it onto her wrist. She doubted she would be asked often as she was now married, and she was not experiencing the same ailing symptoms as Grace.

Susanna, too, in spite of her mother, very boldly accepted her dance card. Adam, Grace, and Cecily were quickly claimed by the vicar and his wife, and Mrs Denham offered Claire and Jack a quick greeting before being helped over to a chair by Peter and Jem.

Claire decided to focus her eyes on the musicians, willing herself not to look around the room for fear she might see him. Anyway, she had nothing to worry about while standing with Jack. He certainly wouldn't dare approach her.

"Oh, no one is going to ask me to dance," Susanna hissed in annoyance. "They all know Mother is such a dragon that she'd chase away anyone who dared approach me."

"Oh, for God's sake," Jack said under his breath. "How ever did you survive two sisters when I can barely manage one?" he uttered to Claire. "Come on then," he urged, holding his hand out to Susanna.

"Oh, you ought to dance with Claire first," insisted Susanna. "It would only be fair."

"Yes, but Claire is not the one whinging at me," Jack retorted facetiously, before grinning at Claire. "Will you be alright for one dance? You might go and sit with your mother?" Jack suggested.

Claire nodded. "Yes, go."

"Thank you, Claire," said Susanna gratefully as she accepted Jack's offer.

Claire did not have a chance to go and sit with Mrs Denham before she was intercepted by a very dapper looking young Jem. He appeared to be wearing an old Sunday best of Peter's, though Jem was quickly outgrowing it. He would be a tall man when he was properly grown up, and even now at fifteen, he stood a head over Claire.

"You startled me, Jemmy," said Claire. "But you look very handsome."

Jem grinned proudly. "I already have my name on four dance cards, you know."

My, Jem was quick. "Do you even know how to dance?"

"Kate has been teaching me," he replied, nodding. "Anyway, this is for you." He pulled a folded note out of his pocket and handed it to Claire. "It's from Mrs Slickson. Something about a present for Mother or something." Jem shrugged his shoulders as though he hadn't been listening to his instructions.

And thankfully so. Claire paled as she knew that this note was certainly not from Mrs Slickson.

"I'd better go and find my first partner," Jem announced, and with that, he was off.

Claire toyed with destroying the note, but she couldn't help herself as she unfolded it. Arthur had approached her brother. Had he managed to capture Jem at a time when his mind was not preoccupied with girls then Jem might have twigged onto his lie.

White always was my favourite on you and look how you have dressed just for me. I have been going mad without you, my lovely Claire.

Claire felt her heart hammer in her chest as all sorts of anger and pain coursed within her. What did he think he was doing? In frustration she ripped the note, first in half, then in quarters, then in eighths, until the words would not be legible. She held the pieces in her hand in a vice grip.

"Well, that was not very nice."

Claire froze, his voice so close that she felt his breath on the back of her neck. "Go away," Claire whispered, her voice sounding so weak and unconvincing.

Arthur casually stepped beside her and tsked. "Claire, you never have such words for me. You are always accommodating to my every whim and desire."

Claire felt her blood run sickeningly cold. They were in full view of anyone paying attention. Especially Jack. Claire only prayed that he was well focussed on Susanna. "You can't say such things to me. I am married."

"Oh, darling," he chuckled condescendingly. "You know you like it when I speak of my desire for you."

"Hush," snapped Claire in a low hiss. Had she ever liked such talk? Much to her shame, yes, she had. She had liked to hear how Arthur had appreciated her. She had believed that such words meant he loved her. But now ... well, she really was one of those stupid girls Cecily and Susanna had been speaking about.

In a swift, yet subtle move, Arthur had seized Claire's left hand, opened her dance card and scrawled in his name before she had even a moment's time to protest. It was the first time she had looked at him, and she saw the look of cunning pleasure in his green eyes.

"I will see you later, dear Claire. I always claim what's mine."

Claire watched in anxious anguish as Arthur sauntered away. She quickly opened her dance card to see where Arthur had written his name, and she nearly lost her luncheon when she saw what dance he had claimed.

CHAPTER 22

The waltz. The dance Jack had specifically requested. Claire panicked as she looked over at Jack, finding him still on the dance floor with Susanna. Had he seen? Claire quickly supposed that Jack would have flattened Arthur with his fists and caused a scene had he been aware of Arthur approaching her.

Should she tell Jack? Claire stressed in anguish. He was bound to find out when Arthur claimed her. His name was on her dance card. She could hardly refuse. To do so would be the height of rudeness. To forget or forgo a partner was simply not done and was indeed a great slight.

But the real question was would Jack believe that Claire had not invited his attentions? She had hardly realised what was happening before Arthur had finished scribbling his name. Indeed, his penmanship was very ill, and spoke of someone in a rush.

Claire quickly retreated towards her mother, not wanting to draw any further attention towards herself. Mrs Denham was sitting alone, as both Jem and Peter had already selected partners. She was watching the festivities with a smile.

Claire sat down beside Mrs Denham, and her mother turned to her. "I cannot believe how grown up you look in that gown, Claire. You are a vision, to be sure."

Claire managed a small smile for her mother. "Thank you, Mama. Jack was really too generous in London."

"A fine man, indeed," noted Mrs Denham. "Do you know, I do not believe his mother gives him enough credit, but that is between you and me," she added quietly.

Claire could have laughed. Her mother didn't know the half of it. "I have never known anyone more decent," she promised.

"Was that Arthur Slickson I saw you speaking to just then?" Mrs Denham asked casually, her voice seeming to rise half an octave in curiosity.

Claire feigned interest in the dancers. "Yes," she said casually, or as casually as she could muster. "He came to offer me congratulations on my nuptials." Another lie. Another sin. When would it end?

"Strange," Mrs Denham thought aloud. "I've never known Arthur Slickson to think of anyone beyond himself in all the years I have known him."

A chill ran down Claire's spine. It seemed a natural defence of hers to speak for Arthur, to tell her mother of a virtue that only she could see, as she had done before their clandestine courtship. But Claire managed to stop herself from telling another lie. She had not always believed they were lies. Claire had obviously been very talented at fooling even herself, along with her family. Arthur Slickson possessed no virtues.

And he certainly deserved no courtesies.

"I quite agree, Mama."

Claire saw Mrs Denham's eyes widen in utter shock. "My!" she remarked. "I know your little attachment ended some time ago, but I never thought I would live to see the day when Arthur Slickson was anything less than a king in your eyes, my dear!"

Claire felt an utter fool and was truly embarrassed by her own ignorance. How ashamed she felt to have sung that man's praises, to have believed his tales so easily. She felt every bit as stupid as the girls Susanna and Cecily had described in the carriage.

Claire could no longer live under his spell. She could no longer lend any piece of herself to the memory of what she thought she have experienced with Arthur. It certainly wasn't love.

Love wasn't cruel. Love wasn't dictatorial. Love didn't come with conditions.

The entire reason she was compromised was because Arthur had led her to believe that physical intimacy was what she needed to do to prove her love for him.

Claire wasn't certain what it was she had experienced, but it wasn't love. She had never been in love, but she did want to be. She wanted to love properly, and she wanted to know what it was like to be loved properly.

Claire watched as the musicians played their final note and the dancers applauded. Susanna was so happy to have danced, and she hugged her brother gratefully. Jack smiled, one of his wide, crinkly smiles that she so enjoyed. She recalled her realisation from the first night of their honeymoon.

Jack wanted Claire to love him.

Though this realisation was only a month old, Claire knew that at the time, she had still believed herself in love with Arthur. She had not thought herself capable of loving another man, even one so good as Jack.

But she could love Jack, Claire thought hopefully. If she tried, if she allowed her heart to feel again, she could love him, and perhaps, be lucky enough to experience love in return.

"I would honestly prefer never to think of Mr Slickson, Mama," murmured Claire. "A childhood fantasy that belongs in my past."

"God help the woman who marries him is all I'll say," Mrs Denham replied. Her tone changed as she tapped the top of Claire's leg. "Now, am I to see you dancing tonight?" she asked.

"Absolutely," enthused Jack, who had joined them from the dance floor.

Claire's heart, which she had thought was quite dead, suddenly flipped in her chest, sending a deep, crimson blush to her cheeks and a flutter of apprehension to her stomach. Claire looked down so that Jack couldn't see the embarrassing colour of her cheeks, and she suddenly realised that she was nervous.

Her husband was making her feel nervous.

"Claire, are you alright?"

Much to Claire's humiliation, Jack knelt down in front of her and lifted her chin with his index finger, bringing her eyes to his. Her heart all but stopped when she realised how close they were, and she couldn't breathe a gasp.

How had she never noticed just how handsome Jack was? His hair was divine, the colour of glossy chocolate, and she longed to tease her fingers in his ringlet curls. His eyes were large and expressive, and the most beautiful shade of hazel. Gold was scattered throughout the iris, while a thin line of green surrounded his pupils. His eyelashes were thick and long, and the sort any woman would long for, and his strong brows were knitted together in concern. His full lips were parted and would reveal a dazzling smile were he not worried. His jaw was angular and strong, reflecting the broadness of his shoulders and the strength in his arms.

"You look hot. Dear Lord, you aren't feverish?" Jack quickly pressed the back of his hand to Claire's forehead to feel her temperature and relaxed slightly when he felt there was none.

"No, I am quite well," she managed, her voice as soft as a whisper. How could she tell him that the reason she had collapsed into schoolgirl embarrassment was because she was finally realising that she liked the way he looked?

"She is a blushing new bride, Jack," Mrs Denham declared, to which Claire willed the floor to open and swallow her. She glared at her mother.

Jack chuckled, though Claire could see that he did not believe Mrs Denham's assessment. A pang of pain his Claire as she realised such a reaction was her doing.

"Does my bride feel well enough to dance with her husband?" Jack asked, playing along.

But as he reached for the dance card on Claire's wrist, an audible gasp escaped Claire as she instinctively snatched it away. Her swift reaction shocked both Jack and Mrs Denham, and she saw an expression on Jack's face that she recognised. It was one of rejection. He stood up and stepped away from her.

"Claire, really!" exclaimed Mrs Denham in a scolding manner.

"No, no, it's quite alright, Mrs Denham," said Jack calmly, in a tone of acceptance, another that Claire recognised.

No, she couldn't stand for this. She wouldn't stand for this.

"I'm hungry!" announced Claire, jumping up from her chair and meeting with Jack so quickly that she bumped into him. He quickly righted her by placing his hands on her upper arms. "Might you take me into the dining room?" she asked.

Jack stared at her quizzically. "Whatever you want," he accepted, allowing Claire to take his arm. He led her away from Mrs Denham and toward the dining room.

The tables were laden with food, as they always were at this assembly, but Claire had no desire to eat. As it was so early in the evening, the dining room was not heavily occupied, and so they had some semblance of privacy for a quiet conversation.

"What strikes your fancy?" asked Jack. "Sweet or savoury?"

"Neither, I'm not hungry," Claire said quickly as she grasped her dance card in her hand before turning on him. "I'm sorry for flinching," she apologised.

Jack saw the dance card in her hand before an expression of understanding appeared on his face. "Claire, I should be the one to apologise. I should not have presumed. I would never take liberties with you."

Her heart flipped again. "No, I promise you it's not that," she assured him. Taking a deep breath in an attempt to quell her nerves, Claire endeavoured to be honest. "Promise you won't be angry."

Her request caught Jack off guard, and he frowned. "What would I be angry about?"

Claire knew her meagre attempt was unjustified. One could not ask such a thing when one knew the topic of discussion would result in a reaction. "While you were dancing, Arthur came and spoke to me," she told him quietly.

Jack's entire body tensed, and he stared down at her with hardened eyes.

"I didn't ask him to, I promise," Claire insisted. "I was dismissive, and I had no desire to speak with him. Before I knew what was happening, he signed my dance card and that is why I didn't want you to see it. I didn't want you to think I had accepted him." Claire opened the dance card and showed it to Jack.

Claire could hear Jack grinding his teeth in anger as he read Arthur's name on her otherwise blank card.

"I am not going to dance with him," promised Claire. "Really, I have no desire to dance with anyone but you." Jack had no idea how much she meant those words. "Please, do not let this spoil our evening," implored Claire. "Do you believe me?"

Jack forced himself to take a breath, and then another, before he said, "Yes." He then added, "I am going to kill him."

"No!" cried Claire, a little too loudly. "No," she said again in a hushed tone. "Please, I don't want anything to do with him!" she declared. "I don't want any thought of him to occupy yours or my mind. I told you because you asked for honesty. But when we walk back into the ballroom, I don't want you to be thinking of issuing him with a demand for satisfaction." Claire shuddered at the very thought.

Jack swallowed as he tried to regain his composure. "Honesty, Claire. I was not intending on killing him honourably," he muttered truthfully. "Honesty, Claire. Do you mean it? You don't want anything to do with him?" He was watching her, looking for any hint of a falsehood, any sign of hesitation.

But as nervous as she was, Claire could emphatically say, "Yes."

Jack's shoulders released some of his tension. The tension then lifted from his facial muscles, and she even saw the beginning of a smile. "If I ask you to dance, will you flinch away from me?"

Claire smiled as she slipped her dance card off of her wrist. Taking it between her hands, she ripped it in half, an action resulting in a hearty laugh from Jack. "Would you look at that? I have no awaiting partners. I am free for every dance this evening."

"Every dance?" Jack arched an eyebrow. "Challenge accepted, my lady."

Jack led Claire back into the ballroom where the couples were assembling for the next dance. Claire spied Susanna standing with Peter, and Jem with a young lady she was not familiar with. She also saw Arthur joining the dance with a lady from the neighbouring parish. Arthur noticed Claire immediately, and looked upon her union with Jack with a sneer.

Had she always thought Arthur handsome? Claire shuddered to believe that she had once thought Arthur beautiful. But now, all she saw in his place was a very small, very bitter man, who had no idea how to behave like a gentleman.

For he so lacked manners, then so could Claire. Height of rudeness be damned. She held up her dance card so that Arthur could see it, before tossing it over her shoulder as she took her place with Jack.

CHAPTER 23

To dance every dance was near impossible, as Claire quickly realised. She had thought she had escaped the first period of her pregnancy relatively unscathed as she had not experienced the nausea that Grace had. However, her energy levels were not quite what they had been. After two dances in a row, Claire was quite exhausted, and Jack happily retreated from the dance floor with her.

Claire found herself looking upon her husband with, what felt like, corrective spectacles. How had she not seen Jack properly? She had looked upon him a hundred times, and yet it suddenly felt like the first. Claire was only glad that Jack had not noticed Claire staring at him as she would have blushed terribly.

Claire was clinging to his arm quite closely, partially for support over her weary figure, but even through the fine wool of his coat, she could feel the strength in his arm. Jack led her over to where Adam and Grace were standing, near the entrance of the assembly hall. A quick search for the duchess surprised Claire, as she spied Cecily sitting down with Mrs Denham in deep conversation.

Susanna was taking advantage of her mother's distraction and was now dancing with Mr Andrews, Ashwood's grocer. Claire knew that Cecily would never have approved such a pairing, but Susanna seemed to be enjoying herself, even if her partner was too old for her. Mr Andrews would have a story to tell down at the tavern that he had danced with the beautiful Lady Susanna.

"I did not attend the assembly last year as Perrie was ill, and now I cannot dance this year. What once was an enjoyable date on the calendar is quickly becoming a disappointment," Grace muttered teasingly to Claire as she and Jack joined them. "You looked to be enjoying yourself, though," Grace observed with a smile.

Claire managed to control her blush. "Yes, Jack is a very fine dancer," she complimented.

Jack chuckled. "Likewise, my dear." Before he paused. "Perrie was ill last year?" he repeated, a sound of alarm in his tone.

Both Grace and Adam nodded.

"I am sure I wrote you," Adam recalled.

"You most certainly did not," retorted Jack. "What was wrong with her?"

Claire, who was still holding onto Jack's arm, felt it tense.

"It was just a little cold," replied Grace. "We had been out in the garden and it had started to rain. We kept watch to ensure it did not become lung fever and she bettered in a day or two." She spoke calmly, like a seasoned mother, and Claire wagered it would be the same tone Mrs Denham would use when she spoke of her children's past ailments.

"Well, how often does this happen? Do children always sicken so easily?" Jack demanded to know, panic evident in his voice.

"Jack," said Claire coolly, but he ignored her.

Grace glanced at Claire knowingly. She knew that Claire was expecting herself and that Jack's reaction was not solely out of concern for Perrie.

"I'll tell you what," Jack said determinedly, turning to look down at Claire. "Any child of ours will not be allowed outside if it is raining. Or at all if it is the least bit chilly."

Jack's statement made Adam laugh. "Well, I am afraid you live in the wrong country, brother," he joked. "You've seen how well Perrie is, and she loves to play in the garden."

Jack was simply vexed, and Claire couldn't help but smile. Jack was concerned for their child. It wasn't even born yet, and the man Jack knew to have sired the child was standing in the same room, and yet he knew the baby was his own. Claire realised that this was indeed the first time that she had thought of her child as theirs. It was not her own, and it was certainly not Arthur's.

Oh, but if God could work wonders to give their child Jack's kind eyes, she would never miss a Sunday sermon.

"I mean it, though," Jack muttered, only for Claire. "There will be no bloody lung fever on my watch."

The music finished and the dancers applauded the musicians once again before they began to prepare for the next dance. Cecily was still engrossed in conversation with Mrs Denham, and Claire watched as Susanna slyly moved to the edge of the dance floor waiting to be asked to dance again.

Claire saw it happen before anything could be done. Her eyes had unwittingly connected with Arthur's, and he was once again looking upon her with a vengeful expression. But then he smiled. Wickedly.

He stood up tall and put on his most debonair grin as he strutted up to Susanna, greeting her with a bow as he bestowed a kiss upon her gloved hand. Susanna, who, despite being two years Claire's senior, was still remarkably sheltered, flushed in her cheeks as she accepted Arthur's attentions.

"Jack," hissed Claire. "You need to stop it!"

Jack followed Claire's line of sight and his face filled with rage. But it was too late. To intervene now would cause a scene and would only embarrass Susanna.

God, Arthur wouldn't dare. Would he? Would he really go after Susanna to spite Claire? Or would he do so, trick Susanna as he had done Claire, to secure Susanna's money? That, after all, was what Claire had lacked.

Susanna deserved so much better. As did Claire. Claire knew that she deserved better, and she hoped that she could deserve Jack.

Jack and Claire were not the only ones to have noticed Susanna's new partner.

"You have not introduced Susanna to Arthur Slickson, have you, Adam?" Grace asked curiously, a tense stare directed at her sister-in-law. Grace had always maintained a fervent dislike of Arthur, and Claire now realised that her sister had always been right.

"No," replied Adam. "And I doubt Mother would have, either. She would not have Susanna acquainted with anyone here."

"I am not one to insist upon separate classes as it would be utterly hypocritical of me, but a man, whether or not he is a gentleman, cannot approach someone of Susanna's rank without a formal introduction!" Grace murmured angrily. "Least of all someone as vain and as intolerable as Mr Slickson."

"I am not very familiar with the man. Is he as bad as that?" Adam asked curiously.

"Worse," growled Jack involuntarily.

Adam glanced at his brother. "Are you acquainted with him, Jack?"

"Well enough," muttered Jack. "When this dance is over, you need to go and get Susanna. She ought to keep as far enough away from that man as humanly possible."

Adam frowned, but nonetheless agreed.

Claire said nothing but was upset at the fact that Arthur had once again done something to spoil their evening. What did he honestly hope to achieve? Nothing could be done, even if Claire wanted something to happen. She was married, and that was that. He could never have her.

As soon as the dance finish, Adam politely brought Susanna back over to their party. She was aglow, her face flushed from dancing so many dances.

Jack startled Susanna by seizing her arm. "What did he say to you?" he demanded to know.

"Who, Mr Slickson?" Susanna gasped, frowning deeply. "Nothing! He introduced himself and asked me to dance, that is all! I was not engaged."

"You are never to speak to that man again!" Jack ordered under his breath, a furious intensity to his tone. "Promise me!" Adam, Grace and Claire had huddled around them so as not to draw attention to the would-be quarrel.

Claire understood Jack's anxiety over this subject, but she knew he would be drawing attention to a feud that Adam and Grace knew nothing about, and would no doubt spark their curiosity.

"Alright!" snapped Susanna as she shook Jack's hand off of her. "Whatever did he do? Shoot your horse or something?"

Claire paled. No, she thought, he impregnated your brother's wife.

"Pardon me."

As if her heart had not already been through enough that evening, it stopped altogether. All five of their party turned around to see Arthur Slickson standing before them, his hands behind his back.

"I am sorry to interrupt. I am merely here to state that the waltz is next, and the lovely Miss Claire promised me her hand at the beginning of the evening." Arthur smiled charismatically as he extended his hand to Claire.

Arthur knew it was a supreme act of poor manners to spurn a dance partner, and he was counting on the fact that Claire would not do so in front of her family. He was also counting on the fact that Jack would not reveal his true hatred in front of his family, so as to protect Claire. Arthur was deliberately goading Jack, and it made Claire sick to her stomach.

But Claire wouldn't stand for this. She felt so ashamed to think of what she had stood for over the years. She had allowed herself to be used, to be so illtreated that she doubted her own worth. She had believed Arthur to be so much better than her that she could never hope to aspire to be good enough for him. But not anymore.

"I am terribly sorry, Mr Slickson," Claire apologised face-tiously before Jack had a chance to explore. "But as you can see, I have no dance card, and therefore, I have not promised any dances." Claire held up her wrist to show that she had none. "You must have me mistaken with someone else. Clearly, I think, as I am no longer miss. But Mrs. And the only man to whom I have promised myself is my husband. I wish you a good evening."

Claire smiled, and it was not forced at all. She smiled at the look of astonishment on Arthur's face as she curled her arm through Jack's and led him away. As soon as they were past Arthur, Jack brought his other hand across to hold hers.

"You did not need to do that for me," he murmured quietly.

"I didn't," replied Claire honestly. "I did it for me."

By the end of the evening, Claire had managed to forget Arthur's feeble attempts to spoil the assembly, and she and Jack had finished the winter assembly with smiles on their faces.

Claire was not at all certain what time it was, but she would not be ringing the bell for a servant at this hour. As soon as she and Jack had made their way into their bedroom, Claire kicked off her slippers which had become mighty uncomfortable after dancing and standing for so long.

Jack walked over to the trunk at the end of their bed and sat down as he began to untie his cravat. He was smiling thoughtfully, as though he was mulling over something enjoyable, and once again, Claire found herself staring at him.

Their room was dark, save for the lamp that Jack had ignited upon entering the bedroom, and so the soft glow of light was flicking across his face. Claire felt her heart flip again, and those all too familiar nerves beginning to settle themselves in her stomach.

But something else began to wash over her, and it was beginning to eclipse any feeling of apprehension. It was desire.

Before she knew it, Claire had crossed the room to stand in front of Jack at the trunk. His face was level at her collarbone, and he looked up at her questioningly.

"Are you alright?" he asked.

"Will you stand up?" Claire asked quickly.

Jack frowned, but obliged. He stood up, and Claire watched as his height quite overtook her own. He was now gazing down at her, wondering.

"No, I changed my mind," Claire stammered. "Sit down."

Jack chuckled as he obeyed. "Am I to hop on one leg next?"

But Claire didn't answer him. She looked into his eyes, and she saw the humour vanish, and a similar look of longing appear. He swallowed, and his tongue wet his bottom lip instinctively.

"Don't move," Claire whispered, as she bent her knees slightly and closed the distance between them. She pressed her lips to his softly, testing the feel of his closeness for a moment, before she kissed him more firmly. Jack was still, just as she'd asked, and Claire was grateful, as she was unsure her heart would be able to take it. Could he hear it thundering in her chest? Claire brought her hand to Jack's cheek, feeling the prickle of his stubble against her fingertips. She released him, allowing her lips to linger on his softly as she exhaled.

Claire then stepped backward from him, feeling her nerves return with a vengeance as she flushed crimson red. She covered her face with her hands, but in an instant, Jack was standing before her, pulling them away with his own.

"Don't you hide your face from me, Claire," he said tenderly. He was smiling at her reassuringly, and he leaned his head down to rest his forehead against hers. "I understand what a leap of faith you just took, and I promise, and I have promised, that I will never force you. But I have wanted to kiss you from the first moment I saw you, on this night three years ago. Can I move now?"

And Claire melted into his arms.

CHAPTER 24

J ack awoke the next morning to the sound of Claire's breathy snores in his ear. It was odd how quickly he had become used to the sounds she made. She was sleeping close to him, nestled up against his chest, her arm strewn across his torso in her slumber.

For what had happened the previous evening, Jack could not care less about Arthur Slickson. Claire had kissed him of her own will. She had looked upon him with a desire in her eyes that he definitely thought he would never see.

It gave him the greatest hope for what might come out of a chance meeting in the library, and a plan that really ought to have exploded into flames. Though, he ought not tempt fate, as they were to announce Claire's pregnancy at luncheon, and that was a key conversation that needed to be believed.

Jack had not realised just how much he had wanted to kiss Claire until he was able to. To hold her in such an embrace was unlike anything else, and he felt lucky. Jack had certainly not considered himself a fortunate man in the emotional sense. But if Claire might love him, or regard him with enough tenderness, then he would be content for the rest of his days.

It truly felt like she might choose him.

Jack had kept to his word, and he had not forced intimacy upon Claire. And he knew that only a few short months ago, waking up with a woman having not had her properly, he would have felt cheated, or extremely dissatisfied. But this was different. It was contentment. Fulfilment.

Jack turned his neck down slightly so that he could look upon Claire's face. She had not washed it, and so the rouge that she had been wearing the night before had smudged, making her look entirely rosy. Her hair, as well, had not been braided, and so it was quite untidy, but he enjoyed it. Jack smiled and laid his head back down on the pillow.

A snore practically ripped itself from Claire's nose which shook her awake, and she looked around in a daze, quickly brushing her hair out of her eyes.

"Oh!" she cried, her voice still thick with sleep. She then turned her head to look at Jack. "Good morning."

Jack smirked. "Good morning. Did you sleep well?" he asked.

Claire nodded as she rubbed her eyes. "I still vehemently deny that I snore, but I do think I heard myself that time," she admitted reluctantly. "I do apologise if I was noisy."

Jack chuckled. "I am quite used to it now. It is my own adverse lullaby."

An amused smile teased Claire's face as she rolled over onto her elbows, one gently resting on Jack's chest. She then used her hands to cup her face as she looked at him.

Jack was startled for a moment at her sudden closeness, her comfort with him, and the very fact that she had such an expression of sweetness that she could have asked him for anything, and he would have consented.

"Where did you learn to dance?" queried Claire curiously. "You are wonderful."

"Oh," uttered Jack bashfully. "I don't know. One attends three or so dozen balls and one learns a step or two."

"I remember thinking you were a wonderful dancer the very first time we danced together," recalled Claire. "I wish I knew the steps to the finer dances that a house like this would host."

Claire did not yet know the family that she had married into. "Mother will take Susanna to London for the Season in April, and we will most likely join in the summer, when both of the children are born. There are always grandiose parties to attend as we watch mothers like mine parade their daughters about."

Claire's eyes widened. "The Season?" she repeated. "Oh, my. How does Susanna feel being paraded about?"

"This will be her third Season, I believe. She is never without callers or offers, but I suppose Susanna is a romantic, and she wants what everyone else does." Jack exhaled with a smile. "You don't watch your older brother follow around the love of his life for his entire childhood, spend the next decade pining for her, before finally marrying her, to settle for anything less."

Claire's face softened with a smile momentarily, before an expression of remorse filled her face, and Jack knew exactly what he had said that had caused that reaction.

"I didn't settle," he promised her.

Claire pursed her lips as her eyes warmed with relief. She leaned forward on her elbows and pecked him quickly on the lips. Jack grinned, enjoying the fact that Claire felt comfortable enough to bestow affection.

Church was not on the mind of anyone within Ashwood House that morning, as evidenced by the fact that it was nearly time for luncheon, and nobody had arisen. Breakfast trays had been sent up, and Jack and Claire enjoyed their tray together.

"Can you tell?" Claire panicked, running from her dressing room into their bedroom.

Jack placed down his copy of The Tempest and looked up to see what Claire was asking.

Claire was wearing a plain, blue day dress, with very little detail. It looked to be one of the dresses she had come with and was perhaps made for Grace some years ago before being passed to Kate. Jack had noticed that Claire elected for simplicity around her mother.

Claire was standing on her side, pulling the fabric tightly across her stomach. She was looking at him in alarm. "Well?" she insisted. "Can you tell?"

If anything, Jack could see the smallest of protrusions, that could easily be attributed to the three pieces of cake each they had consumed at breakfast. When her dress was hanging normally, it would be impossible to tell.

Jack hopped off of the bed and crossed the room to Claire, daring to try his luck. "Well, let me look at you," he mused in a low tone, eliciting a huff from Claire.

Claire put her hands on her hips, still holding the fabric tight against her front.

"Yes ... yes, I think I do see something," Jack teased in a serious tone.

Claire gasped. "Oh, no!" she wailed.

Jack playfully poked her belly lightly. "That's the plum cake," he joked, "and the honey cake is here." He swiftly tickled her at her ribs. Claire flinched and giggled, attempting to swat his hands away. "And what do you know? There's a bit of brioche right here." Jack grinned as he tapped Claire on the nose.

Claire laughed as she rolled her eyes as she went to retreat back into the dressing room. At the door, she paused, and turned back towards him. "Thank you for making me laugh," she said gratefully. "I'm nervous."

"We are having a child, Claire," reminded Jack. "This is a happy day for us. And your family will be happy for us." Mine, too, God willing, he added in thought.

Sunday luncheon was a grand affair, and Claire's whole family had joined the Beresfords in the dining room. Perrie and Kate's infant son, James, were both being cared for in the nursery.

There were at least a dozen conversations being carried on around the table and coupled in with the sounds of silverware on dishes, it was quite a noisy room. Claire, however, was silent, and Jack knew that she was still a bundle of nerves.

He would be the one to make the announcement. He was the proud father, after all. Jack gave Claire a reassuring smile as he stood up from his chair and cleared his throat loudly.

The conversation quickly settled, and all eyes turned to him. Jack unwittingly met his mother's curious stare as she frowned quizzically. Would she be pleased? He didn't know. Jack was quite incapable of pleasing her.

"Pardon my interruption," he began, "but Claire and I have an announcement. We have recently learned that we are to welcome a child."

Silence. Shock.

From everyone but Grace, who, of course, had already guessed it.

And then there was an eruption of joy. Mrs Denham practically threw back her chair and hobbled around without her cane so that she could embrace Claire. Jack received congratulatory handshakes from his brother, Jim Ellis, as well as Claire's two younger brothers. Susanna and Claire's sisters were similarly showering Claire with congratulations and well wishes, and Jack had to smile as he watched Claire experience excitement and anticipation. A child truly was something to look forward to, and Claire naturally had been robbed of that joy for some time.

Jack then made the mistake of looking to his mother. Cecily was still firmly seated, glass of wine in hand, as she was looking on at the scene before her with a cool indifference. Jack was not present when Grace's first pregnancy had been announced, but he would have wagered she would have been a sight more enthused. Even now, as she carried on badgering Grace with silly old wives' tales to ensure a son, she was at least taking an interest. What was she thinking?

"A toast, I think," announced Adam, lifting his glass. "To Jack and Claire, and their wonderful blessing."

The toast was echoed by their guests, save for Cecily, who merely lifted her glass slightly. An intense irritation settled in Jack's stomach as he resisted the urge to openly glare at her. For

God's sake, this was her grandchild. It would be, no matter the circumstances, and she bloody well ought to be overjoyed about it. Or to at least offer an obligatory congratulations.

"Do you have any ideas on names?" Mrs Denham asked enthusiastically.

Jack was unfortunately reminded of the fact that Claire had once told him she had thought about naming the baby after its father.

"Well, if he is a boy, I was thinking of naming him after his father," Claire replied to her mother, as though she was reading Jack's mind.

Jack nearly coughed up his sprout.

"Jack would be a good name, don't you agree?" Claire asked, turning to him.

Jack was quite speechless and was bloody well honoured! The very idea that his son might not only share his surname, but his first name as well meant a great deal.

"Jack's Christian name is not Jack, but John," Cecily interjected coolly.

Jack ignored Cecily and offered Claire a grateful smile. Her cheeks warmed.

"I think Jack or John are both fine names," Mrs Denham said calmly. "And Edward suits both as a second name if either of you are so inclined."

Out of the corner of his eye, Jack saw his mother's posture straighten.

"Yes, I quite agree with that, Mrs Denham." Cecily's tone was oddly firm about that. Jack had half expected her to fight for Peregrine to be in there somewhere.

But then, Jack thought, perhaps Cecily was fond of the name. She had chosen it as one of Jack's middle names when he was born, after all.

"Would you mind if his second name is after my father?" Claire asked him quietly in hope.

Jack didn't mind at all.

After expressing her approval over the name Edward, Cecily removed herself from all conversation for the remainder of the meal, and Jack was becoming more and more irate. Claire was his wife, and she deserved as much respect from Cecily as she bestowed upon Grace. Jack wasn't expecting her to rustle up a bladder to feed Claire, but some politeness would not go astray.

After the meal, the party retired to the drawing room for cards and music, and Cecily surprised Jack by inviting both he and Claire into her parlour. Her tone was serious, and Jack and Claire followed her silently.

The parlour was a room reserved for ladies and seeing as Cecily rarely entertained friends in the country, it was hardly used, but was befitted with an imposing portrait of the duchess if one ever needed to be reminded of their inferiority when being received by Cecily Beresford.

"Won't you sit?" Cecily offered nonchalantly as she took a seat of her own on one of the settees by the fireplace.

Claire had been staring at Cecily's portrait, and did look quite intimidated as Jack took her arm and led her over to the opposite sofa.

"Are you to apologise, Mother?" Jack asked bluntly as they sat down. Claire flinched at his tone.

Cecily's eyes widened. "Apologise?" she gasped. "Why, one only does such a thing when they are wrong, and I am afraid I am unfamiliar with the sensation."

Jack gritted his teeth. Was that supposed to be a joke? "You are to be a grandmother and yet you could hardly charge your glass. I take great offense," he snapped.

Claire was frozen still, and Jack knew it was because she was terrified of Cecily. Jack was too angry to be ashamed.

Cecily rolled her eyes as she shook her head. "Oh, do not be so dramatic. Of course, I offer you both my well wishes for the child's health. My hesitation to celebrate is why I have asked to speak to you both. It is a most serious matter."

CHAPTER 25

Claire felt three inches tall and all sorts of ashamed as she sat frozen on the settee opposite the duchess. Why else would she pull them aside if not to reveal that she knew their secret.

But how? How could she have learned the truth? And what was she going to do? Was there a clause in a marriage certificate that meant unions could be nullified if a wife bears another's child? Would Cecily throw her out?

Oh, dear God, her mother would learn of her shame. Her mama would never look at her in the same way again.

And Jack, dear Jack, who had only tried to help her ... well, she hoped that she would bear the brunt of the trouble here. How Cecily could find fault with Jack's honour, Claire didn't know.

Claire prepared herself, braced herself, more like, and attempted to condition herself not to cry. She couldn't cry in front of Cecily.

"A serious matter?" repeated Jack. "What, pray, have I done now?" he muttered angrily.

Claire wished she could shout at him not to taunt her. Maybe, maybe if Claire begged her, Cecily might keep it a secret.

Cecily rested her hands in her lap and took a breath. "Do you know, I do not appreciate your tone, young man. I am your mother," she said firmly. "And what you have done is precisely why I wanted to speak to you both. Though, I suppose, Claire needn't be here, but I was never privy to these conversations with your father, and I resented it. I thought you might appreciate being in the know, Claire."

Cecily had just directly addressed Claire, but she had no air in her lungs to formulate a coherent response. Claire had no idea what the duchess was meaning, but she nodded, and prayed it was the right response.

Cecily arched an eyebrow as she looked upon Claire. "Good Lord, dear," she said distastefully. "You look as though I have just strangled your cat."

Claire sucked in a shaky breath in an attempt to regain some of her composure. Jack took her hand in his.

Cecily shook her head and focussed her attention back onto Jack. "Jack," she began, "I know you and I have never really seen eye to eye. You are very different to how I imagined you would grow up, and you are living a life far from the one I meant for you."

Cecily paused, and Jack blinked expectantly.

"Indeed, Mother, I might drown in your warmth. Please, don't trouble yourself," he murmured facetiously.

"Hush," snapped Cecily angrily. "I am well aware that the time for a warm relationship between us is passed, and believe you me, I have mourned."

"You have mourned me?" Jack scoffed in disbelief. "Mother, if I wanted to witness absolute rubbish, I'd go down and look at the slop bucket in the kitchen."

Claire could see that Jack was furiously angry, and his anger was not solely fuelled by this one conversation. He had years of pent up pain and suffering inside of himself, which was bubbling to the surface, threatening to erupt.

"Charming," hissed Cecily. "Honestly, why can't you be more like your brother? At least he listens long enough for me to make my point!"

Jack's head snapped, as did something inside of him. Claire winced as she knew exactly what Jack was thinking in that moment. He hated comparisons to his brother. He hated being considered the spare, second best, and not good enough.

"Then make your point," Claire announced forcefully, in a tone entirely foreign to her. She gripped onto Jack's arm and held him tightly. "I will not hear insults directed at Jack that are completely unfounded and unnecessary. If you have something to say about me, then say it!"

Jack slouched back in the settee and glared at his mother, while Cecily looked upon Claire with an expression of surprise. Claire swallowed and braced herself, willing her rush of gumption to stay.

"I may not have always appreciated this, but I do admire you Denham girls. All three of you are very loyal," Cecily noted calmly. "And the two sons of mine who have been so fortunate as to secure your hands are very lucky indeed." She directed the latter part of her statement to Jack tensely.

Though Claire was unsure of what Cecily wanted to speak to them about, her nerves settled a little as her fears of the duchess knowing her secret settled. Surely, she would not pay Claire a compliment if she knew the truth. Indeed, it was the first compliment, and the first real conversation, that Claire had received from or shared with Cecily.

"Though you and Grace do share something in common, Claire," Cecily continued.

Hair colour, eye colour, height ... Claire ran through the similarities in her head quickly.

But Cecily did not leave her wondering for long. "You are both, sadly, extremely poor."

Claire's mouth dropped open and she recoiled slightly. Poor? That was her objection? Did it warrant such a scene as this? Claire already knew that. Grace had been through this already and everything had worked out fine. Before Jack and Adam's father had passed away, he had consented to Adam and Grace's marriage!

"So, this is about money," Jack realised with a scoff.

"Yes, this is about money," retorted Cecily. "You receive a courtesy income from this estate, Jack, but that is not proper means. If your brother felt so inclined, he could suspend it! And he might have to one day in order to provide for his own children. Perrie will need a dowry one day, and Grace has no estate or dowry of her own to facilitate such things. How do you think dukes and earls and marquesses come up with dowries for their daughters? A sum like thirty or forty thousand does not magically appear in one's hand if one so desires it.

"God forbid this next child is a daughter and Adam will need to facilitate two dowries. He's a clever man, your brother, and I don't doubt he knows what he needs to do to ensure this estate remains prosperous, but there is a reason why marrying for money is sometimes a necessity.

"Do not misunderstand me, as I am pleased that you have found some felicity in your union." Cecily gestured between Jack and Claire. "Believe me, I understand desiring that felicity better than you think." Cecily paused and exhaled. "Jack, I say this with kindness, but you may interpret it how you wish. You are a second son who studied a useless degree from one of the best universities in the world. You wasted every opportunity that I served to you on a silver platter in favour of reckless behaviour. Your one chance was to marry rich to create some sort of sustainable life for yourself, but you chose Claire. And now you are to become a father. Do you even comprehend the gravity of this situation? You are living in your brother's house. Every bill, every drink, every woman is paid for by this estate. But this is a living, breathing, child, Jack!" Cecily exclaimed. "A son who will have nothing to inherit, or a daughter with no prospects because she has no money to marry well!"

Cecily stopped, her shoulders slumping as she looked upon Jack helplessly, and Claire got that very impression from Cecily. She felt helpless. She truly didn't know the man Jack was, and she felt helpless to assist the man she thought him to be.

Claire turned to look at Jack, expecting a snide retort, but her heart broke to see him. Gone was his anger and frustration, and in its place was shame and humiliation. He looked ten years younger. He was entirely slumped on the sofa, looking down as though he couldn't meet his mother's eye, accepting that she was right. He wouldn't fight because he accepted what his mother said. Jack had been reminded of his worth by his mother at his every turn, his every failure, and was never taught that it was alright to make mistakes.

"Don't you see what you do to him?" Claire asked accusingly, finding her gumption in spades. "You say you speak in kindness, and yet all you do is call him a failure."

Cecily stared.

"Jack is the kindest, fairest, most decent man I have ever met," Claire declared fervently. "You have spent so long seeing him as what he is not that you have denied yourself the chance to know who he is. He is not a clergyman and never will be! Quite frankly, I could not imagine a more boring existence!"

Claire huffed, feeling her veins flow with a fire that she never knew she was capable of.

"Jack loves to read, and I think devoting himself to one book for the rest of his life would have sent him stark raving mad! Do you know that about him? Do you know he loves to read? Do you know why he loves to read? Jack teaches me lessons that he learns from books. He tells me his interpretations and he understands the written word in a way I will never be able to.

"Jack is selfless, and he cares for others deeply, and the way he cares for me ought to make you proud. He cares for you, and for what you think, Your Grace. You should to be proud of him."

Claire realised that she was standing up and had not realised that at some point during her speech she had leapt to her feet.

Cecily was sitting still, a stoic expression on her face. Her lips were pursed as she breathed deeply.

Claire sat back down beside Jack and stole a glance sideways. He was shielding his face from Cecily with his hand, but he was looking at her with an expression of utter disbelief.

"You are right, Claire," Cecily said finally, nodding her head. "I have spent many years thinking about what Jack has not achieved. As I said before, do not mistake me in believing that I have not mourned for him."

"But he's not dead!" protested Claire. "He is sitting right here!" She did not need to mourn him!

"Oh, for God's sake!" hissed Jack, standing up from the settee swiftly. "I am not a boy anymore, and I will not hear you tell me that I have failed you for the thirty thousandth time. I will not sit here and be belittled in front of my wife." Jack turned to Claire and silently asked for her hand to leave with him, but Claire hesitated.

No. She wouldn't leave it like this. She couldn't. Claire didn't understand why this relationship was irreparable. She felt as though Cecily was meaning to be remorseful, and yet all she did was further remind Jack of his failures.

"Jack, I appreciate that I do not know the man you have become as well as I should. Had you been home in the last three years, I might have had the opportunity!" Cecily said tersely. "And I do sincerely believe Claire's assessment of you. I have never believed you to be of ill character. It does please me that your wife respects you, that she loves you. However, that does not change the fact that a child will be delivered into this world to a father without means to support it. As it stands, you have a wife whom your brother is supporting.

"What am I supposed to think when you consider how you have conducted yourself in years gone by?" Cecily challenged. "I am worried about you! Worried for you! Worried for your wife and your child! If I did not care, I would not have bothered to discuss this with you!"

"Discuss what?" challenged Jack. "You have not offered any solutions. All you have done is explained in excruciating detail what a sack of bloody cow dung you believe your son to be. Do you expect a thank you?"

Claire wondered what would happen if she locked Cecily and Jack in this parlour together, but then feared one of them would light it on fire. Jack hadn't told his mother, or anyone, about his plans for his publishing company. Claire knew that was on purpose. If it failed, as he had a legitimate fear of failure, he didn't want anyone to know.

Cecily huffed angrily. "The solution I was going to offer, darling, is a portion of my trust set aside for your child. Education for a son, a respectable dowry for a daughter. I had my trust earmarked for Susanna, but if I can get her married, and married well, I would happily have a solicitor draw up a new will for me. I won't have my grandchild growing up as a pauper."

Claire looked between Jack and Cecily as they stared at one another. Jack looked a wreck, and Cecily appeared beyond frustrated.

"Tell me, Mother, do you have any faith in me whatsoever?" Jack's voice was suddenly very soft, very fragile, so much so that Cecily recoiled from it.

Cecily remained silent. Her lips parted, but she said nothing.

"Father did," Jack continued quietly. "You may do what you like with your money, but I will take care of my family."

Chapter 26

Claire walked with Jack out of the parlour and back towards the drawing room. Jack looked shaken, and Claire clung onto his arm tightly to let him know that she was there.

Jack stopped abruptly in the middle of the hallway, nearly causing Claire to stumble at the sudden loss of momentum. "Nobody has ever stood up for me like that before," he said gratefully, looking down at Claire. "Nobody has ever said such kind things on my behalf, especially to my mother. Claire, did you mean it? Did you mean what you said?"

Claire's mouth opened with surprise as she saw the genuine uncertainty in Jack's eyes. He truly didn't know if Claire was sincere. "Oh, Jack," she breathed sympathetically. "I meant every word," she promised him. "You have nothing to prove to her," she insisted. "But she will see her folly when you start your business," she added confidently. She placed a hand on his cheek. "I know you will take care of me, and of our child. I have unwavering faith in you."

Jack stared at her in awe for a moment. Claire could see something in his eyes that was being left unspoken, but only for a moment before his gaze dropped and his lips captured hers in a searing kiss. Claire completely lost her footing in the moment and Jack's arms wound around her waist and supported her completely. Claire felt passion from Jack, as though he was giving her everything he had.

When he pulled away, Jack hovered a mere half inch from her face. A shadow cast itself across his face and his eyes looked so very dark and fiery. "You cannot know what it means to hear you say that," he murmured quietly.

Claire quickly realised she was quite out of breath. She exhaled shakily. "We are a team, are we not? I will always find the courage to fight dragons for you ... not that I am likening your mother to a dragon –"

But Jack interrupted her thought with a fit of laughter. He then pressed his lips to Claire's temple and kissed her softly.

"Oh, Lord, do you think she heard?" panicked Claire. They were not so far from the parlour.

"So, what if she did? It's my turn for the next dragon."

The Winter Assembly was always the last social gathering before the winter months set in. Ashwood, like most of England, grew freezing with icy winds and endless rain. Any snow that fell was washed away and would most likely resist sticking to the ground until January.

Before anyone knew, it was Christmastime, and Claire estimated that she was about five months along in her pregnancy, though as far as anyone else knew, she was approaching her fourth month. She was showing noticeably now, though she did try to disguise her size as best she could with heavy winter dresses and sitting at particular angles.

Only Jack had witnessed her proper size. It was something that she had felt she would feel awfully uncomfortable doing, but the more the child grew, the more it felt like Jack's. Whenever Claire pictured the baby as a young boy or girl, she always saw lovely curly hair, dark like Jack's, and beautiful hazel eyes. Though she knew it was impossible, it only made her excited for any future children they might have. And as soon as that thought had entered her mind, it was hard not to think about just how a child was created. She only knew too well.

But as much as Claire could delude herself into imagining that the child she was currently carrying would look like Jack, she found herself increasingly worrying how Jack was feeling. And these worries had begun to make her resistant to affection. Truth be told, as soon as she was beginning to visibly show her pregnancy, she felt guilty every time Jack tried to touch her. Of course, he was never forward or forceful, but she couldn't help but feel ashamed at what he would think if he kissed her and could feel the protrusion of her stomach.

Claire knew that if she asked, Jack would give her an honest answer, but she simply couldn't bring herself to ask him, "Do you ever feel repulsed by me?"

And she certainly would not blame him if he did. Surely the thought had to cross his mind now and again that she was this way as a result of another man.

But every night, without fail, Claire had become accustomed to wearing a pair of flesh coloured pantaloons underneath her night dress as Jack liked to see her stomach. Perhaps it was an answer to her question, but to Claire this felt different to affection.

A few nights before Christmas, Claire and Jack were lying in their bed, and Claire shifted the skirt of her night dress up and over her stomach but making sure her chest was modestly covered. Her rounded belly felt the warmth of the crackling fire and Jack leaned up on his elbow to look at her.

As they already had a name picked for the child if it was a boy, Jack had invented a little game to choose a name for a girl. Using his index finger, he would write a name on her stomach and Claire would try to guess it. She was quite good at the game, though she had rejected all of Jack's suggestions.

"I've been thinking of names a lot today, actually," Jack informed her as his index finger brushed her skin lightly, leaving a trail of goosepimples behind it.

Claire shivered. "Oh?"

"I've finally settled on a name for the publishing house."

Jack had been tucked away with Adam for weeks working on the establishment of the business. Jack told her quite a bit of what was going on, but some of the technical terms were foreign to Claire. Jack was planning on travelling to London in the new year to look at potential locations, which meant that at some point, they would be relocating to London, an idea that excited Claire greatly.

"What did you choose?"

"Beresford Press. What do you think?"

Claire smiled. "I like it. It is simple and professional, and bound to be on the inside cover of every fantastic novel ever written in the nineteenth century."

Jack chuckled. "I admire your optimism."

He liked to dismiss praise, but Claire knew Jack was excited. He had purpose, and it was gaining momentum. The rest of the family were still in the dark about Jack's plans at his behest, but Claire could see Jack's growing confidence every day.

"Now, the other names I have been thinking about." Jack began to draw on Claire's belly, causing her to giggle as he brushed over a ticklish spot he had discovered.

Claire concentrated, and was quite certain the name started with an M.

A ... that felt like an A. R ... and Y?

Mary. The Virgin. Claire thought the she might be struck by lightning if she so much as considered the name. "Mary," Claire guessed. "No."

"What's wrong with Mary?" protested Jack, before he quickly got over her rejection and set to writing another name.

Claire correctly guessed and rejected Agatha, Anne and Emma. None seemed quite like the right name, and she couldn't put her finger on why. She supposed she could only hope the baby was a boy so that she wouldn't have to choose a girl's name.

"Alright, I have one more," Jack said finally.

A straight line. I. But then the letters kept going. Was that an O? V? And going. Y? What sort of name had this sort of combination of letters? U. Claire was certain the last letter was a U.

"What on earth was that?" Claire exclaimed. "I am quite certain you just chose a random assortment of vowels to vex me."

Jack laughed again and shook his head. "No, I assure you, it spelt something."

"What?" Claire asked impatiently.

Jack shook his head. "I thought you were clever at this game," he reminded her.

"You are telling me that you actually just wrote something coherent? In the King's English?"

Jack nodded with a sheepish smile on his face. "Absolutely."

"Well, then! Tell me!" Claire demanded. "What if I like it?"

Jack grinned and extended his arm across her torso as he leaned in to kiss her. The feel of him touching her stomach as he leaned into her caused Claire to flinch, and that horrible feeling filled her stomach. Jack stopped immediately, before laying back down on his pillow. Claire sensed the game was cover, so she pulled her nightgown back down over her stomach. "I truly hope you do like it," he replied, "but I'll tell you another time."

"Sorry," murmured Claire.

"Don't apologise," he assured her quietly. "My brother ... he told me that this time can become very uncomfortable for women and that is why ..." he trailed off.

Claire felt terrible. Jack had not asked her about her reluctance or expressed any particular feeling over it for weeks. This was the first time. And he thought it was because she was feeling physically uncomfortable. And she was, though not in the way that he believed.

Claire had been so worried that Jack would feel disgusted by the feel of her if he tried to kiss her, that she had not stopped to consider any other way he might be feeling.

Say it quickly, Claire willed herself. "Idon'twantyoutoberepulsedbyme!" Claire nearly shouted all in one breath.

"What?" Jack appeared dumbfounded.

Claire forced herself to take a deep breath and found the courage to say, "I don't want you to be repulsed by me."

"Repulsed?" repeated Jack in an alarmed tone. He sat up in the bed, turning properly so that he could look upon her. "Wherever would you get an idea like that?"

Claire flushed crimson.

"Claire, please," begged Jack. "If something is bothering you, tell me."

"Well, I ... I can't help but feel awful every time you try to kiss me, and you feel this." Claire touched her hands to her stomach. "That you might be thinking ... oh, I don't know ... about the stupid girl who has the very evidence of her stupidity poking you every time you try to be near me."

Jack frowned deeply, going as far as to close his eyes and pinch the bridge of his nose with his thumb and fore finger. "Claire, I can swear to you on my life that the last thing I am thinking about when I try and touch you is that you are stupid. And I would certainly never refer to my unborn child as 'evidence of stupidity'."

Claire felt incredibly foolish, though it was not a foreign feeling. She needed to get that through her head. Perhaps her delusions of imagining the baby would look like Jack would help.

"Will you tell me what the last name was?" she asked quietly.

"No," retorted Jack, a smile teasing at his lips. "I'll tell you another time."

Claire sighed. "It better be beautiful and not something dreadful like ... Frederica."

Jack laughed. "Oh, blast. How did you guess it?"

Claire playfully swatted Jack's arm. But he returned his hand to her belly and rested it there for a moment, before he leaned down to kiss Claire softly. She didn't flinch.

At that very moment, she felt a flutter against her hand. Grace had told her that babies kicked inside the womb. Was that what this was? And this time, Jack was the one to flinch.

"What was that?" he asked, alarmed.

"I think the baby moved!"

"Oh my God, is it supposed to do that?" Jack stressed. "Do I summon a surgeon?" He had already leapt out of the bed before Claire could sit up. "Where are my bloody breeches?" he shouted as he tossed a pile of clothes over his shoulder.

"No, no, be calm!" exclaimed Claire. "Grace told me it happens! The baby is big enough to start moving around."

Jack froze as he dropped the clothing that he held in his hand. "That's normal?" he checked.

"Yes," nodded Claire.

"Oh, God, my whole life flashed before my eyes." He slumped down on the trunk and Claire started to laugh. Jack frowned at her, amused. "Just for laughing at me, her name is going to be Frederica, I hope you realise."

CHAPTER 27

"Claire, you needn't have spoiled me thus!" Mrs Denham cried as she wrapped her new satin shawl around her shoulders. "Oh, my, I do not think I have ever owned something so fine!"

Claire had chosen the shawl as her mother's Christmas gift at the dressmakers in London and had been saving it. She smiled widely at her mother's delight.

Claire and Grace had travelled to Mrs Denham's house on Christmas Eve to give their gifts to their family. The Denhams were, of course, joining the Beresfords for Christmas dinner, however Cecily tended to spoil Perrie beyond anything and gifts for others were quite lost.

Claire liked this, however, as it felt like home to be with just her family. Except for Kate. Claire wondered if she ought to run down the street to fetch her. This had been a rather impromptu visit, and so an invitation had not been extended.

"Peter, this is for you," Grace announced, handing their brother a small gift wrapped in brown paper.

Peter frowned bashfully as he accepted the present. He undid the string before removing the paper to reveal a fine, leather box. He opened the box to reveal a steel tipped pen, and a very fine one, indeed. The pen itself was wooden, with gold filigree decoration.

"Adam ordered one of those pens from London for his study," explained Grace, "and he finds it so much more efficient than a quill. You don't need to sharpen them every five minutes. They are not easy to come by, but I thought you might like it."

Peter removed the pen and hefted it in his hand, a small smile of admiration spreading across his face. "I don't really need a pen if I'm going to be a blacksmith," Peter said quietly.

As he held the pen, Claire could see the soot that was caked underneath Peter's fingernails. He was nearly finished his apprenticeship with Jim. He would indeed be a blacksmith very soon. He would be able to open his own forge and earn a living with the trade.

Had their father lived, Peter would have no doubt learned Edward Denham's trade as a tailor. But Grace knew, as they all did, that Peter had a cleverness inside of him that went beyond what was expected for his life. He was quiet when it came to his intelligence, and he never advertised a desire for anything more, most likely out of respect for Jim.

Had their father lived, Claire was certain that Mr Denham would have seen Peter's potential and found a way for him to attend a proper school, a day school or somewhere he could stretch his mind. As it was, Peter was educated at the church like the rest of his siblings. He was lucky to have such natural intelligence.

"What you use it for is entirely up to you," Grace replied, "but I hope you get some use out of it."

Peter wouldn't say it, but Claire could see that he was monumentally pleased with his gift. She truly did hope he found some fulfilment with it.

As the gift exchange concluded, and Jem had already run off to find a friend to use his new tennis racquets, Claire happened to follow him by looking out the window. She gasped, and was thankfully quiet, as no one asked her what was wrong. Standing across the street, leaning nonchalantly against a wall, was Arthur.

What on earth was he doing? How had he known she would be here? What did he want her to do? As these questions flooded through Claire's head, she suddenly realised that any one of her family members could look out the window and see him. Especially Grace. After what had transpired at the assembly, she could not have Arthur hanging around and arousing Grace's suspicions. Claire needed to get him to leave, but in order to do so, she needed to leave the house for a legitimate reason.

Kate. Of course.

Claire suddenly got to her feet, drawing her family's attention. "Mama, I am going to run down to the forge to fetch Kate. It is not a family gathering is she is not here." Of course, Jem had already abandoned them. Claire had not asked. She was married now, and she did not need her mother's permission.

That did not mean there would not be any objection.

"We'll send the carriage on," Grace decided. "It's far too cold to be walking."

Claire blasphemed in her mind. "It's a five-minute walk, not a five-mile walk," she protested. "Besides, I like the winter air. It's refreshing."

"In your condition?" Mrs Denham added disapprovingly. "I think not, Claire. I think sending the carriage is a fine idea."

Claire wasn't about to be told. "I will return shortly with Kate. I have made the walk a thousand times, even in winter." She walked stubbornly over to the cupboard where her coat had been stored.

"Peter, go with your foolish sister," insisted Mrs Denham reproachfully.

"No!" cried Claire, a little too quickly. "I am perfectly capable of going by myself. A baby does not prevent me from walking. I will return soon." And Claire left before she could hear any further protestations.

The Ashwood carriage was waiting outside of the Denham house for Claire and Grace. Claire smiled at the driver and the footman politely before she continued on her way down the street towards the forge. She wrapped her coat tightly around herself to keep out the intense chill of the wind and stole a glance sideways to make certain that Arthur was following her.

He was.

Claire felt sick as an awful feeling of guilt filled her stomach. What was she doing? Oh, what would Jack say if he knew what she was doing? Claire knew she was only trying to protect her secret from her family, but why did it feel so wrong?

Her legs seemed to have a mind of their own as she walked, and they took her off into the woods before she could reach the forge, towards the spot where she had once rendezvoused with

Arthur. She could hear his footsteps now, the sounds of twigs snapping following along behind her.

When they were concealed from the road, but not so deep into the woods, Claire turned on him. "What do you think you are doing?" she snapped angrily, doing her best to stare at him with hard, no-nonsense eyes.

Claire had expected Arthur to smile at her, to say something wicked or suggestive, but instead, he stood quite defeatedly, and a safe distance from her. His expression was pained, and his green eyes were sad.

"I am sorry," he uttered, in a way that suggested he was sorry for a lot more than merely waiting for her outside her mother's house.

Claire was startled.

"Claire, you cannot know how sorry I am," Arthur continued. He didn't move from where he stood, keeping the same level of distance between them. "Haven't you ever made a mistake? This is, without a doubt, the biggest mistake I ever will make. Because of it, I lost you. And I should be angry with you, I know it. I should be angry that you couldn't wait five minutes for me to comprehend what you had told me before you went and got yourself married ..." Arthur trailed off, the frustration in his voice rising.

Claire closed her eyes to stop herself from shouting out an expletive so loudly that everyone in the village would hear her. "No," she practically growled. "I will not be blamed in your apology. That is not how an apology works."

Arthur nodded, conceding. "Yes, yes, you are right, of course. I am sorry," he apologised again. "It is not you I am angry at, but myself. I lost you, Claire, and I cannot fathom it. You were mine and I let you slip through my fingers."

Claire searched in desperation for any hint of falsehood, but she couldn't find it. Arthur appeared truthful, and genuinely remorseful, and her eyes involuntarily welled up. Just because she was angry, it did not mean it did not still hurt.

And it also didn't mean that she did not care. She couldn't eliminate her compassion. The moment those feelings began to settle in her stomach, Claire ceased to trust herself. She couldn't understand what was happening, and even if Arthur was sincere, she knew it was wrong to be conversing with him. Jack would be furious. He hated any mention of Arthur, so much so that Claire had never really told him about what had happened to her. But she would tell him this. She had to, didn't she?

"Oh, Arthur, I cannot hear this," Claire exclaimed, exasperatedly. "I cannot trust you. I cannot trust a word you say. I don't know what you want from me. Do you want me to forgive you? Or do you want me to betray my husband?"

Arthur didn't answer, instead he pulled a small, wrapped package from inside of his coat and extended it out to Claire. "I never got to congratulate you," he murmured. "Please, take it. Happy Christmas."

Claire tentatively closed the distance between them for the briefest of moments before she flitted back to her original position. For a small parcel, it was weighty, and Claire was curious. Arthur had never given her a Christmas present before. He had never wanted to draw suspicion from his mother. What was this for?

"Open it, please," Arthur urged.

Claire spied him cautiously before unwrapping the present. Inside the paper was a black, leather box, not too dissimilar to the one that Peter had just received, except instead of a pen, inside the box was a beautiful silver rattle. The handle was moulded like a flower stem, and the two bells hung off of silver rose buds. It was, without a doubt, one of the most beautiful things Claire had ever seen.

She could not mask her delight at the gift, and Arthur took a step towards her.

"There is a place to engrave the child's name," he explained. "Of course, if you would like, you could return the rattle to me when the child is born, and I will have its name put on there for you. I wanted you to have it now as a token."

"A token of what?"

"Friendship," replied Arthur simply. "We were always good friends, weren't we?"

Claire's momentary pleasure dissipated as she closed the lid on the box. "No, Arthur. We were never friends. I was ..." she paused, struggling, "I was hopelessly in love with you, and you knew it. You preyed upon me. We were never friends." Taking a breath, Claire added, "I cannot accept this." She held the box out to Arthur. She really didn't understand what he was trying to do. For all she knew, he could be sincere, but Claire did not have enough trust left in her to believe in the good.

Arthur sighed. "Claire, please, I know I have made unforgivable mistakes. I am paying for them. I have lost you, and I understand that. But this child –"

"– has nothing to do with you. This child is my husband's," Claire interjected forcefully. She had never spoken to Arthur this was before, and she was amazed that her voice hadn't faltered.

Arthur exhaled, frowning. "I understand that is what will be circulated, obviously." Arthur sucked in a breath. "Claire, I know what you think of me, you have told me as much. But I cannot live with myself if my ... if this child has nothing from me. Please, take the gift. You can tell Beresford you bought it yourself, or you sent for it. He doesn't have to know it was from me, but I will. And I hope you will see, Claire, that this gift comes with no obligation. I only hope that you will see things from my side, and perhaps we might find a friendship in the future ... one that suits us both."

Claire stared at him in confusion. What did he want from her? Did he wanted to be asked to Ashwood for tea? But then, Claire thought, was this perhaps a good way to make peace? Peace with her past for her future. It was hard not to associate Arthur with thoughts of her heart disintegrating, even though she had already realised that she had never truly been in love with him. That did not make the pain any less real.

"I need to call on my sister now," Claire announced, placing the rattle in the pocket of her coat. She made the decision then and there that she would tell Jack about this meeting. She had done nothing wrong, and Arthur hadn't done anything inappropriate. Jack would make what he would of the rattle. If he chose to throw it out the window, Claire would understand. "Thank you for the rattle," she said obligatorily. "It was a nice thought." That was more sincere. It was a lovely rattle; the loveliest Claire had ever seen.

Arthur smiled now. "You are very welcome," he replied. "Run along now, Claire. Be seeing you."

Claire moved swiftly past Arthur, looking back over her shoulder as she made her way towards the street. He was watching her with a calm smile on his face. The minute she was back on the street, she hurried towards the forge.

Having taken longer than three minutes to fetch Kate, Claire was subject to a lecture from her mother. Apparently, marriage did not make one exempt from being scolded by one's mother. But after Mrs Denham had seemingly gotten over Claire's tardiness, they did enjoy the rest of their afternoon.

Claire, however, felt a burning heat on the back of her head, as though her coat was staring at her from the cupboard, taunting her with the knowledge that the rattle was inside her pocket. She felt guilty for having it, and guilty for questioning Arthur's motives. She knew it was foolish to trust him, but he had never made any sort of gesture like it before, and Claire wondered if he truly did want his blood to possess something fine.

All she knew was that the minute she confessed the day's events to Jack, all would be well.

In preparation for the festivities the following day, Claire asked for a tray to be brought up to their room for their supper. Jack was not in the bedroom yet, but Claire was not prepared to dine with her sister and have Grace ask any follow up questions as to why she had taken so long to fetch Kate.

Jack arrived three minutes after the supper tray did and looked very pleased at the offering. He kissed Claire's forehead as he sat down at the table beside her and helped himself to a sandwich.

Claire stole a glance over her shoulder. Her coat was laying atop the trunk. She had not yet removed the rattle from her pocket. Just as she was about to work up the courage to tell him, Jack spoke first.

"I have something to ask you."

His tone was quite sombre, and it startled Claire, as he did not sound at all pleased as he had been not a minute ago when he had seen the sandwiches.

"Is something wrong?" Claire asked involuntarily, her mind starting to race. Oh, God. Had someone seen? Had they sent word? Claire forced herself to be sensible. She was not in the wrong. She hadn't done anything to be ashamed of. And she would be telling Jack about the meeting anyway.

"No," replied Jack, "though I am afraid my request is quite morbid."

Claire frowned as she listened intently.

"Shortly after my father died, I left for London," he started. "You know this, of course. But my father died on the twenty-sixth of December, three years ago the day after tomorrow." Jack was staring down at his plate as a chill ran down Claire's spine. "He is buried on the estate, in the family tomb. This year will be the first that I am in residence on the anniversary. My mother will visit at some point, as will Adam, Grace and Susanna." Jack took a breath. "I want to see him," he said decidedly, before his eyes flicked to hers. "But I can't do it alone."

Claire hadn't realised the anniversary of Peregrine Beresford's passing was so near. As she looked into Jack's eyes, she could see the raw pain, the residual grief, and the fear that he felt in asking her. Claire knew in the moment that she could not burden Jack with any news of Arthur.

"Of course," she said, nodding. "Of course, I will go with you."

CHAPTER 28

Christmas went relatively smoothly, and a good time was had by all. Even Claire managed to forget about the silver rattle which was still hidden in the pocket of her coat above stairs. But not entirely.

The day after Christmas was a more sombre affair. Gone was the joy of the season, and in its place was a house in mourning. Of course, the house was no longer in full mourning, or even half mourning, but it was a day of reflection and remembrance

Seeing Jack deeply saddened only increased the guilt she was feeling in the pit of her stomach. But she couldn't upset him further. She could not make this day about her own foolishness. Jack had asked for her help, and by God she was going to give it.

Claire wished that she knew Jack's father, even a little, so that she might have something to say about him that might bring Jack comfort. Grace was the only one who really knew the duke outside of his family, and Claire remembered her sister telling her about reading Dante's Divine Comedy to Peregrine during his last weeks and days.

Such an anecdote was the inspiration behind Jack's Christmas present from Claire. She had not realised the significance of the day after Christmas, only while they were in London, she had procured a copy from a print shop. She was certain Jack had a copy somewhere, but she thought he would appreciate it, nonetheless. And he had. He had spent an hour on Christmas night reading to her from Dante's Inferno.

Cecily left for the tomb early, according to Adam, and on this day she wore her mourning attire. Susanna followed her mother an hour later, and Adam and Grace journeyed down with Perrie at noon.

Claire busied herself with some embroidery while Jack quietly read. She knew that he would not want to interrupt anyone, especially his mother.

"My father wanted to read this in its entirety before he died," Jack said suddenly, after a long while of silence. "I think, as he came to grips with his own mortality, he believed that reading through the three stages of this book, Inferno, Purgatorio and Paradiso, the paradise being Heaven, that it would cleanse his soul."

Claire abandoned her embroidery on the seat cushion next to her. "What a powerful tale," she murmured.

"Indeed," agreed Jack. "Did you know I studied Dante at Cambridge?" he asked.

"No, I didn't," replied Claire. "I don't really know much about him." She definitely felt very ignorant about a lot of things. Her world was very small compared to Jack's.

"Dante Alighieri is perhaps the most famous poets to have ever lived," Jack informed her softly. He closed the book and sat up on the bed so that he could look over at her. "In his Comedy, he writes of his final guide through Heaven, the symbol of beatific love and divinity, and her name was Beatrice. We were taught that Beatrice was a real person, a girl whom Dante met only twice, but he fell in love with her at first sight and carried his love for her always. I remember thinking at the time how could one person so affect another after one meeting."

Claire smiled serenely. "She must have been quite an extraordinary lady for Dante to consider her so perfect."

"I always thought he must have been a little mad," admitted Jack, "but then, I didn't know until it happened to me, and I found that perhaps we all are a little mad."

Jack's eyes narrowed with a glimmer of intensity and Claire recoiled slightly. He was speaking of her. Why would he think such things about her? "How could you ever equate me with someone divine?" Claire stammered; her unease evident in her voice.

Jack surprised Claire but chuckling. "I struggle to believe there is anyone truly divine, Claire," he replied honestly. "What I meant was I understand how meeting someone who is meant to be important in your life can change you. The night you danced with me was the night Dante began to make sense to me."

Claire struggled to believe she could have made such an impact on what was, perhaps, the most foolish night of her life. All she could think about was being noticed and ravished by Arthur that she had not taken much notice at all of Jack. It only made her wish that she could go back and force herself to listen to the warnings of others.

Claire's eyes flicked to her coat, which was still strewn across the trunk at the end of their bed. She needed to return the rattle. She should not have accepted it. She would return it and be done with it, with him.

"Will you come down with me now?" Jack asked.

Claire sucked in a breath and nodded. "Yes, of course."

The Ashwood estate was very large, but Claire did not realise just how large it was until it came time to walk to the family tomb. It was well past the gardens, the stable, and through a small wood before they came to a large pond. Claire had not realised there even was a pond on the estate. Adjacent to the pond was a large, marble cathedral, or what looked like a cathedral.

Jack told Claire quietly that it was modelled after Parthenon, though obviously not the scale. Claire had no idea what the Parthenon was, but looking upon the tomb, she could imagine it.

It was a very serene place by the water, and Claire thought it very restful. There were no sounds around them save for the tread of their boots through the grass.

Claire held Jack's hand tightly as they climbed the few steps up to a series of marble columns. Through the columns was a heavy door that Jack pushed open. The hinges squeaked from disuse. Jack let go of Claire's hand momentarily to light a candle which illuminated the large room. It was quite plain, save for the wooden crucifix nailed to the wall. There was another set of doors which Claire assumed would lead them through to the place where Peregrine was buried.

"My father's great-grandfather had this tomb erected," uttered Jack, "consecrated, everything. I don't want to end up in here."

Jack opened the next set of doors and led Claire through, though he stopped very close to the doorway and stared ahead with a hard expression on his face. This room was much larger than the first and contained several stone sarcophagi. Cold, rectangular boxes containing the people who had once ruled over this estate.

On the end of each was the name of the duke, his date of birth, and his date of death. Jack fell silent, and Claire took back his hand and squeezed it tightly. They walked together to the last sarcophagus, and Claire looked down at the epitaph.

6th Duke of Ashwood

Peregrine John Clarence Edmund

BERESFORD

February 6 1751 – December 26 1806

Jack was frozen still as he stared. His face was almost contorted with a conflict of grief and anger. "I don't know what to say ... what to do," Jack whispered, almost inaudibly.

"When I visit my father at the church," replied Claire, just as quietly, "I converse with him, and every time I go back, I pick up where I left off. I could be chatting to him about something banal that I know he would not care for, or I will be telling him about something important. What would you tell your father?"

Jack was quiet again for several minutes, before he suddenly said, "You will be happy to know I am finally reading the Divine Comedy." He actually chuckled, a laugh that was thick with emotion. "I never got through it when my professor set it, and it was through sheer luck I got through the course, but I was given it as a present by my wife, who might possibly be ..." he paused, "... is my Beatrice."

Claire's heart swelled and shattered at the same time. She knew what those words meant, and to be privy to such a heartfelt, vulnerable conversation was important. To be seen in such a light was a deep privilege, and one that Claire knew she did not deserve. Not while she was in possession of the rattle, which, at this very moment, was still in the pocket of the coat that she was wearing. Claire knew that she couldn't hurt him. She wouldn't allow Jack to be hurt again.

She reiterated her conviction from this morning. Claire would return the rattle, and she would never be led, swayed, or tricked by Arthur again. No matter his intentions with his gift, Claire could not and would not give him the opportunity to get into her head and spoil what she had been so fortunate to find.

Jack left Claire alone later that afternoon to work with his brother, so Claire stole away into the lady's bedroom in their suite. She sat down at the untouched writing desk and produced the rattle, still in its leather case, and placed it on the desk beside the sheet of paper she was going to write on.

Dear Arthur, Claire began, before immediately deciding against the term of endearment. She crumpled the paper, but then decided it wasn't destroyed quite well enough. Claire ripped it to pieces and threw it into the fireplace. She got out a fresh sheet and began again.

Mr Slickson,

Yes, Claire decided. That was better.

I am writing to you to return your gift. While generous, it is unwanted and inappropriate.

I kindly ask, Claire crossed out "ask", demand, and she pressed a little too hard with her quill and darkened the ink, that you refrain from any form of correspondence or communication in the future.

Should you meet me in the street, I ask that you treat me no different to anyone of whom you view as an indifferent acquaintance and I shall do the same.

I wish you good health and happiness in your future.

Claire Beresford.

Claire's hand, she knew, was not her best, but her writing was legible, and any gentleman would receive and take heed of such a missive. She signed the letter positively because she did not want to wish harm on anyone. She did sincerely hope that Arthur may find someone for whom he would move mountains. It would not be her, and Claire had long accepted that fact.

Claire folded and sealed the letter, addressed it, and took it and the rattle box out of the bedroom. Claire entrusted the letter to Mr Cole, who was discreet when it came to the interests of the family. And the minute it was out of her hands, Claire felt relief.

It was gone, and she could move on.

Or so she thought.

The morning of the first of January, during a family breakfast to celebrate Adam and Grace's third wedding anniversary, the post arrived like it usually did. Letters and cards arrived as they always did, only this time, there was something for Claire as well. A letter and a parcel. From Arthur.

Claire rarely received letters. The last few years of her life, ever since her father died, really, had been spent tending her mother's house, and so she had never had time for friends who would write her.

Everyone was occupied with their own post. Jack, in particular, was reading correspondence from a man in London who was looking into printing presses for him, and so Claire quickly broke the seal on her letter.

The letter was short. So short, that he had only written four words.

Until we meet again.

Claire knew what would be inside the parcel, and she felt sick to her stomach to look at it.

CHAPTER 29

"On the ground floor there is a very comfortable drawing room and sunroom, a dining room, a parlour, and a sizeable study and library. There is a master's suite of rooms, as well as three additional bedrooms above stairs. Downstairs boasts a generous kitchen as well as servants' quarters."

Jack looked around the Mayfair townhouse with admiration. It was, of course, not as large as Ashwood House or Ashwood Place, but it was a sizable family home in a desirable and safe part of London that he could afford. The rooms were large and bright, and the location was ideal, and very close to the space he had leased for his publishing business.

The house was comfortably furnished, but there would be some pieces that Claire would need to choose. The minute his mind naturally shifted to Claire, Jack felt a pang of guilt in the pit of his stomach.

"I think this will do nicely," Jack told the leasing agent. "And it was two hundred guineas per annum?"

The agent nodded. "Yes, milord. I shall have the contract drawn up for you post haste and sent to Ashwood Place."

"Thank you." Jack was led out of the house and the agent locked the door behind him.

The two gentlemen separated, with the agent climbing into a hired carriage and Jack walking on foot back towards Ashwood Place. Jack hoped that the news he had secured a home for their relocation to London would please Claire. He needed to return with good news, or something that would endear himself to her.

He had been a right coward for nearly two months now. In fact, it was now March, which meant that it had been two months since Jack had seen Claire. Jack had written to her, of course, and had received some brief replies, but he knew he had done wrong.

Jack had been in London for business. He had spent the last eight weeks procuring equipment, renting his business space, hiring a few printers, and finally securing a home. While it was only a thirty-mile journey from London to Ashwood, Jack had been reluctant to make the trip knowing he had left Claire poorly. Poorly was perhaps an understatement. They had quarrelled for the first time, and Jack had been a right ogre to Claire. He had stormed out of the house that very hour.

January 2, 1810

Two months earlier

Jack had observed Claire's odd behaviour for nearly two full days. She seemed on edge and nervous, anxious even. He would have attributed it to her condition, however whenever they talked of the baby, she never seemed afraid.

Something else was bothering her.

Before dinner that evening, when everyone had gone upstairs to change, Jack let himself into Claire's dressing room. She was alone and had not rung the bell for a servant to help her. She was sitting at her dresser fiddling with something in her hand. It was small and silver, and as it moved, Jack heard a soft twinkling sound, as though there were small bells attached to it.

"Claire?"

Claire had obviously not heard him enter the room, and she jumped from fright. She turned in her chair to face him and she placed a hand on her chest as though she was trying to settle her pulse.

"I do apologise," he uttered. "I should have announced myself."

"No, no, don't be silly," Claire assured him. And she smiled at him in earnest, and Jack felt his chest tighten.

Lord, she was beautiful when she smiled. She was beautiful all the time anyway, but he loved to see her smile. He had realised some time ago that he loved everything about her, only he had not yet mustered the courage to tell her. That all too frightening fear of rejection plagued him. He teased it, though, often writing it on her belly during their name game, but Claire could never work it out. She was trying to spell a name and was quite convinced that Jack was writing something in Ancient Greek.

But her smile was not as full as it would usually be, and this brought Jack back to his senses. "Claire, what's wrong?" he asked tentatively.

Claire stowed whatever it was she was holding on the dresser, and Jack looked upon it quizzically. It looked like a rattle, perhaps. It had been many years since Jack had seen one. The last he could recall was Susanna's when she was an infant. Had Claire sent away for one?

"There is something I need to talk to you about," Claire began softly, planting her hands in her lap.

Jack felt his stomach seize as he sensed a seriousness in her tone. "What?" he asked nervously.

"Please, don't be angry," Claire begged, her voice breaking as she looked up at him, and her eyes quickly became glassy with tears.

A sickening feeling of dread fell over Jack as he thought the very worst. He could see it all over her face. Guilt. She had done something to feel guilty about, and Jack already knew what she was going to tell him. She had gone and done it. She had gone and done it and now she was going to leave him.

"What?" he asked again, though this time, however, he spoke through gritted teeth and nearly spat venom.

His change in tone made Claire flinch. "Please," she said again desperately. "It's Arthur, he –"

But that was enough for Jack. He heard that man's name, he could see the guilt all over Claire's face, and he knew what had happened. How? When? What? A thousand questions flooded Jack's mind, all bringing with them an overwhelming feeling of absolute irate fury, all of them making him feel violently ill.

"Do not finish that sentence!" he ordered furiously, and Claire began to cry.

"Jack, please!" Claire cried. "Arthur –"

"Stop!" hissed Jack. "I won't hear it. I won't hear it!"

Jack had continued to shout at Claire for the next hour as he packed, compelling her to be quiet as she cried and tried to explain but he wouldn't hear her excuses. He couldn't hear what she did. He didn't want to live with the picture of it burned into his brain for eternity. As it was, he was livid with her, and livid with himself that he had allowed himself to get so carried away with the idea of a perfect family, and a perfect marriage.

He was always second best, and he had chosen a wife who could never love him.

A letter arrived for Jack shortly after he arrived in London. It was from Claire, and was addressed very poorly, the ink having run from her tears. Jack was still in a foul disposition and had furiously thrown the letter into the fire without reading it.

A letter from his brother arrived shortly after asking after the situation, and Jack had written him briefly explaining that he was in town making preparations. Adam had made no mention of Claire, which Jack deduced to mean that Claire had kept their quarrel to herself. Jack wouldn't out her. He had honour even if she did not.

What he hated most of all was that his feelings were unchanged. For whatever maddening reason, Jack still felt the deepest love for Claire, which was hurt more than anything.

Claire wrote twice more that week, and by the time the third letter arrived, Jack's tore the letter open in frustration.

Jack, she began.

Seeing as you have responded to Adam's letter, I am assuming that you haven't broken your hand and are incapable of replying to me. So, I must, instead, conclude that you are still too angry with me to even listen, or read what I have to say. That will not stop me writing it down every day and sending it to you until you write back to me.

The more I think about it, the less I realise that I have done wrong. I tried to tell you the truth and you wouldn't let me speak. By your reaction, I can imagine what you believe has taken place, but I must state vehemently that this is not true.

What I was trying to say was that Arthur and I spoke on Christmas Eve, when Grace and I went to visit my mother to deliver Christmas gifts. He was waiting outside of my mother's house and I spoke with him so that he would leave and no draw attention. He gifted me a silver rattle which I returned.

I didn't tell you about it because you asked me to accompany you to your father's tomb and I didn't want to cause you any pain at an already troubling time.

On the first of January, I received a short missive from Arthur, as well as the rattle returned. Arthur stated that he would see me again. I felt terrible that I had deceived you, but I believed I was doing the right thing in protecting you at a time of grief.

I then decided to confide in you, to tell you the truth and to ask for your help, but you immediately thought the worst of me. And I cannot blame you for that. You married me in my state, and so it must not have taken much for you to believe me capable of something so sordid.

But I am sorry I didn't tell you the truth straight away. Aside from this falsehood, I have not committed any sin.

Please respond to this letter at your earliest convenience.

Your wife,

Claire.

Jack had read Claire's letter through another half a dozen times to make certain that his fears were not realised. For the briefest of moments, Jack felt pure elation, followed swiftly by relief. She hadn't betrayed him. She wasn't leaving him.

And then reality had set in quickly after when Jack realised what a true brute he had been. He had behaved appallingly, and he had made Claire feel cheap. He had allowed his own insecurities to manifest and warp a situation that might have been easily handled.

Jack wanted to return to Claire, but he quickly became too afraid. He allowed weakness to settle in, and his insecurities to continue to plague him. Claire hadn't been intending on leaving him, but after the way he behaved, he wouldn't blame her if she did.

Jack thought that by staying away, he was letting the dust settle, and Claire's animosity cool. But he knew he was simply being a coward. If he faced her, Claire could leave him. She could declare that she would never love him after the way he'd made her feel. He wasn't strong enough to handle it. Would he ever be?

Jack had replied to her letter immediately, apologising profusely for his reaction. He had continued to write frequently as he carried on with his business in London, informing Claire of the goings on in hope that it would excite her. She had loved London, and he was praying that when he did finally return, she would be excited.

Jack sent Claire one final letter that March, telling her of the house he had secured. He described it in as exciting detail as he could, going so far as to suggest that she look in catalogues for any nursery furniture items that she might want to send for.

But as his business was now concluded, Jack knew that he needed to return home.

CHAPTER 30

I t was the eighth Sunday that Claire had attended church alone. Of course, she was never alone, but Jack was not there.

He was not there because they had quarrelled. Or rather, Jack had refused to listen to Claire long enough for her to explain her side of the story, or even the story in general. It had also taken four or so letters before she had received an apologetic reply from Jack.

And that was weeks ago.

He had still not returned.

Claire had never felt more isolated in her life. She was in a house full of people who couldn't know what she was experiencing, and the one person who had promised to be on her side wasn't.

Jack didn't trust Claire, and she did understand why. She had allowed herself to be compromised, but that still didn't mean Jack's flight to London didn't hurt. Jack could believe the worst in her and Claire had the reason why tucked underneath her dress.

What was worse was that she had needed to pretend that all was fine. She had perfected her false smile, and had assured Grace mainly that she was fine, and was in regular contact with Jack while he conducted his business in London.

Cecily, who was still not privy to Jack's plans, had made a few comments about Jack slipping back into old habits when she thought Claire wasn't in earshot, but she had heard them, and she had to admit that it had crossed her mind, too.

If Jack knew the truth, and was sorry, why hadn't he come home to ensure that she was alright? The name Giulia Panetta kept haunting her, and Claire was unsure what she would say or do if she found out that Jack had reverted to his old ways. Would she be expected to permit them? He had promised her that he would never take a mistress, but had he changed his mind?

These were all questions that she longed to ask him if he ever deemed it necessary to show his face.

At the conclusion of the service, Claire excused herself to go and make a contribution to the collection box. It was getting harder and harder to get up and down, particularly after an hour of sitting on those uncomfortable wooden pews. Claire didn't know how Grace was managing it considering she had mere days or weeks to go before the birth of her own child.

She rubbed her sore back before she unfastened her money purse to make a donation.

"Are you alright, Claire?"

Claire was startled as someone else dropped a handful of coins into the box quickly after her. When she looked up, she saw Arthur's green eyes watching her curiously.

"Leave me alone," Claire whispered in reply.

"It seems that is all that husband of yours is doing lately," countered Arthur coolly. "What has it been, two months, or three, since he has last escorted you to church, or anywhere? And in your condition, my, my," he tsked.

Claire had become an unwitting participant in a correspondence with Arthur since Jack had left for London. He wrote her love letters, really, messages of affection, care, and curiosity after the baby. Claire had ignored his letters, or responded with brief requests for them to cease, but if she didn't reply, he happened upon her in the street as she visited her mother or accosted her in church as he was now.

And as much as Claire didn't want to be receiving correspondence from Arthur, she couldn't deny that it was nice to read kind words. In comparison, the letters from her husband boasted the number of ruddy printing presses he had acquired, and it did nothing but infuriate her.

Nevertheless, Claire knew that the letters were wrong, and would only cause more friction, which she believed was one motive of Arthur's. What she wasn't certain of was his endgame. What did he hope to achieve? She couldn't marry him. He wouldn't have any claim over the baby. If anything, all he could really achieve would be Claire's ruin, which was what stopped her from scratching his eyes out.

"You look beautiful today," Arthur continued softly, a smile teasing at his lips. "You know I always loved you in white. Is that why you chose that dress?"

Claire frowned in poor temper. "No," she said flatly. "I chose it because it is one of the few that fit me at my current size. Do not flatter yourself. Your head is big enough."

Arthur chuckled, an impressed expression upon his face. "How ever could Beresford leave you?" he wondered aloud.

"Is that a joke?" Claire practically hissed. "Why don't you ask yourself that same question because you managed it, too, or don't you remember?"

"Too?" repeated Arthur. "So, he has left you?"

Claire bit her tongue, annoyed that she had allowed her temper to get the better of her. What plagued her now, really, was that she didn't know if her words were the truth. Jack could have well left her. Perhaps that was what kept him away, and the letters of business were a sham to cover it up.

"Claire," Grace murmured, joining their conversation as she linked her arm through her sister's. Grace looked between Arthur and Claire curiously, not apologising for the look of disdain she gave to Arthur. "We are leaving. Come along," she urged.

"Your Grace," greeted Arthur, almost slyly, enjoying Grace's disapproval as he tipped his hat and bowed to her. "How well you look."

"Do pass along my best wishes to your mother, Mr Slickson," Grace said tersely. "On behalf of Mrs Denham, also."

Mrs Slickson was not in church today and hadn't been on the days that Arthur had intercepted Claire as he had.

"Mother is only too happy to hear how well her former servants are doing," Arthur replied in a menacing tone, a clear attempt to put Grace in her place.

But Grace was poised and practised in receiving such taunts. Cecily had prepared Grace well for her first jaunt into London society. She did not crumble as Claire would in being chided so.

"Forgive me, Mr Slickson, but green is not your colour," Grace said apologetically, but without sincerity.

Arthur furrowed his brows and looked down briefly at his clothing. "I am not wearing green, Your Grace."

"Oh, I was not referring to your attire. Good morning." She smiled sweetly, before leading Claire away from him and towards the church doors where the congregation were exiting. "I do not like that man," Grace hissed under her breath. "What was he doing talking to you?"

"Mr Slickson was making his donation as I was," replied Claire quietly.

"I feel like he has taken a bit of an interest in you these last weeks, or are my eyes deceiving me? I have never seen him pay a bit of attention towards you before now. Well, aside from the assembly, of course."

And she wouldn't have. Arthur had been very careful to appear aloof during their secret courtship. He was now breaking all the rules.

"Has he? I hadn't noticed," replied Claire as they met with their family.

Grace was immediately claimed by Adam, who had taken to fussing over her, and so she was not able to ask Claire anything else.

Claire received two letters in the morning post a few days later. One from Jack telling her about a house that he had leased for them, and one from Arthur, detailing how lovely she looked at church on Sunday.

Claire abandoned Arthur's letter quickly for Jack's. A house? This was the first time he had written to her about something other than the preparations for the publishing company. He had leased them a house in London. Jack went on to describe the rooms, and his plans for what needed to be done. He even suggested that Claire begin to source nursery furniture that she liked.

Jack clearly planned for Claire and their child to accompany him to London. He wasn't set on abandoning her, then. That much was clear. But then, nothing felt clear. Not until he returned and explained.

Claire stashed the letters in her pocket and decided to go back up to her bedroom. The stairs were getting harder and harder each day and looked very much like a mountain today. The baby kicked her right in the ribs as if to mock her lethargy.

No sooner had she climbed the first step did Cecily appear at the top of them. She looked upon Claire with an expression of relief. "There you are, Claire!" she exclaimed. "Hurry up! It's Grace's time!"

All of her unsettled emotions vanished to the back of her mind as her focus shifted to her sister. Claire had been present for Perrie's birth, but this felt different, incredibly so. Claire used the bannister to pull herself up the stairs as quickly as she could, before she hurried after Cecily as swiftly as her legs would carry her.

As Claire and Cecily rushed down the hallway, Claire could see Adam pacing outside of his and Grace's bedroom while holding Perrie on his hip.

"Did you send for Mrs Denham?" Cecily asked as they reached the door. "And the doctor?"

"Yes," replied Adam, an anxious and pained expression upon his face. "I should be in there," he said insistently. "This is my bloody house, my wife, my child ..."

"No," said Cecily firmly. "Even if it wasn't how things are done, you are far too nervous and will only put stress on Grace. She has a big job to do. It is not comfortable pushing one of those out." She nodded to Perrie. "You wait here, and I'll let you know when you have your child."

"Mother," Adam said tensely. "It's early. The doctor predicted the end of March and it is only the eighth. Will Grace be ..." Adam couldn't finish his sentence, and Claire could see the true fear in his eyes.

And the minute that thought entered Claire's mind, fear set in for her as well. Oh, God. Was her sister in danger? Would ... would Claire be in danger, too?

"Grace will be just fine," promised Cecily, putting a comforting hand on Adam's arm.

"Mother," Adam said again, more forcefully this time, his hazel eyes watering. "I don't care a wit if it's a boy or a girl, I just need everyone in that room to be healthy and stay healthy."

His voice was cracking on nearly every word and Claire needed to leave. As she pushed open the door to the bedroom, she heard Cecily reply, "I am not about to let anything happen to either of them, I promise."

Cecily followed Claire inside the bedroom and closed the door behind her. Inside, Grace was pacing in front of the fireplace, her maid, Ruby, flanking her with her arms outstretched to catch Grace if she fell. Susanna was pulling back the covers on the bed.

Grace suddenly stopped, placed her hands on her waist and threw her head back as she moaned, clamping her eyes shut. "Oh, Lord, that was a big one," she complained, before she continued to walk.

"Grace, come and lie down," suggested Cecily.

"No," rebuffed Grace. "I need to stand. I need to walk."

"Ruby, how close are the pains?" Cecily asked.

"About six or seven minutes apart, Your Grace," replied Ruby. "She says she was having the pains all night but didn't say anything."

"You saw Adam, didn't you?" Grace huffed as she stopped to lean against the mantle. "They were intermittent, and I knew if I woke him, he'd be in a panic. At least this way he has had a proper night's sleep."

Claire's mouth opened as she realised just how impressed with her sister she was. Claire didn't yet know the pain, but she couldn't imagine suffering in silence just so her husband could be fully rested. Claire's next thought was that she would wake Jack the minute her pain began so he could suffer alongside her.

Claire then wondered if that would even be possible considering she had no idea of when he was planning on returning. For all she knew, she could be sending him a missive to London to let him know that the child had arrived.

"Alright, well, your mother has been sent for, and the doctor," Cecily announced. "You can tell us when you are ready to get into the bed."

Grace nodded as she winced, leaning her head against the mantle now as another wave of pain hit her. She let out a long, excruciating moan and cried as it left her. "Oh, that one was awful!" she complained weakly. "And it came faster."

Claire watched, half in fear, half in awe, as her sister soldiered through a dreadful labour. Grace was strong, and she bore every wave of agonising pain for hours.

Mrs Denham and Kate had arrived, and by the time that the doctor had entered the room, Grace was in bed and pushing. Grace was covered in sweat, her dark hair slick against her forehead. Susanna was wiping her forehead every ten seconds it seemed as she pushed harder and harder, veins appearing out of nowhere to show just how hard Grace was working.

Claire and Mrs Denham were either side of Grace, holding onto both of her hands. Every time Grace pushed, she nearly broke all the bones in their hands and Mrs Denham was forced to give her hand to Kate.

"Mama," whined Grace, "I'm tired. It hurts." Grace was exhausted and pale, and looked as though she had absolutely nothing left to give.

"I know, darling, I know," comforted Mrs Denham. "You are doing so well."

"Push, Your Grace," instructed the doctor. "I can see him."

Grace found a strength within her to obey, and she cried with all her might.

"Oh, my goodness," gasped Susanna as the sound of a newborn crying filled the bedroom.

Grace collapsed into a heap and started to cry as she pulled her hands from both Kate and Claire and reached out in front of her, anxious for the child to be given to her.

Cecily took the baby into her arms as she was holding fresh linens to allow the doctor to finish with Grace. Claire looked up at the grandmother to see tears streaming down her face as she smiled at the new baby. Cecily quickly placed the bundle on Grace's chest. As soon as she had her baby, Grace wrapped him safely in her arms.

"It's a boy?" Grace asked weakly as she tried to crane her neck to look.

"No, dear," replied Cecily, still brimming with happy tears. "She's a perfect little girl."

Claire couldn't help herself either. She cried as she watched Grace immediately bond with her baby. The pain she had endured through over the last several hours vanished and it was swiftly replaced by a look of true love, a look that told Claire that Grace would do it all over again. Claire instinctively hugged her belly protectively.

"Well, what do you know?" murmured Cecily. "Lamb's bladder doesn't ensure a boy."

Grace gasped. "You actually fed me bladder?" she snapped.

"What does it matter?" Cecily said dismissively. "Who cares a wit? We have another perfect little girl in the family." She cooed over the newborn and stroked her head gently.

As Cecily pushed back the linen slightly, Claire could see that the new baby had quite a lot of dark hair, just as Perrie had when she was born.

Grace shook her head. "Will someone go out there and put Adam out of his misery?" she asked, and Ruby dutifully left Grace's side to go to the door.

No sooner had the door been opened did Adam burst in, not waiting to hear what Ruby had to say. He raced over to the bed, practically pushing Susanna out of the way to sit down beside Grace.

His eyes were not for the baby, not at first. Adam's focus was solely on Grace as he looked over her with a husband's worry. Adam then looked to the doctor, who was now standing by the basin and washing his bloody hands. "Is the duchess alright?" he asked desperately. "Are they both alright?"

"Yes, Your Grace," confirmed the doctor. "The duchess did excellently, and the new babe has a good set of lungs. You're not to worry."

Adam kissed Grace with relief and broke away with a smile. "Thank God," he declared, before he could finally look down at their new child. Adam gently kissed the top of the baby's head as well. "Who do we have here? Is it a boy or a girl?"

Grace smiled up at Adam tearfully as she said, "It's Lily."

Adam grinned. "Welcome, Lily."

"Lily," both Cecily and Mrs Denham said at the same time. "I love it," then added Mrs Denham.

"Perrie was named for our fathers," Grace surmised quietly. "And now Lily is named for our mothers."

"Oh," gasped Cecily, holding a hand to her chest. She appeared truly touched.

Tears fell freely down Mrs Denham's face. Kate hugged their mother.

"Cecily Ellen Beresford," clarified Adam.

"Did I hear that right? We have a Lily?"

Claire's head snapped around at the sound of a voice she recognised.

Chapter 31

Jack entered the bedroom tentatively, and Claire observed that he was holding Perrie, for perhaps the first time. She had never seen him hold her. He carried his niece on his hip.

His expression was reserved, and Claire didn't know how to feel for a long moment. He was returned. She had seriously considered, up until receiving his letter regarding the house, that he might very well elect not to return to Ashwood. Up until she had broached the subject of Arthur, they had been such a pair, such a team, and Claire had truly felt as though it might be different.

She knew very well what he wanted from her, and Claire believed that she would one day be able to give that to him. But whether Jack liked it or not, Claire had a past, and a very painful one, with Arthur, who at this point in time, was making it very difficult for Claire to have a future. She had never shared any of her experiences with Jack, and perhaps that was what had been holding her back from fully trusting him. Ought not she be able to share these experiences with her husband?

But the moment she had even mentioned his name, Jack had assumed the worst of her, and he had abandoned her. Claire decided that Jack could call it business all he liked. But she had been alone these two months with nobody to talk to. Her world had shrunk exponentially since becoming with child, and though that was not Jack's fault, leaving her without the chance to properly explain was.

Jack had left, and Arthur had fully taken advantage of that fact. It was attention she no longer wanted or desired, and it was something that her husband ought to know. But what would happen if she brought up the subject of Arthur again? Would he publicly disgrace her as a whore this time?

Jack did not trust Claire. He had made that perfectly clear. But now, Claire feared, she did not trust Jack. And she was loathe to feel such a way, for up until that argument, Jack had been her perfect champion.

Jack's hazel eyes settled on her, and he offered her a small, yet well-meaning smile. Claire did not rise to greet him. Partly because she had been supporting her sister for hours and hours with a weight the size of a large pumpkin under her skirt, and partly because she was angry. Mostly because she was angry.

"Jack, when did you return?" Grace asked lethargically. "You never told us you were coming back today. Did he tell you, Claire?"

"No," Claire replied quickly.

"No, I didn't tell anyone I was returning today, though I am happy to have made it back for the birth." Jack placed Perrie down on the bed, and she immediately crawled across the bed-clothes to her mother.

"If you delayed much longer, you might have missed the birth of your own child," Cecily said disapprovingly.

"I would not have missed the birth of my own child, Mother," retorted Jack.

"Enough," ordered Adam, as Perrie began to peer over the blanket that her sister was wrapped in.

"What is it?" Perrie asked curiously as she extended her index finger to poke the baby.

Claire couldn't help but smile. Her sister was in absolute raptures, and Adam appeared to be the proudest father there ever was as he looked over his two daughters, and the wife he adored.

"She's a baby," answered Grace softly. "She's your sister. You must be very gentle."

Perrie obeyed her mother, and gently stroked the top of Lily's head, seemingly enjoying the feeling of the tuft of dark hair.

"You are the oldest now, Perrie. You will always have a little sister to look after," Adam told his daughter tenderly.

Claire could not help but look up at Grace then and knew that her own parents must have said the same thing to her when she and Kate, and even Peter and Jem were born. Grace always endeavoured to look after her, and it was now ... now that she was feeling wretched and alone, that she wished she could run to her older sister like she had done so many times over the years.

"Can you give Lily a kiss?" Grace prompted, lifting Lily a little higher to Perrie.

Perrie leaned down, and very softly placed a kiss on Lily's forehead, prompting a big smile and a very sweet giggle.

"Alright everyone," Cecily said to the room. "I think it time we give Adam and Grace a little privacy with ... Lily." She almost whimpered as she said the name. Claire really admired how touched the duchess was for such a gesture.

"Would you like us to bring you anything, Grace?" Mrs Denham asked. "Something to eat or drink, perhaps?"

"Oh, yes, I wouldn't mind," Grace replied, nodding her head.

"I'll see to that, Mrs Denham," Ruby interjected, before the maid turned back to Grace with a smile. "Congratulations, Grace."

"Thank you, Ruby," said Grace appreciatively.

As Ruby left, everyone but Adam and Perrie moved to follow. Kate claimed Claire before Jack had a chance to, and she helped Claire to her feet. Claire quickly slipped her arm through her sisters and walked with her out into the hallway, purposefully avoiding her husband.

"I can't wait to have another child," Kate whispered to Claire. "I hope it does not take as long as it did for us to be blessed with James."

Claire recalled it had taken nearly three years of marriage, perhaps a little longer, before Kate had announced that she was finally with child. "I am sure it won't take so long next time," she assured her.

Kate smiled, and rubbed Claire's forearm. "Nevertheless, it is your turn next. And at least you can be certain that Grace did not choose the name you wanted." She lowered her voice. "Something tells me that your husband would never approve the name 'Cecily'."

Claire tsked. "Don't be wicked," she scolded, albeit playfully. "I think Grace chose well." Claire, on the other hand, really had no idea what she would name a daughter.

Cecily arranged for a late supper, though Kate needed to excuse herself to get home to feed her baby. Without her sister as protection, Jack deemed it safe to approach Claire.

Claire's arms hung listlessly at her sides as Jack met her on the landing.

"Might we talk?" he asked quietly, and only for her ears. "Perhaps in our bedroom?"

Claire merely nodded, and Jack excused them from supper, before they walked silently in the direction of their bedroom. Jack opened the door once they had finally reached it, and Claire's nose immediately turned up at the slight musty smell.

It had been two months since she had shut the connecting door, however. She had been sleeping in the adjoining room. She had not wanted to be in this bedroom alone.

Jack seemed to smell it as well, and he immediately went to one of the large windows and pushed it open, letting in a cool breeze from the clear night outside. "That's better," he murmured. Then he finally turned around.

Claire was still standing by the door rather awkwardly. After not being in this room for so many weeks, she suddenly felt like a guest. Though, after not having seen her husband, either, for so many weeks, she feared feeling like a stranger.

"Claire ..." he began, rather helplessly. Jack's brows her furrowed, and she could see the appearance of shame upon his face. But he didn't continue.

But Claire wouldn't listen to an apology he couldn't even begin. "Arthur has been writing me," she interjected instead. "Some weeks I have received a letter every day. Some are every other day. Love letters, letters of admiration, letters inquiring after my health and the health of the child. And when I do not reply, he finds some place to happen upon me. In the street, in church, and I do not know what he wants or expects from these interactions, but I wanted to tell you in full before you run away again thinking I am some sort of frigid, inconstant whore." Claire spoke quickly, her voice thick with emotion, and shaking quite considerably.

Jack flinched at the last word, though he looked very pained to hear her entire speech. But he didn't interrupt, and he did listen.

"I haven't known what to do," Claire continued vulnerably, her voice breaking as her eyes involuntarily filled with tears. "He won't leave me alone and I don't know what he wants from me. But I haven't had anyone to help me. I have had nobody to talk to because ... because ..." A sob escaped Claire's throat. Claire took a deep breath in an attempt to compose herself. "Jack, for three years of my life, Arthur was my whole world, and I thought myself in love with him. Even though I know now it wasn't real, that does not mean the pain vanishes, and ... and I want to be able to talk to you. I thought you were on my side, but the moment I needed you, the moment I tried to be honest with you, you thought the very worst of me. And, believe me, I can understand why you would think the worst of me, as I know the condition you found me in was less than respectable, but I thought ... I thought you held me in higher regard."

Claire wiped her eyes with her sleeves as tears fell.

"I have no excuse," murmured Jack, holding out his hands. "I was a jealous cad, and the moment you mentioned his name, I thought I'd lost you. I thought I'd lost you to him and I was furious, furious with you, furious with myself. I should have listened to you, I know. The moment I read your letter, I knew what an utter fool I had been."

Jack anxiously rubbed his hands together as he took a shaky breath.

"I was jealous," he said again, his eyes finding her with an ashamed sincerity. "I've always been jealous of him; from the bloody moment he took you away from me at the first assembly. And I couldn't bear to listen to you speak about him for fear you would tell me that you wanted him. I couldn't hear it. I couldn't survive it. It's a fear that has lived in my mind this whole time that you would leave."

"So, you left instead?" Claire uttered.

Jack hung his head, supporting it with his hands. "I do not think you a ..." but he couldn't say the word. "Claire, when I saw the guilt on your face when you tried to tell me about ... him ... all my fears were realised. I thought I'd lost you to him, and I knew I would always be second best."

Claire knew that was Jack's innermost fear and insecurity, and she did understand how it would be so affected by Arthur's constant presence.

"Why has it taken you so long to come back?" Claire demanded to know, her voice stronger. "I wrote you weeks ago."

"Because I am afraid," he stated. "I am a coward and I am afraid." Jack exhaled as he closed the distance between them, standing not four feet from Claire. He did not reach for her, however. "I was, and still am, afraid that you would leave me now that I am returned. I almost felt as though I was delaying the inevitable.

"You have never told me that what you felt for him wasn't real," Jack continued softly, "and I realise that I have never allowed you to speak of him, of your experience, without making you feel awful or uncomfortable. Had I set my pride aside, I would have known this. Claire, I cannot tell you how sorry I am for leaving you. I am sorry for leaving you alone, and for leaving you unprotected. I am sorry for abandoning you, and breaking your trust, and for allowing my own stupid fears to affect you so."

Jack surprised Claire by sinking to his knees and looking up at her.

"I have unburdened myself on you time and again, and you have listened to me and comforted me, defended me. My God, Claire. Can you ever forgive me? I will be better, I promise."

Claire's lower lip trembled uncontrollably. She believed Jack's sincerity. But did he trust her? She had just confessed everything to him, and he had not said a word. "Do you trust me?" she whispered.

"Yes," breathed Jack, "I do. I trust you, Claire. And I hope that I can once more have your faith."

"And what about Arthur?"

"You will leave him to me," said Jack firmly. "And I will do what I ought to have done months ago when my first message did not sink in. But Claire," Jack reached out for her hand, and was very relieved when Claire did not deny him, "I want you to talk to me. I want to you feel as though you can tell me anything. I make you a solemn vow, here and now, that I will never walk away from you again."

Chapter 32

Claire did not know what Jack said, or what he had done, but the letters from Arthur soon ceased after Jack's return from London. Shortly after their reconciliation, Jack had left to call upon Arthur, though Claire knew it would be anything but a social call.

Claire and Jack spent the following four weeks finding their place in the other's life again. The ease of the friendship that they had shared did not magically reappear, and before there could be familiarity, there was awkwardness and uncertainty.

But Jack did try. He was attentive and present, and he never, not once, walked out on a conversation. He invited Claire to speak about Arthur, and after some convincing, she had divulged exactly what had transpired over their three years of supposed courtship.

Claire told Jack of her infatuation with Arthur, beginning in childhood. She told him how she used to dress especially nice for church when she was but ten years old in hope that Arthur would notice. Claire explained how this infatuation had become her silly idea of love, and how it had culminated in Arthur kissing her for the first time on the night of that fateful winter assembly.

Arthur had convinced Claire that it was a courtship, and that it must be kept secret. His mother wouldn't approve, and if she were, she needed time. Claire was too naïve to understand that chaperones needed to be present during a respectful courtship, and that what she was engaging in was a reputation ruining tryst. Claire had fallen head over heels in love with Arthur, or what she had believed to be love at the time.

Over the years, he would tell her that he doubted her love, or that he needed to be convinced, and Claire believed him completely, fearing for his insecurities. This was how he had convinced her that she needed to prove herself in a more intimate way. Claire had known it was wrong to be engaging in such affairs outside of marriage, but Arthur had always told her that they would be married when he had convinced his mother.

The moment she had revealed her pregnancy, Arthur had spurned her, and Claire realised that she had been monumentally fooled. And that was why she could not understand why Arthur refused to leave her alone. If he didn't want her, why did he keep interfering?

Jack dutifully listened to her tale, even though Claire knew he hated every moment of it. She couldn't know exactly what he was thinking, but she truly hoped he was not wondering how on earth she could be so persuaded.

But he never said any such thing. Instead, he brushed her cheek with the backs of his knuckles and uttered, "I am so very sorry this happened to you. There is a special place in hell for men who illtreat women."

Claire and Jack began sharing a bedroom again shortly thereafter, and slowly they began to return the friends that they were before Jack had left for London. Although, Claire did sense something was different. She found Jack hesitating at times, often before he spoke, or if he looked to be thinking over something. It was as though he had something on the tip of his tongue and couldn't yet say anything.

Claire feared asking him what was on his mind. Jack had refused to tell her what has transpired between himself and Arthur, and she worried that Arthur had been cruel. She didn't want to hear that Jack was doubting the trust that he had put in her.

By Claire's calculations, she was in her eighth month of pregnancy when it came time to christen Lily. She felt as big as a horse, and she found her dress to be entirely unflattering, and yet she was forced to attend as Grace and Adam had asked her and Jack to be Lily's godparents. Of course, Claire was honoured and would carry the title with pride, only she wished she did not feel so much like a peddler pushing a heavy cart.

April had been unseasonably warm thus far, and Claire felt quite hot and bothered as she tied her bonnet ribbon under her chin. Her skin was glistening with sweat.

Jack appeared behind Claire in the mirror and smiled. It immediately annoyed her just how dashing he looked in his fitted coat and breeches. He certainly did not look like a whale.

"Why must you look like that?" she huffed.

"Like what?"

"That!" insisted Claire. She turned around to look up at him. "You are very handsome, and you know very well."

A sheepish grin appeared on Jack's face as he received Claire's backhanded compliment. "My, I am sorry. Though it is nice to hear that my wife does not find me abhorrent."

"My cheeks are chubbier," complained Claire as she covered them self-consciously. In fact, everything about her person felt swollen. Even her fingers. Perhaps this was her punishment for escaping the nausea that Grace had suffered through.

"Claire, you are very beautiful, and you know very well," Jack countered, using her own words. Claire softened momentarily before he spoke again. "Even if there is a little more of you," he added teasingly.

Claire gasped, but could not help but laugh as she swatted him playfully. "I do not think there is much longer to go," she revealed. "Some weeks, I think, and then he or she will be here."

"And yet we are still to decide on a name for a girl," murmured Jack.

"I know you have a favourite. Only you refuse to tell me," accused Claire. Something else that they had resumed since Jack's return was their little game in which Jack wrote names he liked on her belly and she attempted to guess them. It was something she was glad for, and it greatly made her feel close to Jack despite her fears. Feeling such a closeness to him was unlike anything she had ever experienced, and she had not realised just how much she needed him until he had returned.

Some of the names were easy to guess and dismiss, but he kept coming back to the one name she could not figure out. The one full of vowels. He clearly liked that one, or else he would not suggest it so often.

"If only you would learn to spell," teased Jack in reply.

Claire rolled her eyes. "I am convinced you have plucked it from some obscure book as it is certainly not English. It ends in a "u", does it not? What name ends in a "u"?"

"You really want to know?" Jack asked, raising his brows in question. He looked at Claire intently, inspecting her.

"Yes," she insisted.

"I couldn't bear if you dismissed this one," he continued, his voice softening.

Claire willed herself not to make a face, hoping the suggestion wasn't awful. But her curiosity reached its peak. What name could be so important? "I am certain I'll like it."

Jack smiled, but before he could open his mouth, the mantle clock chimed. "I will tell you after the christening," he promised.

Claire groaned.

CHAPTER 33

Claire lost all feeling in her legs as they buckled underneath her, her wrists catching her before she fell to the ground properly, saving her belly from any trauma. Her breaths were shallow and panicked and she felt as though she were going into shock.

From the corner of her eye, she could see Arthur walking away, leaving her on the ground, but Jack was quick to kneel before her, placing his hands under her arms to lift her to her feet.

"Do you need a doctor?" Jack asked tersely, and Claire dared to look up at him.

"How could you do it?" Claire rasped tearfully. "How could you challenge him?"

She could see the mistrust as plain as day in Jack's hazel eyes. Were she not so frightened, so unnerved, she would have been furious.

"How could I not?" he countered angrily. "That man laughs at me!" he hissed. "And he has no respect for you."

"And so, you would kill him for it?" Claire exclaimed, almost shrilly. She wiped the tears from her eyes with her fingers. "Or you would die because of it?" Her voice broke at the very thought.

Jack's lips pressed firmly together. "Did you plan this?" he snapped. "Did you arrange to meet him? Did you mean to steal away to him? Tell me so at once."

Claire's hand whipped across Jack's cheek before she knew what she was doing, but she could not regret it. "No!" she cried emphatically. "No, I never planned anything! I never asked for anything! I was hot!" Claire insisted. "I told you so in the church. I needed some air and he was here without my knowledge. He accosted me and owing to the fifty-pound gourd I am carrying; I was not quick to get away! Though I tried to push him away from me. I did try."

Claire's hands fell to her sides as she looked up at Jack, truly unknowing what else she could do prove herself.

"You begged my forgiveness," she whispered. "You asked for my faith. You told me you trusted me."

Claire watched as Jack's face softened, and his eyes filled with guilt and remorse. He nodded in concession, and said, "You're right. I did ask that of you. I do ... I do trust you, Claire. All I know is I rounded the corner and saw you ... with him. I wasn't paying much heed to what your hands were doing. I'm sorry. I made a snap judgement."

"I don't think you do," said Claire tearfully, as she shook her head. Claire felt a pain her chest, not unlike the pain she felt keenly the day that Arthur has spurned her in September. Only this pain made her previous suffering feel like a tickle.

Claire's heart ached immeasurably at the realisation that perhaps Arthur, and the mistakes that she had made with him, would forever haunt her. He was stopping Jack from loving her, and in that moment, Claire realised that she wanted nothing more than for Jack to love her.

Properly love her. Passionately, mercilessly, foolishly and ardently love her. Claire wanted Jack to love her the way that she had fallen in love with him. Utterly, and without realising, Claire had become completely his. Claire's vision for her future had changed. She saw Jack. She saw them as terrific friends, the team they had been, and yet so stupidly in love with one another that they were the envy of all. She saw their children, the ones they would share together, and they would be raised in a loving home knowing nothing but care and compassion for their dreams. They would grow together, take care of one another, and be the other's champion. And yet there was an unyielding mountain in the way of Jack becoming Claire's.

Just as Arthur had taken everything from Claire once, she felt him ripping this life away from her, too. Jack didn't trust her, and there was nothing she could do to change it.

Claire was resigned, and yet her heart didn't waver. "I love you, Jack," she whispered. "I don't know if that means anything to you, but if it does, I ask, nay I beg you not to fight him tomorrow. Please. I can live with you not trusting me. It will kill me, but I can live with it. But I cannot live with the thought of you dying because of something so foolish as jealousy."

Jack's eyes widened and he stared down at Claire, seemingly searching her face for a sign of something. Claire looked up at him with furrowed brows, unable to discern what he wanted.

But then, Jack brought his hands up to cup her face and a smile, a relieved smile spread across his face.

"You don't know if it means anything?" he asked in disbelief. "My God, Claire. It means everything. You mean everything to me. You are my life now. No one ... no one has said that to me before."

"Well, now they have," breathed Claire.

Jack brushed away a lingering tear with his thumb. But then one of his hands dropped to her stomach. Just as he had done so many times before with their name game, Jack began to write. Only this time, he spoke aloud.

"I," he began, tracing a straight line on her belly. "Love," he continued, and Claire's chest tightened. "You," he concluded, finishing with the letter "u", the letter that had her so convinced Jack was coming up with the most obscure name on earth.

But had he been writing that declaration this whole time? Claire trembled as she tried not to stammer. "You love me?" she repeated.

"I do," Jack confirmed.

Despite having heard a declaration before, this felt like the first time someone had ever spoken those words to her. They loved each other. It had been declared, and before God. Near God. They were adjacent to his house, after all. Surely, surely this could only mean that they might move forward. Perhaps all hope was not lost as she had thought only moments ago.

"You won't fight tomorrow?" Claire asked it as a question, but she really meant it as an order.

Jack shook his head. "No, I won't fight tomorrow," he complied. Jack leaned down but stopped himself just shy of Claire's lips. "I love you," he whispered. "And I trust you."

Claire's breath caught in her throat as he finally closed the distance.

Claire wasn't sure what had woken her up, but her eyes fluttered open sometime in the early morning. She reached out across the bed to feel for Jack, as perhaps he had woken her up, but Claire soon realised he was not there, and that his side of the bed felt quite cool.

It took a moment for Claire's sleep fatigued brain to realise what that meant, and she suddenly sat bolt upright in the bed. She anxiously searched their dark bedroom for any sign of Jack, but she didn't see him.

"Dear God, no," she whispered as she threw back the bedclothes. Claire raced as quickly she could possibly carry herself into the dressing room, and found it empty, though she saw Jack's night shirt strewn over the back of a chair. He had already been in to dress. He was gone. "No!" Claire cried. She nearly broke the mantle clock as she read the time. It was just before six. When she threw open the drapes, she saw the morning fog and the lightening sky as the sun prepared to rise. "No!" Claire cried again, nearly screaming the word. Claire dropped the clock on the floor as she ran to the door. She forced herself to run, and she clutched at her belly as she moved as quickly as she could towards the family bedrooms.

Her heart thundered and her tears blurred her vision. Claire panted and breathed erratically, but she found the will to push herself until she reached her destination. Claire opened Grace and Adam's door so forcefully that the door swung open completely and the handle smashed into the wall behind, making a cracking noise.

"Help me!"

Claire heard Grace gasp, and Adam automatically leapt out the bed in a defensive stance, positioning himself between Grace and the door, before he registered that it was Claire who had infiltrated their chamber. Adam immediately illuminated the lamp on their bedside table and the room began to glow.

"Claire!" exclaimed Grace, who climbed out of bed quickly. "What has happened?" Grace reached Claire and pulled her into her arms.

But it wasn't Grace that Claire needed. It was Adam. Claire looked past her sister to her concerned husband. "Please," implored Claire. "You must go to Jack. He has challenged Arthur Slickson to a duel at dawn and he is gone. You must stop him."

"What is all the commotion in here? It sounded like a herd of horses was thundering down the halls," Cecily entered the bedroom wrapped in a silk robe, her hair out and combed. She frowned upon the scene before her in confusion.

Adam disregarded his mother's question. "What do you mean Jack has challenged Arthur Slickson? Why would he do such a thing?"

Claire cried out in exasperation as she was certain her heart was going to burst. "GO!" Claire screamed. "Or I will get on a horse myself!" she threatened.

Adam nodded, and immediately entered into his and Grace's dressing room to change. Claire impatiently wished he would go in his night shirt for all she cared.

She rested her forehead against Grace's shoulder as she tried to calm herself, but it wasn't working. She cried, out of fear, out of anger, and for a lack of knowing what else to do.

"What would possess Jack to enter into a duel with this man?" Cecily demanded to know. "Do we know him? Who is he to Jack?"

"Not to Jack," murmured Grace as she rubbed Claire's back. "Claire," she whispered. "Claire, tell me. Tell me what happened."

Claire sobbed, and she couldn't speak for fear of hyperventilating. Grace quickly helped Claire to an armchair by the embers of the fireplace. "He ... told ... me ... he ... wouldn't ... fight!" Claire struggled to say in between sobs.

"Adam will stop him. Don't fear," promised Grace.

"But why is he fighting?" Cecily demanded to know, with a sound of fear in her voice that Claire had never heard before.

"Because ... of ... me!" Claire exclaimed.

Adam stormed out of the dressing room; an ensemble barely thrown together.

"Adam, you bring him back." Cecily spoke almost viciously in her demand.

Adam left the bedroom without saying a word. Despite knowing that help was now on the way, Claire cried harder. How she prayed Adam reached Jack in time.

"Claire, what happened with Arthur Slickson?" Grace asked, her voice tender, but wary. She knelt down on the floor before Claire and placed her hands on Claire's knees.

Claire couldn't speak, and all she could do was put her hands on her stomach.

She heard Grace inhale a gasp, as Grace uttered, "Oh, dear Claire. Please Lord, let me be wrong," Grace whispered, before she asked, "Claire, is Jack the father of your child?"

Yes. In every way that mattered. But in the way that Grace meant? Claire shook her head.

"Oh, good God," Cecily all but hissed, and Claire felt her distain like a slap across the face. "How long after you managed to trick my son into marrying you did you spurn him for another?"

"Cecily!" snapped Grace.

"I never spurned him!" Claire exclaimed, finding her voice between sobs. "Please," she said, her eyes meeting her sister's. "Please understand. Arthur preyed upon me for years. I was led by him, tricked by him, and he made me believe that I had to perform certain acts in order to prove myself to him. I found out that I was going to have a child before Perrie's birthday party. When I told Arthur, he rejected me, and ... and that was the night that I met Jack for the second time. He happened upon me when I was in quite a state and I told him everything. He knew everything. And he offered to marry me to save me from ruin."

"Oh, my goodness," gasped Grace as she cupped a hand over her mouth.

"I love Jack," Claire insisted vehemently, looking up at Cecily and flinching at the hard, disapproving expression on her face. "With every breath in my being, I love him. He is a good man, the best I know, and I don't know what I'll do if anything happens to him."

Her heart seized on the last word, but the pain began to suddenly radiate through her, centralising in lower abdomen as warm gush of liquid began to pour down her legs. Claire clutched her stomach as she cried out in pain.

Grace stood up abruptly as she realised what was happening. "Oh, Lord. We must send for the doctor!"

"You must send her to her mother's house," countered Cecily. "Though I would not wish this shame on my friend."

Claire felt that pain more keenly than she did the wave of agony that flowed through her body at that moment. She couldn't bear to see the look on her mother's face.

"Cecily!" shouted Grace. "She is my sister, and your son's wife! She will have a doctor as she is going to deliver a child today."

Cecily stood over Claire, and she looked up at her mother-in-law fearfully. "Jack knew everything?" she said through gritted teeth. "He knew you were ruined? He knew were to have another man's child? He still offered to marry you?"

"Yes," rasped Claire. "He said it was the right thing to do. He wanted to save me, and he promised that if we married, this child would be his. Ah!" Claire cried out as she closed her eyes tightly and endured her next pains. "He promised to look after me, and I love him."

"Foolish boy," hissed Cecily angrily. "If anything happens to my son ..." she began but couldn't finish her sentence.

Yet Claire could imagine what she would say, and she did not blame Cecily in the slightest.

CHAPTER 34

Jack waited in the clearing, the one where he had followed Claire to months earlier during their brief engagement. He had sent a trusted servant the night before with a letter for Arthur, instructing him to meet Jack here.

Jack had taken a mahogany box from Adam's study, containing pistols which had once belonged to his father. As the challenged, Arthur had the right to choose the weapon, and Jack had come prepared. Jack did not take Arthur for a swordsman.

He had no second. Jack knew that he should have brought his brother, but that would mean telling him Claire's truth, and he wasn't prepared to share their secret. Jack would negotiate. He would allow Arthur the chance to repent. But if he refused, then Jack would go through with the duel.

Claire had asked him not to fight, and he had told her he wouldn't. But he hadn't promised. A lie was surely better than a broken promise. Jack had everything to fight for. Claire had told him as such when she had confessed her love for him. She would never comprehend what that meant to him, to know that someone loved him, preferred him, chose him. Jack would protect her with his life, and if that meant facing a pistol to stop Claire's harassment then he would do it.

Jack watched as the sunrise shone through the trees, and the fog began to lift in the clearing. He hadn't slept the night before. He had been watching Claire, memorising her, before he had written a will, leaving everything he had to her. The will was on her writing desk, and Jack truly hoped that he would return before she even woke to hide it so that she need never see it.

Jack's horse, which was tethered to a nearby tree, lifted its head as the faint sound of galloping hooves echoed through the woods. Jack could only hear one horse, and he wondered if Arthur, too, was alone.

His question was soon answered as Arthur entered into the clearing on horseback, his green eyes settling on Jack coolly as he dismounted. He was alone and dressed in his best finery.

"No second?" called Arthur as he tied his own horse to a tree branch.

"Likewise," replied Jack. "But I will offer you the same courtesy." Not that he deserved it. "I demanded satisfaction from you, and if you do not swear on your honour this minute to leave my wife in peace from this day on, then I will have you face me, or you will forevermore be known as a coward."

Arthur chuckled and shook his head as he all but strutted towards Jack. "I won't apologise for claiming what is mine."

It was meant to be a taunt, but Jack could not be goaded. As he stared into the cold depths of this man's eyes, Jack saw no threat. He saw a weak, reprehensible man determined to secure a plaything. Jack felt no jealousy, and instead looked upon Arthur Slickson with pity. He was a man who resorted to cons to trick women into favouring him. He could offer nothing of substance from within himself. He had nought but a handsome face to offer, and even then, it was bruised terribly courtesy of Jack the previous afternoon.

How many women had he preyed upon as he had Claire? How many children were stashed across the country? Was Claire the first to reject him?

"She is not yours, Slickson," uttered Jack. "And she never will be again. You make a mockery of yourself every time you attempt to contact her. I will say again, repent, and you leave here as you are."

"What will you do if the child looks like me?" jeered Arthur. "Will you drown it? Drop it? Pretend it came to untimely end with an infant illness?"

A cold chill ran down Jack's spine at the very thought. The very notion that Jack would ever harm his child was unthinkable. His son or daughter would be raised in spite of the man who had sired him.

"What is your weapon?" growled Jack.

Arthur smiled. "Pistols. I trust you brought them."

Jack fetched the pistols and shoved one of them into Arthur's hands. Both men stood before each other, watching the other load. Jack's heart was racing, in fear, and in anger. But his mind shifted to Claire as both men began to pace away from each other.

How he loved her. If he lived, if he was allowed to live, how he would love her, and love their child. He wouldn't let any harm come to them, especially, Jack thought, as he turned to face Arthur, him.

"On the count of three," Jack shouted across the field as he raised the barrel of his pistol. He noticed his hand shaking with the energy of the moment. How he wanted this man gone, but could he take a life? "One –"

But the sound of his opponent's pistol blasted through the air, and Jack felt a burning sensation rip through his arm. The shock of the blast knocked him on his back. As Jack craned his neck to see his arm, he saw that his white shirt was stained with blood. He inhaled a staggered breath as he saw Arthur start towards him pistol raised, as he prepared to take a second, more fatal shot.

"Coward!" shouted Jack with as much might as he could muster. "You could not face me like a man?"

At the mention of cowardice, Arthur stopped, and his left eye twitched. Jack pushed himself up, climbing to his feet, though his injured left arm hung uselessly beside him. Jack raised his pistol, his chest heaving as pain radiated through his body. Arthur waited, watched, all but glaring at Jack as he stood motionlessly.

Arthur had taken his shot. He could not take another until Jack had fired, lest he be labelled a coward. And if a second shot proved fatal before Jack had fired, it would be murder, and Arthur would be hanged.

Jack cocked his pistol and aimed, before he pointed his gun in the air and fired into the morning sky. An expression of genuine shock spread across Arthur's face as he realised what had happened.

Jack couldn't do it. He couldn't stare into a man's eyes and take his life, no matter who he was. "I could have killed you," he stated quietly. "I could have killed you, and it would have been ... lawful." In a sense.

Arthur had quickly paled, and Jack believed that he realised this. Arthur had just realised that he had, all of sudden, come mere seconds from meeting his maker.

"I won't fire into the sky again," promised Jack. "My aim will be true, and I will not show you mercy. From this day forth, my wife is a stranger to you. You have no reason to ever approach her or my family. You do so, I will see you right back here. Do I make myself clear?"

Arthur's eyes dropped to Jack's arm. Jack could feel the blood seeping from his wound and running down his arm, and he wasn't sure for how much longer he would be able to stand with conviction.

"Are you satisfied?"

"Am I?" countered Jack.

"Have her then," sneered Arthur, as he promptly turned his back on Jack and swiftly fetched his horse. No sooner had he climbed atop his steed, did a third man join them in the clearing. Arthur did not stay, as he immediately kicked in his heels and forced his horse into a quick gallop.

As soon as Arthur was gone, Jack fell to his knees weakly as his brother practically leapt off his horse. Adam was half dressed and entirely in anguish as he raced to the ground beside Jack.

"Oh, good God, I'm too late," hissed Adam as he inspected Jack's torso for injuries, before his focus settled on his bloody arm. "Why would you not tell me about this?" Adam snapped as he positioned his arm around Jack's waist to lift him. "I would have been your second! Or I would have bloody stopped you."

Adam heaved Jack to his feet, and Jack felt as though he left his stomach on the ground. He felt very faint and Adam did not pester him with any more questions. "I need to get you to a doctor."

Jack was not entirely certain how he made it onto the horse, but he and Adam rode for the doctor's house nearby. He charged hefty fees for some of the parishioners, which was why they often had to seek alternative care from nearby London. However, the doctor was not at home, and it was his wife who answered the door.

Jack couldn't hear what was being said, but Adam had managed to convince her to allow them inside. She was a good, dutiful woman who assisted them with water and bandages. Adam assisted her in cleaning Jack's wound, before he packed it with cloth and bandaged it tightly until they could see the doctor for proper treatment.

The bleeding had stopped, and although Jack still felt quite nauseous, he did not feel as though he was going to faint. After a spoonful of laudanum to manage the pain, Adam paid the woman for her charity, as well as her discretion, and he and Jack left the house. Once Adam had assisted Jack back onto the horse and they had started back towards Ashwood House, Adam spoke.

"Tell me at once what this was about," Adam demanded to know. "Claire came into our bedroom this morning absolutely hysterical demanding that I stop you from fighting. She seemed to think that this was because of her."

In his blood loss haze, Jack hadn't questioned as to why his brother was there. How had he known where to find Jack? He hadn't left a note.

"How did you find me?"

"I was riding towards the Slickson's home before I heard the shots. I rarely have poachers on my land, so I knew it had to be you. What is going on between Claire and Arthur Slickson? I know that Grace was suspicious about your union in the beginning, and I know she grossly dislikes the man."

Jack hadn't meant for Claire to find out he had fought, though with his arm wound, it was now inevitable. She had sent Adam after him, and Jack knew that her sister would be asking the same questions that Adam was now asking. Claire would have told the truth. Jack felt certain of this. It was almost startling how certain he felt that Claire would confess their secret to save him.

"You are not to breathe a word; do you understand me?" Jack made his brother swear.

Adam frowned, but nodded. "You have my word."

As they rode, Jack confessed everything, right from the very beginning. From discovering Claire crying in the library, to proposing to her, marrying her, forging a friendship and a partnership, and everything else that had happened to get them to where they were now.

Adam listened intently, an expression of pure shock on his face as he took in every part of Jack's story. "You ... the baby is not yours?" he managed to say after Jack had finished relaying his tale.

"The baby is mine in every way that matters," Jack said with conviction. "Do you understand that, Adam? I won't ever have anyone doubt that this child is mine. No one will ever treat my son or my daughter as anything less than a beloved member of our family."

Adam nodded slowly. "You are a better man than I, Jack," he decided. "I really don't know what I would do if it was Grace."

"The difference is that Grace has always been yours. I bloody married you myself when you were children," Jack said impatiently. "Claire hasn't always been mine, and for a long time she was a victim of that man. But I knew there was only one thing I could do, only one right thing to do. Claire is safe, and I am going to love them both for the rest of my life. And by some miracle, Claire loves me, as well. We are to be a family, and I need you to treat Claire as you always have. She has not changed, save for growing into her own person. She is kind, loyal, beautiful, and she sees something in me that nobody else does."

Adam looked upon Jack with pride and offered him a reassuring smile. "You are going to be a terrific father," he declared.

Ashwood House came into view, and their horses trotted through the open gates. Jack hated to think what awaited him inside the walls. Claire was going to be furious.

"I hope so."

"Well, you are going to find our sooner than you thought," replied Adam. "The doctor is here," he revealed. "That was why he was not at home. He was sent for early this morning by Ashwood House as it was Claire's time."

Jack's heart stopped as he aggressively pulled on his horse's reins. "What?" he hissed.

"I did not want you to ride recklessly and risk injury," said Adam defensively. "I know from experience that labouring takes hours and hours, so we did not need to rush."

Oh, good God. Was it early? Was it dangerous? Had he brought this on? Jack panicked as he leapt off his horse, not bothering to tether it to anything. He held his injured arm as he ran towards the house, bursting through the front door so violently that he nearly took it off its hinges. Jack could hear Adam racing behind him.

Jack's adrenaline helped him to bound up the stairs, and just as he was about to head in the direction of his and Claire's bedroom, he saw a housemaid racing in the other direction carrying cleans cloths.

"Are those for Lady Claire?" Jack shouted after her. "Where is she?"

The maid turned around, startled, before she replied. "Milady is in the duke and duchess' bedroom, milord." Her eyes then widened as she saw the blood on Jack's shirt. "Oh, dear Lord, are you alright, milord?" she cried.

But Jack didn't answer her. He raced past her and ran towards Adam and Grace's bedroom. Jack knew that it was customary for the father to wait outside the birthing room, but he didn't want to. He needed to see Claire.

"Jack, you ought to change!" Adam shouted after Jack.

Jack ignored his brother as he burst into the bedroom, immediately spying Claire in the bed wearing her nightdress. She was covered in sweat and was flanked by both Grace and Susanna on either side of the bed. The doctor was tending to her, ensuring that she was modestly covered, and his mother was standing near the end of the bed.

"Claire!"

Claire cried out helplessly when her blue eyes found Jack, but it was Cecily who spoke first.

"Oh, thank you, God," she declared. Were Jack not positive that his mother would have preferred to drink poison, he could have sworn that she smiled at him.

"Jack, your arm!" exclaimed Susanna. "What happened?"

"I cut myself shaving," Jack muttered as he raced over to the bed, kneeling down at Claire's side. He placed a hand on her clammy forehead, and she leaned into his touch. "I'm sorry, I'm so sorry," he whispered. "I'll explain everything, I promise, but it will all be alright."

Claire nodded as her face began to contort with pain and she screamed an unholy scream.

"It's moving quickly ... but ... oh, dear God," gasped the doctor from the end of the bed, "it's a footling. The child is backwards."

CHAPTER 35

"A footling?" exclaimed Jack, feeling immense horror at the tone of voice the doctor had used. He could see the appearance of anguish on the man's face, and Jack knew that he ought to be very afraid. "What is there to do? How do you ensure this is safe?" he demanded to know.

The doctor pursed his lips and thought seriously. "It is childbirth, milord. It is never safe, particularly for children who are born early."

Claire whimpered in between her pains and she reached for Jack. Susanna made way for her brother, and Jack sat down on the bed beside Claire, taking her hand with his good arm.

Cecily gasped, and covered her mouth with her hands. She was near the doctor, and so could see what the doctor was seeing. "Oh, good Lord, it really is a foot."

"Mother!" hissed Jack, as he turned his attention back to Claire's panicked face. She was bright red and slick with sweat. The veins in his forehead were practically bulging. Her eyes, though, were so fearful, and so in need.

"Alright, alright," the doctor said under his breath. "I've delivered a footling before."

"Did the child survive? Did the mother?" panicked Grace. "Susanna, please, send a note to my mother," she urged, and Susanna obeyed immediately, retreating to the writing desk.

Claire squeezed Jack's hand, but Jack noticed how the doctor did not answer the question. Jack did not know much about childbirth at all, but this was obviously not how it was supposed to be.

"Everyone quiet!" ordered the doctor as Claire screamed through another pain. Claire tried with all her might to push, but the doctor looked dissatisfied and concerned. "The child won't deliver spontaneously. It needs help. First the knees," he murmured.

Jack tore his eyes from Claire, and he looked to his mother. Cecily had her eyes trained on the doctor's hands as he manipulated the child. She was watching in shock, before she gasped. "Oh, oh, two legs," she cried. "Ten toes."

"Now the shoulders ..."

Claire screamed as the doctor manoeuvred the baby again, her wails laboured and exhausted.

"Alright, everyone off the bed, I will need some room," the doctor then instructed seriously, and from where Jack was sitting, he could see the legs of his child being supported by the doctor.

His chest seized, but he obeyed.

"Doctor, the cord ..." Cecily uttered fearfully.

The cord? What cord?

"What about the cord?" stammered Grace as she climbed off of the bed.

"What's wrong?" sobbed Claire.

"Nothing, milady," replied the doctor. "This is the last of it, time for the head, and then she's here."

She. It was a girl. They had a daughter.

Jack watched as the doctor manipulated their daughter for the last time to free her head, and then she was born. His momentary joy all but dissipated when Jack realised that the baby made no noise.

A cord, a bloody, fleshy cord was wrapped around the baby's neck, and no sooner had Jack noticed it, the doctor unwound it. Her skin and lips were turning blue as the doctor laid the baby down on the bed.

She was tiny, lifeless, and Jack stared at her helplessly. No, this couldn't be it. The life lost today was not meant to be her. If it was to be anyone, it should have been him.

Claire cried again in a way that Jack had never heard before. It was the cry of a mother.

"Come on, little one," uttered the doctor as he leaned over the baby, shaking her and tapping her gently. He lifted her back and supported her head and patted her back, increasing the pressure.

Slowly, very slowly, the blue of her skin began to fade, and the newborn pink materialised. And then she cried. And it sounded like the gates of Heaven.

Jack sank to his knees and Claire whimpered as the baby was placed on her chest before the doctor returned to the end of the bed to conclude the birth. Claire pressed her lips to the baby's forehead and cried tears of happiness as their daughter began to settle.

Jack felt his own tears falling down his cheeks as he got back up to his feet to kiss her as well. She had hair, a tuft of white blonde, though it was matted down. Jack didn't care as he kissed her for the first time. He laid his hand down on her tiny back and felt the softness and fragility of her skin.

"Congratulations, Claire, Jack," wished Grace, who was still quite shaken from the ordeal. "She is undoubtedly perfect."

"Indeed," added Cecily reservedly. "You were very fair when you were an infant, Jack. I think she has inherited some of your features," she noted, approaching his side of the bed and noting the baby's hair.

Her tone was not entirely sincere, and Jack knew in that moment that his mother was aware of the secret. She spoke for the benefit of the doctor, but Jack couldn't discern her true feelings. Regardless, he did not care. The child was healthy. Whatever his mother thought meant nothing to him.

Susanna returned after sending the note to Mrs Denham, and Adam accompanied her, tentatively approaching the bed to look upon his new niece.

"A girl, is she?" Adam smiled, and clapped Jack on the back. "Congratulations, brother."

Jack couldn't help but smile with pride as he looked back down at Claire cradling their daughter.

"Do you have a name picked out for her?" asked Susanna curiously.

Claire and Jack exchanged a glance. "I feel I suggested two thousand girls names, but Claire never liked any of them," replied Jack.

"Well, I always knew, girl or boy, she would be named after you," Claire murmured lethargically as she traced around the baby's lips with her forefinger.

Before the doctor left, he tended to Jack's arm properly, and placed it in a sling. Jack was lucky that the bullet had not grazed his bone, and that it was a flesh wound. He would need to keep it clean in order to keep it free from disease. The packing and bandaging applied by his wife had stopped the bleeding and had allowed Jack's body to clot naturally to stem the bleeding.

Mrs Denham arrived with Kate, Peter and Jem in tow, very alarmed as to the urgency of Susanna's missive, but were relieved to find that all was well by the time they reached Ashwood. They were informed of the circumstances of the birth, and Mrs Denham had needed some water to calm herself.

She fussed over Claire and the baby, and they all had a turn of holding her, cooing her, and rocking her.

Jack didn't complain, but he was anxious for his turn.

By the time everyone had departed, and Adam and Grace had retired to another bedroom, it was nearly nine o'clock in the evening. Jack finally was able to hold his daughter in his arms, or rather his arm, sitting in the bed beside Claire as they both looked down at her.

She was a perfect, tiny little thing. Her features were so small, pink and delicate, and the minute he touched his finger to her palm, she wrapped her little hand around him. This child was brand new, faultless, and without sin or injury. No one had harmed her, no one had hurt her, and she had never known pain or suffering. Her life had just begun, and Jack felt it in his bones that it was his responsibility to ensure she grew up in a wondrous place of opportunity.

Jack's attention was grabbed by the sound of Claire's soft snores, and he saw that she had fallen asleep, a look of true exhaustion on her face. They had yet to speak properly, and they would, but Claire needed to rest.

Jack carefully got up from the bed and carried the baby over to the armchair by the fire that was crackling away. Jack sat down slowly as he cuddled the baby into his chest. He was not yet an expert on how to handle children and doing it with only one arm was not easy.

She was clean now, and her hair was dry, and Jack could see the true blonde of it in the firelight. She was, indeed, very fair, but her beauty was all her mother. Clearly.

"You will never know a day where you feel unloved, little one. That is my promise to you," Jack whispered to her.

At that moment, the door to the bedroom opened quietly. Jack looked up to see his mother entering, balancing a tray against her hip, before she shut the door behind her. Cecily first looked at the bed, before she spied Jack by the fire. She carried the tray over to Jack and set it down on the small table between the armchairs. She had brought some sandwiches.

"I thought you might be hungry for a light supper," murmured Cecily as she sat down in the chair beside Jack.

"Thank you," replied Jack awkwardly. It was a very strange notion indeed to be witnessing thoughtfulness from his mother.

"Jacqueline Beatrice Beresford," Cecily uttered, testing the name on her tongue. "Well, I know where Claire got Jackie from. From whence does Beatrice originate?"

Jack thought back to the conversation he and Claire had shared while reading the Divine Comedy. They had talked of Beatrice's divinity, and how Dante had painted her in such a way as she had affected him so. Claire had refuted her own divinity, but they could both agree that Beatrice suited their angel.

"A book," was all Jack replied, and Cecily managed a small smile.

"But, of course." Cecily rested her hand on the arm of the chair and took a deep breath. "Jack, I will not pretend I approve of Claire's actions. Were it Susanna, I do not know what I would do," she said honestly. "But I do not condemn her. Believe it or not, I do understand what it is like to be young and in love, and to make decisions that you otherwise wouldn't."

Jack frowned at her. "Claire does not need your approval, Mother," he said icily, though he had a hard time believing that his mother had ever been young and in love. From his experience, his parents had barely tolerated each other while his father had been alive.

Cecily nodded in concession. "Yes, you are quite right. She doesn't need my approval. "But regardless of that fact, I know you understand that this secret of yours cannot go beyond those who already know it. You and Claire, Adam and Grace, and myself. We are the only ones who know the truth, and that is as far as it shall go."

Jack gritted his teeth but forced himself not to tighten his gentle grip on his daughter. "She's not even twelve hours old and you are already concerned about her ruining your position?"

"No, you misunderstand me," retorted Cecily. "My concern, I assure you, is for her," she clarified sincerely. "I know you think me heartless, Jack, and I know I have given you plenty of ammunition to fuel this belief. But I can see that she is yours, in every important way, and therefore, she is my granddaughter, and I would never let a vicious rumour ruin her chances."

"You would see her as you do Perrie?" asked Jack sceptically. "As you do Lily?" Jack had been witness to his mother fussing over Perrie in particular with the sort of affection he had never seen.

Cecily nodded with conviction. "I will escort her upon her debut, and I will present her to the queen myself," she declared determinedly. But her expression changed to one of regret, to one of sadness and concern as she uttered words that Jack had never thought he would hear from his mother. "Jack, I am sorry," she said in earnest. "I have grossly underestimated you, and I am ashamed." Cecily looked into Jack's eyes with nothing by truth. "I made a judgement about you many years ago, and I have never allowed myself to see you as anything but. I held your mistakes against you, and I used them as proof of my own judgement. I never encouraged you, or supported you, or helped you to become a better man. And yet in spite of this, in spite of me, you have grown into a truly decent man.

"What you did for Claire, when you owed her nothing, is perhaps the most selfless thing I have ever heard of. When Claire confessed this, I felt such incredible pride to have you as my son.

And as I felt this pride, I felt such grief and remorse at the fact that I did not know that this was the man that you are. I didn't know you, and that was entirely my doing.

"I know I have not been the kind of mother that you deserve. I have not been the sort of mother that I would have wanted for myself. I allowed my own demons to poison me for a very long time, and I, as a result, lost all three of you for a time. But I know that I hurt you the most. I lectured you, I scolded you, and I never forgave your mistakes. I know exactly how I made you feel, and something wicked inside of me prevented me from comforting you.

"It might be too late, and it might not mean anything to you, but I want you to know that I am eternally grateful for you, and I am so very proud of you.

"You are bright, you are kind, and you are decent, and I know, I know that you will achieve great things. Your father knew this, too, and I wish I had listened to him years ago.

"When I thought you might be hurt today, you might be killed –" Cecily voice cracked, and she quickly composed herself. "I couldn't bear it. The very idea that you could be lost to me before I even really found you was unthinkable. I love you, Jack, and I always have in my way. But I am determined to be better ... I am determined to be more like you."

Were Jack not so determined to remain upright for the sake of his child, he might have passed out on the floor. Pigs would fly before he had ever thought he would hear such words from his mother, and yet the fragility of her tone of voice told Jack that she meant every word.

She was sorry. She was proud. And she loved him.

Jack couldn't help it as a tear rolled down his cheek as he stared at his mother. He didn't know what to say. After so many years of resentment, he was lost for words.

"I will leave you with her," Cecily announced quietly as she rose from her chair.

As she went to leave, Jack felt his chest lurch. He had hated his mother for as long as he could remember. He could not remember a time when she had ever approved of him. While he sometimes behaved poorly to spite her, Jack would have been lying if he had ever said that he didn't want his mother's approval. Of course, he wanted it. No child wanted to be unloved by a parent.

"Mother," said Jack softly.

"Yes?"

CHAPTER 36

Claire awoke with the start when she heard her baby crying. Jack, too, who had been sleeping while sitting upright beside her, nearly fell off the bed in fright at the sound.

Claire was not at all certain of what time it was, but it was very dark in the bedroom. Jackie had been placed in the basinet beside the bed, the one that both Perrie and Lily had used.

"Don't you get up," Jack urged, as he leapt out of the bed and raced around to the basinet. Claire watched in admiration as he had a rather pleased smile on his face as he collected Jackie from her basket. Jack appeared to be handling delicate china as he lifted the baby with his good arm, slowly bringing her grizzling form over to Claire's waiting arms.

Claire took her tiny child into her arms and admired her briefly before starting to feed her as her mother had shown her earlier. As she suckled, Claire enjoyed the feeling of Jackie's soft, fine hair tickling her arm. It nearly appeared silver in the darkness.

Claire then realised that this was the first time that she had Jack had been alone with their daughter. Throughout the day, there had always been one family member or another present to offer advice or to teach her what to do. As much as Claire appreciated their help, she did want time alone with Jack in order for them to get to know their child.

Furthermore, she wanted time alone with her husband to talk to him. Childbirth had not prevented her from noticing the bloody shirt he wore when he had entered the bedroom. He had been shot.

"Claire, I am so proud of you, you know," murmured Jack as he watched them, returning to his place in the bed beside her. "I don't think I've ever been more terrified in my life before today."

Claire glanced at him. "I know exactly what you mean," she replied. Those few moments when Jackie had been blue had felt like hours. And she would never resent the sound of her baby crying. "But my fear began much earlier this morning."

Jack nodded slowly, grimacing.

"Jack, you promised me you wouldn't fight," Claire whispered.

"No, no," replied Jack quickly. "I never promised. I told you I wouldn't, but I didn't promise."

Claire frowned deeply. "Are you trying to tell me you are without guilt because you merely lied?"

"No," sighed Jack. "I lied to you, and I apologise. I should not have told you I wouldn't fight when I had every intention of going." Jack leaned back against the bedhead. "Claire, he dishonoured you ... and for the last time."

Claire felt the blood leave her face, and she was thankful for the darkness. Was Arthur dead?

But Jack seemed to sense her horror. "We both fired," he continued, "his shot landed, as you see. I fired into the air. I demanded satisfaction and I received it."

Claire was genuinely shocked to hear that Jack had fired into the air, but at the same time, she was incredibly relieved. Duels were a barbaric practice, and she saw no honour in them as many gentlemen did. But the idea that Jack could have fired at someone on her behalf was sickening.

"I think I could have lived with it," Jack decided quietly. "Had he accosted you, touched you ... I think I could have lived with it had we simply moved to London had begun our lives as the three of us. But I went because not only did he dishonour you, I did as well." Jack softly brushed some hair out of Claire's face and tucked it behind her head. His hand then dropped, briefly grazing her collarbone before landing beside her. "I doubted you, and I hate that my first reaction was to doubt you."

"Did you believe that you owed me a sort of debt?" whispered Claire.

"Claire, I owe you everything," Jack said vehemently. "And at the first test of my honour, I failed."

Jackie pulled away and fussed quietly, and Claire quickly covered herself as she brought the baby up to her chest and began to rub her back as her mother had instructed.

"You owe me nothing," Claire assured him. "If there was ever a debt, it is mine –"

"Oh, Claire," hushed Jack, shaking his head. "I mean what I say when I claim that I owe you everything. When I think about the sort of man I was, the path I was on, even the day before we met again at Perrie's birthday ..." Jack tailed off, unable to finish his thought coherently. "I can be proud of the man I am today, and I never thought that ever possible. My mother ... my mother is proud of me."

Claire could hear the pride in his voice, even though he sounded as though he was in disbelief. It pleased her greatly that Jack's mother could see him as he was, and not who she believed him to be.

"Whatever the circumstances that saw us join together, Claire, I can say vehemently that I am eternally grateful for you," declared Jack. "Even more so as I never thought it would be possible for me to feel as I do." Jack turned his torso to look on her intently and Claire's breath hitched in her throat.

At that very moment, they both laughed when they heard Jackie, with her beautiful timing, release the gas from her belly. She made a satisfied sound and Claire began to settle Jackie in her arms.

"I am certain you must have felt it, too, one time or another, when you looked upon Adam and Grace. My brother, oh, how I envied him. Not Grace, of course, but I envied his clarity, his certainty that Grace was his future." Jack smiled. "I hoped for us, of course I hoped. But I never thought it would feel quite like this. I don't think there is anything I would not do for you and our baby. I love you endlessly, with the certainty I have always wanted. And the minute I heard Jackie's cry; I was lost to her. I will never fail you again, I swear it to you."

Claire felt his sincerity in every word, and she knew that she would never have to fear the sort of abandonment she had felt all those months ago. Jack loved her properly, the way a man ought to love a woman, wholly, passionately, and faithfully. For how many years had she longed to be loved this way? Claire didn't know.

Claire lessened the distance between them but stopped just shy of Jack's lips. Instead, she uttered, "I can take a lot, Jack. I have done. But I won't be lied to. You lied to me before, and that can't happen if we are to enter into this together." She spoke with a smile on her face, but she did mean every word. She wondered if Jack would remember the words he had said to her during their brief engagement, when they had made an agreement to be honest with each other.

Jack exhaled a breathy chuckle. "Touché," he agreed. "No lies," he promised. "If I plan on doing something utterly foolish, I will forewarn you."

Claire rolled her eyes as she pressed her lips to his, enjoying his closeness with nothing between them. They were husband and wife, with their daughter between them. After everything they had been through, Claire felt as though their life was about to begin.

"You are the first man I have ever loved," Claire declared when they parted. "And you will be the last."

"You are the first woman I have ever loved," replied Jack, "but I am afraid you are not the last." With a wicked grin, he leaned down and pressed a soft kiss to Jackie's forehead.

The news of Jackie Beresford's birth spread around the village like wildfire, as news of any kind tended to do. Cecily was instrumental in describing the traumatic and dramatic scenes of Jackie's early arrival, and Jackie's tiny size at her first church appearance supported Cecily's claims.

Claire never heard a word in question, though she would wager nobody would dare go against the dowager duchess.

In the weeks that followed, in between the sleeplessness and the feelings of incompetence at three o'clock in the morning, Claire and Jack settled into parenthood well, and were more than ready to move their little family to London, much to the dismay of their entire family.

Claire had to admit that she was sad that Jackie would not grow up in the immediate vicinity of her cousins, but their adventure in London was important to Jack, and he was ready to establish his publishing house. Claire thought, however, that even if Jackie could not grow up seeing Perrie and Lily every day, that she would have to make do with the siblings that Claire hoped to give her, and soon.

Claire and Jack were to leave for London at the same time as Cecily and Susanna. Susanna's foray into society had been delayed due to Jackie's arrival, but Cecily would not keep her at home any longer.

Susanna was now three and twenty, and Cecily was determined to have her married by the season's end. Susanna was a prize, and could afford to be choosey, but her age worried Cecily. Susanna, however, did not care a wit. She, like Jack, had grown up with a brother who showed her how a man ought to love a woman. Susanna would not settle, and Claire completely understood. She did wonder whether or not Susanna would meet someone in London this year. But Claire hoped that if she did, he would love Susanna as she deserved.

"Jack, you cannot bring all of your books to London," Claire scolded as she rocked Jackie back and forth.

They were in the library with an open trunk, and Jack was going through the shelves choosing which titles to take with them. Their new home had a library, though it was not as well stocked as Jack would have liked.

"Think of the poor horses," she appealed. "They cannot tow such weight."

Jack smirked. "Well, I shall have to buy my favourites again, won't I?" He restored the books that he was deliberating between back on the shelf as they were interrupted by a knock on the library door.

Both Claire and Jack turned to see Peter standing rather awkwardly in the doorway. Claire smiled at her brother but looked upon him quizzically. He was dressed very nicely, indeed, and it was not even a Sunday. He perhaps looked as grown up as he ever had, despite being only nineteen. His dark hair was combed, and his hands, which were normally caked in charcoal, were scrubbed clean, and holding what looked to be a new hat.

"Sorry to disturb," he said apologetically.

"Not at all, Peter," replied Jack, abandoning his task. "Did you need something? Or are you here to visit with Claire?"

Claire had received Kate that morning already, in what had been a farewell tea. "Shall I ring for some tea? Or some sandwiches, are you hungry?"

"No, no, do not trouble yourself," refused Peter. "I actually came to speak with Jack." Peter fidgeted with his hat nervously.

Claire frowned. "Do you want me to leave?" she asked.

Peter shook his head. "No, it's alright."

"What can I do for you?" Jack asked curiously.

Peter took a deep breath, bit his bottom lip for a moment, before uttering, "You could give me a job."

Both Jack and Claire stared at Peter openly, and colour filled Peter's cheeks.

"Right," he uttered bashfully, "well, you would react like that." He shook his head as some conviction returned. "Don't get me wrong, I am grateful to Jim for his time and effort in training me as his apprentice, but you both know I fell into that position because of his charity. I have a brain in my head, and I've never had a chance to use it. Tell him, Claire," Peter urged. "I did well in school until I had to leave. I am very good with numbers, I understand arithmetic better than anyone ... and I thought that with a new business, it might do to have someone who knows numbers well enough to manage the finances.

"I can do more than ... I am capable of more ... I want more for myself. I've wanted an opportunity like this ever since I had to leave school, and I never thought it would come. I am no fool, and I have the ambition to succeed. Please, I want to come with you to London. I want to be a man of business ... I know I can do it."

Peter returned to looking thoroughly embarrassed, and Claire could not shield her pride. What it must have taken for her brother to come here today, to leave Jim when he had been so good to him. Claire had always known Jack was clever, too clever to be in a profession where his mind wasn't inspired. When Jim had taken Peter on, it was because the Denhams had not been able to afford an apprenticeship for him.

Had their family had the finances, Peter would have done very well in university.

Claire looked to Jack and nodded eagerly. "He is right," urged Claire. "Peter is terribly clever –"

But her appeal did not last long as Jack interrupted her. "It just so happens, Peter, that I am rubbish with numbers." Jack grinned as relief washed over Peter. "I'm honoured that you've come to me, and if you are willing to work as hard as I am, then I will be pleased to have you at the helm with me."

Peter nodded, quite awestruck. "Yes, of course," he promised.

"And there is a bedroom in our house in London for you, so your mother will not have to worry about you in bachelor's lodgings."

Peter beamed. "London ... I'm going to London." He practically skipped in the air. "Thank you," he said gratefully. "Thank you. I will not let you down."

"You ought to pack, Peter," urged Claire, "and break it to Mama." And Jim, she thought sullenly. Perhaps Jem could take Peter's place?

Peter nodded, grinning, before turning on his heel and hurrying from the library.

Jack and Claire exchanged an amused look, and Claire smiled widely. "Thank you."

"Are you ready?" posed Jack.

"For London?" queried Claire.

"For forever."

EPILOGUE

F our Months Later

August 1810

It was a gamble, of course. Jack had never published a novel before. He was a vociferous consumer of the written word, and so when he had read this manuscript, he had been enthralled. By his own taste, he knew it was a worthwhile read.

The paper had been purchased for his printer at great expense. Peter, in his analytical way, had advocated for a thinner, cheaper supply of paper, but Jack knew that the ink would bleed and would make the book illegible. In establishing the publishing house, Jack had burned through a great majority of the capital that his father had left him.

The gamble had been taken on a female author, which made his first run of seven hundred and fifty copies a great risk indeed. It was an unfortunate fact that many people frowned upon female authors, and it being Jack's first project, he was putting Beresford Press at risk before it had even begun.

Whatever the sex of the writer, Jack paid no heed. It was the talent he cared for. Though, he did know that one day, years from now, he would tell his own daughter that the first book he ever published was written by a young woman, just like her.

Jack had wanted a legacy, one of which he could bequeath, and in this act, he was forging one. If she wanted it, Beresford Press would one day be owned and operated by Jackie.

"It is official," remarked Peter, as they watched the printers operate the machine. "We are in print."

Jack smiled, quite in disbelief that in a short while he would be holding the physical copy of a book that beared the Beresford Press name. His name. "Thank you for doing this with me, Peter," Jack said gratefully.

Despite being only nineteen, Peter looked as though he had grown so much older in these four months they had been in London. He carried himself with pride and confidence, and he wore an expression of true happiness and contentment. Jack had not known Claire's younger brother very well before now, but he was consistently impressed by the cleverness of young Peter Denham.

"Thank you for taking me on," replied Peter.

Jim had been gracious in supporting Peter's decision to go to work for Jack. Mrs Denham had been the one to grieve the decision as she was losing Peter without even a wedding to show for it. The pain of the loss was eased slightly by the knowledge that he would be living with Jack and Claire and would not be left to wander the streets of London alone.

"Jack?"

Both Jack and Peter's heads turned at the sound of someone calling his name. Jack recognised the voice instantly, before he saw the rosebud pink silk figure making her way across the printing floor.

Susanna wove around the machine and the workers effortlessly as she made her way to the stairs. She had walked this route many times this summer, and by the way she was striding with purpose, Jack would have wagered that their mother had pushed her one too many times today.

Despite her advanced age in the world of debutantes, Susanna Beresford was still the jewel of the season, a true prize. She was beautiful, accomplished, and fabulously wealthy with perhaps the best connections in all of London. She possessed the most sought-after hand in the country and was never without an invitation.

Cecily was in her element as she meticulously commanded every ballroom she and Susanna entered. She was an expert manipulator in every social scene, and if she was to have her way, Susanna would be engaged in the next few weeks as the season ended.

Susanna marched up the stairs and met Jack and Peter on the landing. Her blue eyes were wide with emotion, and her cheeks were reddened from exertion. She carried a parasol but was without a bonnet.

"He proposed!" exclaimed Susanna.

Jack stared at Susanna, trying to discern whether or not she had come to tell him the good news, or whether she wanted him to be outraged. Either would be difficult as he had no idea of whomever this gentleman was. There were so many of them sniffing around Susanna's skirts while dreaming of bank notes.

"Congratulations?" bid Peter, as though he was asking a question.

Susanna huffed. Jack then realised that he ought to be outraged.

"The audacity of the man!" he cried.

"Exactly!" agreed Susanna enthusiastically. "Lord Bertram has been an acquaintance for perhaps three weeks, and I use the word "acquaintance" generously. We have danced twice, and he has called thrice, though I have barely received him, and only at Mother's insistence. And this afternoon he declared passionate love for me!" Susanna scoffed and shook her head, folding her arms impatiently across her chest. "This is not what it is supposed to be like," she added determinedly, "and I am not imagining anything. I've seen it. Twice. I know what one is supposed to feel, supposed to look like when they are bound to the person whom they shall marry."

Peter quietly excused himself from the conversation, and left Jack and Susanna to speak.

Susanna was still quite in the dark about how Jack and Claire's relationship had begun, as was everyone besides Cecily, Adam and Grace. This did make Jack feel some guilt in how his sister was including his marriage as something to aspire to.

While Jack knew that he had been fortunate as to have found love within his marriage, it had not begun that way, which was not to say that Susanna mightn't have the same luck.

But he knew that Susanna would never take such a chance. Susanna wanted what her elder brothers had found and would settle for nothing less, which Jack sincerely admired her for. Many a terrible and unhappy match was made during these seasons purely for financial gain. Jack wouldn't see Susanna unhappy.

"What did you say to Lord Bertram?" asked Jack. "I hope you were gentle. Despite a lack of affection, it still takes courage to propose to a woman."

Susanna rolled her eyes. "Lord Bertram is not very bright," she informed him. "We were walking in the rear garden. Mother allowed it despite the fact that I informed her I believed I was coming down with typhus."

Jack couldn't help but laugh.

"He asked me to marry him nearly as soon as we were alone, and I knew I needed to get away from him, so I pretended to faint. Unfortunately for me, Lord Bertram believed I swooned for him, and he took my reaction as an acceptance. I told him "no" emphatically, and he told me that he would give me some time to think it over as "women can be fickle with their decisions"." Susanna hissed angrily. "I then told him that I needed some fresh air, and so I left him to go to the front garden. He didn't seem to question it despite the fact that we were already outside. I fled then and climbed into a hackney and asked to be brought here."

Amusement left Jack's face. "You took a hackney alone?" he scolded.

Susanna frowned irritably. "Really, Jack, please see my dilemma," she appealed. "When Mama finds out that I have rejected yet another suitor, she will lose her already thin patience. The season is almost over. What if she forces me to marry Lord Bertram?"

"You know Adam will never allow you to be forced into anything. And neither shall I," Jack promised her. "Despite what Mother may think, Adam has the final say on any potential husband of yours."

Susanna huffed. "I know I ought to be happy that Adam can protect me from these sorts of men, but nothing makes me feel more powerless then knowing that I have no control over the man I will marry."

Jack did not know what to say to that, because he knew that Susanna was exactly right. She had no choice in her husband. She could not accept a man and marry him without Adam's permission. They both knew that their brother was not the sort of ogre who would refuse Susanna her happiness, but Jack realised his own position was so much easier because he was a man.

"Are you coming to the faire on Friday?" Susanna then asked quietly. "I would appreciate a guard, and if you and Claire were to bring Jackie then I know that Mama would be considerably distracted."

Jack had asked Cecily when Jackie was born whether or not she would treat his daughter the same as she treated Perrie and Lily. Cecily had declared that she would, and it was her interactions with Jackie that were really helping to mend the two-decade long fracture in Cecily and Jack's relationship. Cecily adored Jackie, and proudly showed her off to whomever would listen.

"If it will help you, then yes," Jack confirmed. He had planned to work, but Jack then supposed that Claire deserved a day out at the faire. He had not treated her to many of the sights this season owing to his efforts at the publishing house.

Susanna smiled with relief. "Thank you," she said gratefully. "The season is nearly over."

Susanna sent a note home to let Cecily know that she would be dining with Jack and Claire that evening and that Cecily was welcome to join them. Jack and Peter ensured that the printing was working successfully on the paper before they decided to retire for the day. Jack would have had conniptions otherwise if the ink had bled through to the other side of the paper after he had spent a fortune on it.

The house that Jack had leased for his family in London felt very much like home already. Really, it was the first home of his own that he had ever had, and Claire thrived in running it.

Upon returning home, Peter and Susanna went into the drawing room while Jack ascended up the stairs to find Claire and Jackie in the nursery. It was in coming home to their nursery each day that Jack had discovered Claire had a beautiful singing voice. She often sang to Jackie when she was alone, and Jack had enjoyed teasing her about her nightingale singing voice and its contrasting snoring of a nighttime.

"Lavender's blue, dilly, dilly, lavender's green,When I am king, dilly, dilly, you shall be my queen;Call up your men, dilly, dilly, set them to work,Some to the plough, dilly, dilly, some to the cart;Some to make hay dilly, dilly, some the thresh corn;Whilst you and I, dilly, dilly, keep ourselves warm."

Jack smiled as he heard the song and pushed open the nursery door. Claire was rocking Jackie in a chair, and she smiled at Jack when she saw him enter the room.

Jack wondered if there would ever come a day when he would not stare at his wife, as she simply astounded him at some point every day. A glance, a smile, or a word, and he would be stunned by her beauty and utterly perplexed as to how he had been so fortunate.

"Jackie learned a new trick today," Claire informed him excitedly. "She can sit up by herself."

Jack grinned as he leaned down and kissed Jackie's head. "My clever girl," he mused. Jackie was still awake, though she was settled in her mother's arms. Jack then lifted Claire's chin and pressed his lips to hers softly, lingering for a moment, before he pulled away. As he did, he saw Claire's eyes darken ever so slightly as she lost her momentary composure, and Jack couldn't help but smile with satisfaction.

Jack took the baby from Claire and lifted her into his arms to look upon her properly. She fussed a little at the movement, but soon settled as she looked up at the familiar face of her father.

Jackie's eyes were wide and inquisitive but were not the same blue as they had been when she was born. They had begun to change, and in some lights, Jack could have sworn they were green. Her hair was still wispy, still the same shade of white blonde, and just long enough for a tiny ribbon, which his mother liked to fix whenever she was tending to the child.

To those who knew, there was a resemblance to Jackie's blood father. And perhaps that resemblance would continue to grow.

Jack would not deny that this very fact would have deeply affected him at one point.

But it didn't anymore. Not at all. Whether Jackie's eyes were green or purple, it made no difference to Jack. This baby was his, and she would be his daughter always. Blood did not make a father, but love.

Arthur had married. Perhaps a month after their duel. Jack and Claire had read about the marriage in the newspaper over their breakfast. He had married and heiress and was on an extended honeymoon on the Continent. The latter information was not found in the newspaper, but in a letter from Grace who felt she ought to mourn for the poor wife in question.

Claire had expressed similar sentiments, and Jack saw no evidence of grief in Claire whatsoever. Instead of wondering over it, Jack had asked Claire, sharing his worry with her in keeping with his promise to be honest.

"I have no reason to grieve," Claire had assured him, "for I have everything I could ever want."

Jack and Claire had since lived happily in London as husband and wife properly, getting to know one another all over again as they learned how to be exactly what the other needed. It was the happiest Jack had ever been, and he often thought every night, before he fell asleep with Claire in his arms, that he would endure it all again if it meant he would end up here with her.

"Susanna is here for dinner, and so might Mother," Jack informed Claire as he knelt down on the floor, still holding Jackie.

"Susanna is here without your mother presently?" clarified Claire as Jack nodded. "Oh, dear. What happened?"

"Aunt Susanna tried to fend off a marriage proposal from a man she dislikes," Jack said in a cooing voice as he sat Jackie up on the floor. "Are you going to show Papa your new talent?"

Claire quickly knelt down on the floor beside him as Jack tentatively removed his hands from Jackie's body. Sure enough, she stayed sitting upright, staring up at her cooing, proud parents with a perplexed expression.

"Poor Susanna," said Claire sympathetically. "I suppose she must be relieved she had made it through the season unattached."

"I don't think Susanna would mind being attached to someone she genuinely cared for," replied Jack. "But I truly wonder if our family could be so lucky a third time," he mused, turning to Claire.

A smile teased the corners of her lips. "I suppose we should consider ourselves lucky then."

"Oh, I do," promised Jack. "Do not you worry about that."